GHOSTS, GARTERS, AND GRIMOIRES

EMERALD CITY PARANORMAL COZY MYSTERIES

THERESA CRATER

Ghosts, Garters, and Grimoires

Emerald City Paranormal Women's Fiction

Copyright © 2025

Theresa Crater

Print ISBN: 979-8-9927156-3-7

Cover by Karri Klawiter

Crystal Star Publishing

P.O. Box 223

Lafayette, Colorado

USA

www.crystalstarpublishing.com

 Formatted with Vellum

CONTENTS

Chapter 1   1
Chapter 2   10
Chapter 3   17
Chapter 4   24
Chapter 5   34
Chapter 6   45
Chapter 7   53
Chapter 8   63
Chapter 9   72
Chapter 10   87
Chapter 11   97
Chapter 12   105
Chapter 13   113
Chapter 14   121
Chapter 15   133
Chapter 16   142
Chapter 17   154
Chapter 18   161
Chapter 19   168
Chapter 20   179
Chapter 21   187
Chapter 22   193
Chapter 23   202
Chapter 24   212
Chapter 25   221

About the Author   227
Also By   229
Acknowledgments   231

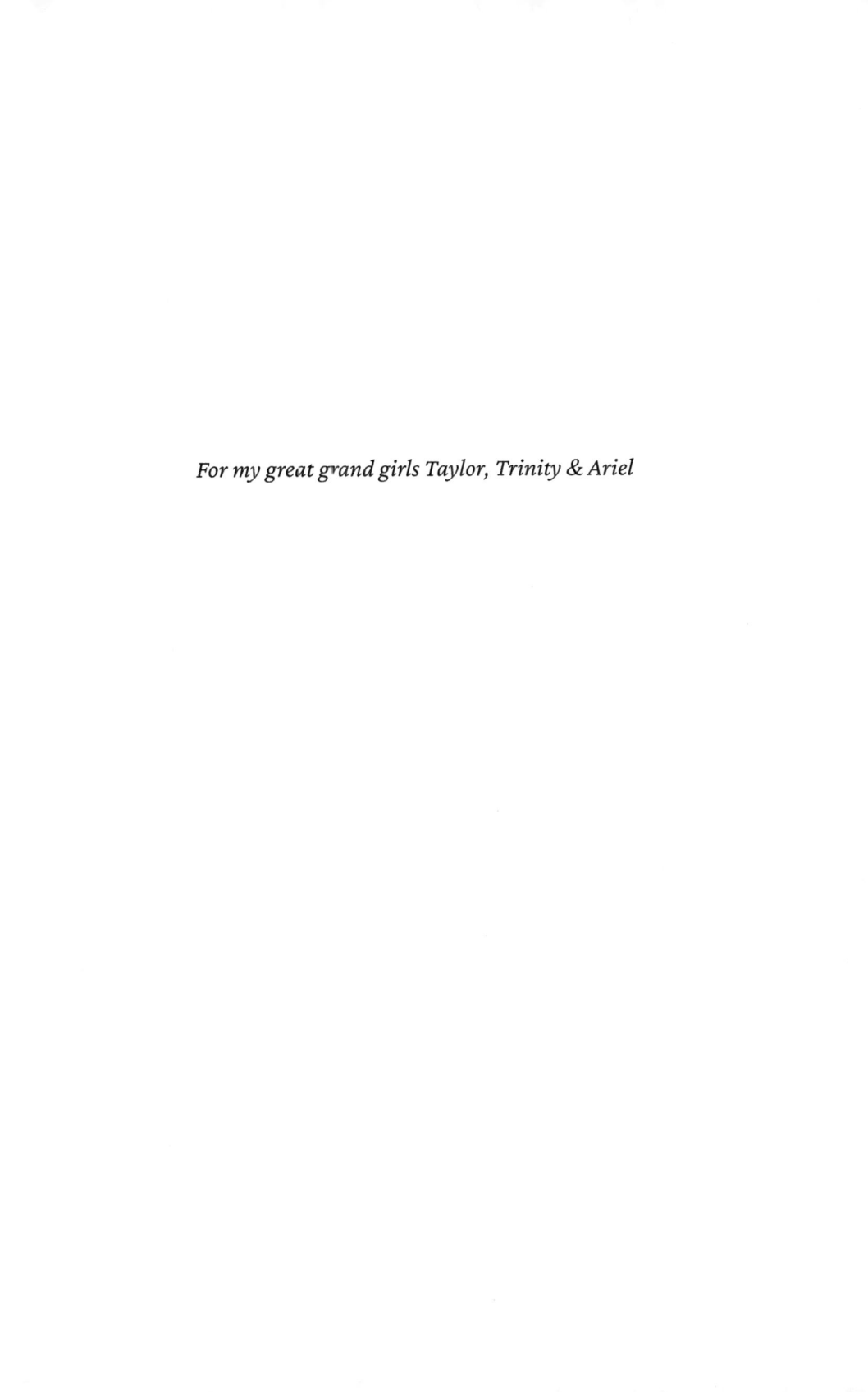

For my great grand girls Taylor, Trinity & Ariel

CHAPTER

ONE

Dana Preston knew she couldn't adjust her bra while she stood in the reception line greeting the rich and powerful of Washington State. But she dearly wished she could because the underwire was digging into her ribs and stabbing her every time she took a breath. And these blasted heels. Why had she let the image consultant talk her into five inches? "It's just for a couple of hours," Nicolette had said. "You're in good shape." But her feet ached, her back hurt, and she was sure she felt a blister forming on her heel.

She smiled again, then realized her jaw was clinched and she probably looked like she was going to take a bite out of the person in front of her. She made herself relax her face and shook hands, trying to remember the name of the donor. There were so many. It had surprised her how many nitwits wanted to contribute to her husband's campaign for the U.S. House of Representatives. Next in line came Baldwin Cress, the owner of Galactic, who had been especially generous. His name was easy to remember. He shook hands with Kevin and emphasized his priority in Washington. Once Kevin was occupied with the next person, Baldwin caught her ear. "I appreciate your help with that writer."

Walter Pearce had been Baldwin's top author, writing best-selling mysteries with a multi-million-dollar movie contract. Unfortunately, his plots turned out to be based on the murders he himself committed. Or hope to commit. Dana and her two friends, Skye Yarrow and Laurie Olson, had found the evidence to convict Pearce. John Newman, Laurie's new boyfriend—was that the right word to use for a relationship at their age? Anyway, John had dubbed their group 'the posse.'

"It was a pleasure to see Pearce convicted, sir," Dana said soft voice that wouldn't carry in this noisy ballroom.

"I'm sorry for the"—he hesitated, maybe searching for the right word—"inconvenience he put you to."

"It was no problem," Dana said. Then immediately wondered why she'd dismissed being beaten up and held at gun point as no problem. Why did she placate the top one percent of the one percent?

"Your discretion was highly valued." With this, he walked away to talk with others at the top of the heap, in this case Winton Foster, owner of CyberCoast Technologies. He was accompanied by the French actress, Sabine Tourneur, the latest big star in Hollywood. Dana wondered what Nicolette would say about her outfit.

How in the world she'd gotten herself involved with all these glittering people? It made her itch. Much like the stiff collar on the blouse that matched the brocade skirt Nicolette had picked out. "It matches Kevin's tux perfectly," she'd gushed. Who knew campaigns had to have image consultants anyway?

The athletes came next. Blast the man for expecting her to know their names. He should have gotten his son for this part. Minh not only knew who they were, but he could quote statistics, talk about what team they were on before their current one. Plus, her son looked great in a tux. Suddenly, Marcus Robertson floated up behind her as if by magic and whispered a name in her ear. He hovered there, continuing to supply all the information she needed to make it through the throng of quarterbacks, basketball centers, and semi-famous hockey players. Kevin's campaign manager Marcus was worth every penny of his eye-popping salary.

After the parade of athletes, Dana dredged up a smile for the lesser endowed millionaires who circled like carrion birds, waiting to make a deal with the likely next representative from Washington State. Her feet were numb and her bra was probably drawing blood by now. Not that she was well endowed like her friend Skye, but after the kids, well...

She took out her previously crisp handkerchief—the lace now drenched, the linen crumpled—and pressed it on her forehead and under her nose. She wished she could put it down her front to sop up the perspiration, but that would be in the newspapers the next morning. "Horses sweat," she remembered her mother saying, "ladies perspire." How her Vietnamese immigrant mother had picked up that phrase was beyond her. Dana wasn't having hot flashes. Not like poor Laurie, who was finally getting to the other side of that business. It was just plain hot in here. With all these bodies competing for time with Kevin, the air conditioner couldn't keep up.

Dana decided she was going to drive home tonight. She'd almost let Kevin pressure her into staying. "There's an extra bedroom in the suite. The breakfast tomorrow is important and you can help with the white-collar donors," he'd wheedled.

Honestly, instead of people, Kevin only saw dollar signs. He hadn't been like that when they'd met. They'd been interested in the same causes—income equity, better health care access, cleaning up the environment. But politics had changed him. She'd had enough. Plus, he thought she was only good with the "little people" and not the rich and famous? She snorted.

Kevin shot a disapproving glance at her.

Snorting wasn't lady-like? Dana frowned at him, then turned her head and smiled at the next person in line, a round-shouldered heiress weighed down with three strands of pearls and an emerald pendant. Marcus supplied the woman's name.

Once everyone had come through the reception line, some twice Dana suspected, Kevin put his arm around her and smiled for the photographer who suddenly appeared. Dana didn't have time to rearrange her face before the flash went off. "Go mingle," Kevin ordered, his breath a hot whisper in her ear.

She almost left then and there, but her stomach growled. Best not to drive back to Seattle when she was this hungry. She'd eat some of this expensive food, then leave. Dana turned to Marcus. "Thank you. I would have made so many mistakes without your help."

"My pleasure, ma'am. Do you need anything else?"

"I'll be fine. I'm sure you have better things to do than babysit me."

Marcus shook his head. "You are a brilliant attorney and an asset to the campaign, if you don't mind me saying so."

Dana's hand went to her heart. She felt a rush of warmth for this young man. "Thank you, Marcus. You know how to make a person feel appreciated."

"I mean it." He tilted his head toward a passing waiter. "The smoked salmon and spinach swirls are to die for."

"Good tip." Dana followed the waiter and took two from his tray. She thanked him and walked into the crowd, polished them off quickly and picking up a glass of white wine. It would be safe to drive in another hour if she only had one. Maybe two. It had been a night.

She moved through the glittering fundraiser, the scent of expensive perfume, champagne, and ambition lingering in the air. The room hummed with the clinking of glasses, laughter, and the low murmur of half-whispered gossip. Two older women stood near the champagne tower, their voices a refined murmur. They didn't notice her. Dana didn't need Marcus to recognize Eleanor Winslow, with her elegantly coiffed silver hair and a posture that spoke of old money and social dominance. She wore a brooch shaped like a falcon, a subtle nod to her late husband's aerospace empire. Eleanor whispered to her companion, "Isn't that Sabine Tourneur? My God, she's even more stunning in person. I heard she's dating a European royal, but you didn't hear that from me."

Her friend adjusted a large sapphire ring on her finger. "She must be playing the field. Word is she has connections to a certain billionaire with ties to defense contracts." Her voice was laced with amusement. Her eyes glinted with satisfaction as she took a slow sip of her cocktail, savoring the weight of the words.

Dana moved on. Two waiters lingered near the edge of the room, trays balanced effortlessly in their hands, their crisp uniforms blending into the elegant backdrop of the fundraiser. She picked up some stuffed mushrooms to munch on, then grabbed a few honey-drenched figs. The wiry man in his early thirties nodded as she thanked him. She took a few steps away and heard him say, "That man by the bar? Ex-intelligence, definitely. You can tell by the way he keeps scanning the exits."

The second waiter, with salt-and-pepper hair whose sturdy build suggested he could have bartended in the wild west, gave a slow nod. "Yeah," he muttered, glancing at the bar again. "You can always tell. They can never quite turn it off." The two of them cast another look toward the man, trying to appear inconspicuous but failing just enough that anyone truly paying attention would notice.

The younger man said, "Wonder what a guy like that is doing here."

Handing a fresh glass of champagne to a passing guest, the former bartender gave a slow nod. "Nothing good."

Dana moved just behind two women who observed the crowd. She had no idea who they were but was starting to feel a guilty pleasure eavesdropping. Did that make her a bad person? She dismissed the pinch of conscience. As soon as she left Kevin's side, she'd turned invisible to these people, like the ghosts she used to see but nobody else could. Only Kevin mattered, it seemed, which suited her just fine.

The first woman leaned in, her pearl earrings catching the light. Her platinum-blonde hair was swept into a flawless chignon, and her burgundy gown hugged her slim frame a little too tightly. "Did you see Margot's dress? I swear it's the same one she wore to last year's gala," she whispered behind a manicured hand, her voice laced with mischief.

Her companion nodded, her diamond bracelet clinking against her champagne flute. Her face was smooth, framed by a sleek auburn bob that hadn't changed in a decade. She pursed her glossy lips before delivering her verdict, her tone utterly matter of fact. "I don't care what anyone says. Botox is an investment, not an expense."

Dana wondered what had elicited this random comment until the younger woman smirked, lowering her glass. "Margot's invested heavily." The two dissolved into giggles, their laughter delicate but edged with cruelty, like a pair of well-dressed vipers enjoying the evening's entertainment.

Good Lord, Dana thought, *I wonder what they said about me.*

She stepped back and started toward the door. She'd heard about enough, but her way was blocked by Senator Howard Langston. He stood with the practiced ease of a man used to commanding rooms. His tailored navy suit hugged his broad frame, the gold cufflinks at his wrists gleaming under the chandelier's glow. He stood beside another man, the CEO of an international company, but Dana couldn't recall his name or any more details. They exchanged pleasantries and Dana took a few more steps past him.

Senator Langston must have thought she was out of hearing range, but his deep voice carried the weight of authority, even when lowered to a whisper. "You didn't hear this from me, but there's talk that the contracts Kevin's pushing aren't exactly...above board."

Dana paused near a marble column, pretending to check a message on her phone, her ears attuned to their murmured words. This was the first she'd heard of Kevin having questionable connections. With a start, she realized this didn't come as a surprise. She glanced back at the two.

The CEO smirked as he swirled amber liquid in his glass. His black tuxedo was sharp, but his posture was relaxed—too relaxed, as if he already knew the game was rigged in his favor. He had the look of a man who never hurried but always arrived first. His graying beard was trimmed to perfection, and his dark eyes gleamed with amusement. "Winton Foster and Baldwin Cress in the same room?" he mused, scanning the crowd. "That's either a sign of the apocalypse or the start of the most expensive rivalry in history."

"But Senator Whitmore isn't here. Wonder why?" The senator watched the two men, then said, "Notice how the real money's in the back corner?" he murmured, barely moving his lips. "That's where the actual deals are happening."

The CEO arched a brow. "There's a lot of foreign wealth moving around tonight. Some of it might not be welcome in the States."

Senator Langston chuckled, the sound low and knowing. "If I were Kevin, I'd be very careful right now."

They clinked glasses, their expressions unreadable, then melted back into the crowd, their conversation already lost to the hum of the night.

Something in her stomach twisted. Foreign money. Rigged contracts. Deals happening in the back corner. The casual way they spoke about it, as if this was just another night of expensive whiskey and whispered corruption, sent a chill up her spine.

She let her gaze flick across the room, following their line of sight. Baldwin Cress. Winton Foster. Kevin working the room with his politician's smile, unaware—or maybe all too aware—that he was standing in a jungle of predators.

A slow breath. A sip of champagne she'd picked up as a prop. She moved again, but before she could slip away, she noticed a man and a woman standing near the bar. An instinct told her to pause and listen. Dana didn't recognize them, but something about their presence set them apart from the usual donors and socialites.

The man stood with one hand wrapped around a glass of bourbon he had barely touched. He wasn't working the room like the other power players. Instead, he observed, his steel-gray eyes flicking between groups. His posture was casual, but there was an edge to him, the kind that made Dana instinctively classify him as someone used to being in control, even in rooms where he wasn't supposed to be. But the way he adjusted his cufflinks, a restless flick of his wrist, made her think he wasn't entirely at ease here.

The woman, on the other hand, was perfectly comfortable. She surveyed the room like she had been born into power, her midnight-blue gown complemented her rounded figure, her graying auburn hair pulled back in a soft bun. She leaned in, her voice low but edged with amusement. "I know he's an idiot, but he's our idiot." She swirled the wine in her glass.

Were they talking about Kevin? Dana wished she knew their names.

The man exhaled, the tension in his jaw almost imperceptible. He spoke near the older woman's ear, his voice just as quiet but weighted with something heavier. "We need the White—" His sentence cut off the moment his gaze flicked past the older woman's shoulder and landed on Dana.

His expression shifted in an instant, transforming from cool calculation to effortless charm, as if the previous words had never existed. "Mrs. Preston," he said smoothly, lifting his glass in a subtle toast. "May I say you look ravishing tonight." His lips curled into a smile, his perfect white teeth on prominent display

All the better to eat you with, my dear. The line from the children's story ran through her head, but Dana didn't flinch. She noted the speed of his recovery. Too fast. Too practiced. Whatever they had been talking about, they hadn't wanted her to hear it, but she'd heard enough to surmise they were talking about the president.

She returned his smile, tilting her head slightly, her grip tightening on the stem of her champagne flute. "That's very kind of you, Mr....?" she paused.

The man chuckled softly, exchanging a glance with his companion before extending his hand. "Blackwood. Damien Blackwood. And this is Ms. Olivia Mercer."

Olivia nodded, her hazel eyes assessing, though the polite curve of her lips never wavered. "A pleasure."

Dana accepted the handshake, feeling the weight of secrets. And then there was that feeling—the kind she had learned never to ignore. That instinct, sharp and insistent, telling her that tonight wasn't just about money or power.

Something bigger was at play.

"Nice to meet you." She gave them a nod and ducked behind the next group of sharks—err, donors—finally reaching the exit and making her escape. Dana felt like she'd walked through the kitchen of a greasy spoon and picked up a layer of oil. She'd have to jump in the shower when she got home.

TWO

Dana tiptoed down the stairs in the predawn to get some coffee and enjoy it on the deck before the kids woke up. Of course being teens, she'd be lucky if they woke up before lunch. Her tortoise shell cat Lele ran past her, probably dreaming of hunting mice. In the living room, she stopped dead. Marcus Robertson sat slumped in the chair next to the window. What was Kevin's campaign manager doing sitting in her house at this hour?

She pulled her silk robe tighter and gave him a closer look. "Marcus?" she whispered.

He didn't move. Maybe he was asleep. Still dressed in a tuxedo. Had he drunk too much champagne and passed out? But why here? She appreciated his help last night and felt a warmth for him, but Kevin had hired him recently. She didn't know him that well. Had Kevin given him a key to their house? That seemed unlikely. A glance at the door reassured her the lock was intact.

"How did you get in? Has something happened?" she asked in a normal tone, hoping to rouse him and not her children.

Marcus's eyes opened, but he didn't answer. He just stared at her, his expression shell-shocked.

Then she noticed something red on his jacket. And it wasn't a handkerchief in his pocket.

Was that blood?

She stepped closer. "Marcus?"

He raised a hand and reached for her.

She stopped just out of reach, a little creeped out. Then she saw it. Two bullet holes bright red against the stark white of his shirt. He'd been shot in his chest. That meant he was—Dana didn't want to finish that thought.

Looking down, she noticed Marcus's hand was not quite solid. Dana eyed him up and down. His whole body was translucent.

Marcus was a ghost.

Her shoulders fell and she stared up at the ceiling. "Not again."

Dana turned on her heel and stalked into the kitchen. *Oh my God. I'm a monster,* she thought. She'd just turned her back on poor Marcus. But why did she have to keep seeing ghosts?

The first time she'd seen one had been after she'd almost fallen to her death from the top tier of the Galactic Globes. But the woman who had fallen to her death had appeared in the hospital and followed Dana around until she and her two friends had discovered who had murdered her. Had word gotten around on the other side that she was the ghost detective?

Dana chided herself. A young man might be dead. A nice young man, a good soul. She grabbed a bag of strong French roast beans already ground and poured them into a filter, then put it on top of her favorite mug. She went through the process methodically, filling the kettle, waiting for it to boil, all the while thinking that by the time she went back into the living room, Marcus would be gone. Maybe it had all been in her imagination. Or a dream. She'd been half asleep after all.

She snorted. Fat chance. Still, hope springs eternal.

The kettle sang. Dana grabbed it before it made too much noise and poured. What if Marcus was gone, though? How would she figure out what had happened? Impatient to check, she tapped her fingers on the counter and watched the brown stream of wakefulness fill her glass mug. She leaned down to inhale the aroma, then opened the refrigerator. No oat milk today. She deserved half and half. Steeling herself, Dana walked back into the living room and there he sat. Clear as day.

Well, transparent.

For Pete's sake. Whoever Pete was. She'd never figured that out.

Dana took a gulp of her coffee and burned her tongue. She swallowed fast, dancing in place. It was just gross to spit it back into her cup. She blew over the surface and risked another sip. Better.

She considered the ghost. Dana felt sad but decided to give herself a pass for not feeling devastated by the death of this man. After all, she'd met him maybe twice. It was terrible. He was young and all, but she thought she was done with the ghost-seeing business since Kimberly had moved on. Well, there had been the girl in the antique shop, Anastasia Nikolaevna Romanov, but she'd dismissed that as a one-off. Was this getting to be a regular thing? Maybe Jade, Skye's wife, could help rid her of ghosts. Jade's family had a long history in Santería.

Marcus slumped in the chair and stared at her. Then she noticed another red dot in the center of his forehead. She jumped. This time her coffee sloshed over, burning her fingers. She switched hands and shook her fingers. What had poor young Marcus done to become the victim of a professional hit job? Wasn't that how the pros did it? One shot to the head, two to the chest?

She might as well ask. "What happened to you, Marcus? Who did this?"

"Help," he whispered, reaching for her with his pale hand.

Then he disappeared.

Dana blew out her breath. She stared at the now empty chair. Was it too early for something to be on the news? Glancing at her wrist out of habit, she remembered she'd stopped wearing a watch almost a decade ago. Risking waking the kids, she switched the television to a local station. It was five-thirty Sunday morning. Some overly caffeinated woman beamed into the camera. "No accidents this morning, but traffic is slowing southbound from 85th already. Northbound is backed up starting at Boeing Field."

Dana wondered why there was so much traffic on a Sunday. Must be some game at Lumen Field. She hit mute and went back to the kitchen for more coffee. Lele followed her, curious what all the excitement was about. When she got back to the living room, a reporter stood in front of the capitol building in Olympia. Maybe this was it. She turned up the volume.

"Late last night, the body of Marcus Robertson was found near Capitol Lake in Olympia. Mr. Robertson was last seen at a fund-raising event for Kevin Preston's campaign. Robertson had recently been hired as Preston's campaign manager in his run for the U.S. House of Representatives. The police have no suspects this early in the investigation."

Dana grabbed her phone and called Kevin, but it went to voice mail. She tried again with the same results. The third time, she left a message telling him to call her. Kevin would probably wait until after he'd spoken to everybody else. Bastard.

Lele jumped on the windowsill and was staring out, fixated on something. Probably a bird. She hissed, jumped down, and ran up the stairs. What was that about? Then came a knock on the door.

Dana flipped back the curtain just enough to get a peek at two news vans unpacking cameras in front of her house. No, no, no, no, no. This wasn't happening. She wasn't even dressed yet.

Whoever was on her porch knocked again.

Dana cinched her robe at the waist—it was too thin for a cameo appearance on the news—and opened the peephole in the door. Before she could get a word out, the reporter asked, "What do you know about the murder of—"

"No comment. This is private property. Please leave." Dana slammed the peephole shut. Vultures.

Then the tears hit. She collapsed on the sofa, cradling her head in her hands. Marcus had been nice to her. Nicer than Kevin, that was for sure. She remembered the reassuring feel of him standing behind her, solid but unobtrusive, feeding her names and little tidbits of information so she wouldn't look like a complete dufus. And he'd been so young, at least by her reckoning. She'd reviewed his resume. A recent graduate from Harvard's Kennedy School of Public Policy. A promising career ahead of him. Had Kevin said something about him being engaged? She couldn't remember.

Dana blew her nose and got to her feet. Listening for any noise from the kids but hearing nothing, she took a quick shower and put on a pair of sweats, then headed downstairs to the kitchen. She should eat some breakfast, but instead just drank more French roast and had a piece of toast, trying to remember everyone who'd come to Kevin's fund raiser. The motive was most likely political. That seemed obvious. With all the changes in the White House and Congress, the possibilities flooded her mind. Immigration, funding for the environment, loss of civil rights, firings of federal officials. The country was in an uproar and the list went on and on.

But what if it hadn't been political? Maybe somebody had used the event to disguise a personal vendetta and send the police on a wild goose chase. They'd have to investigate Marcus's private life. Check out his family history. She needed more than toast for this heavy lifting. Dana stir-fried some veggies and crumbled in tofu, added spring onion, garlic chives, and basil, then sat at the counter and ate. Lele sniffed for chicken sausage. Finding none, the feline registered her complaint with a loud meow, then walked out of the kitchen, her tail straight in the air like an exclamation mark. Dana looked down. The cat's bowl was full.

"Diva," she whispered.

She tried to wait for a decent hour to call Skye but wanted to catch her in case she might be heading in to work at her family's magical shop, Star, Stone & Flower. It was almost six-thirty now. The teens were still asleep.

"Yeah?" Skye's answered, her voice drenched in sleep.

"You know how I thought I was done seeing ghosts?"

"Oh, no."

Dana heard a whispered, "What's happening?" from Jade.

"No emergency," Skye whispered to her wife. "Go back to sleep."

Dana heard bedclothes rustling. A door close. Then Skye asked in a normal tone of voice, "Okay, what's going on?"

Dana told her about the ghost of Marcus showing up and everything she knew so far about the shooting.

"You saw him early this morning. Do they know when he was shot?"

Dana paced as she talked, trying to recall if the news had mentioned a time.

"You still there?" Skye asked.

"Yeah, I'm just trying to remember. I don't know what time it happened."

"Have you seen him again?"

"No, just the once. He reached out and asked for help, then disappeared." Dana wrapped her free arm around her middle.

"Before you panic, see if he comes back. Maybe he came to you right after it happened and he was trying to reconnect to the world of the living. Before he realized he was, you know, dead."

Dana stopped in front of the kitchen island. This hadn't occurred to her. "Maybe," she said.

"Don't make it our problem yet," Skye said.

Dana felt a tight knot in her stomach loosen when she heard the words 'our problem.' She had friends. She didn't have to face this alone.

"I'm going back to bed. I've got the day off. But call if you need to," Skye said.

"Thanks." Dana ended the call and put her phone on the island. She decided to wash the dishes and tidy up, then check to see if the

15

news vans had left. Best not to encourage them with too much curtain flapping. The hot dish water soothed her even more and her shoulders dropped. She finished up and walked back into the living room.

Marcus sat there in the same chair.

THREE

The ghost just stared at her, not saying a word. Dana stared back. He grew more solid the longer they looked at each other.

"Marcus, I'm so sorry this happened. It's not fair. Not fair at all."

He nodded.

So, he could hear her. "Can you tell me what happened?"

He touched his chest.

"Yes, you were shot in the chest and—" she flinched "—head."

Marcus stiffened, his spectral form flickering like a flame caught in a sudden gust. His hands jerked up to his head, his entire form tensing, shoulders locking.

Dana winced in sympathy. "Do you know who did this?"

Marcus stared down at his bloodied shirt, then looked up at her, eyes wide.

He must still be in shock. You were supposed to wrap a person who was in shock up in a blanket to keep them warm. Rub their hands. But Marcus was a spirit. She couldn't use any of these remedies. Maybe if she kept talking it would bring him more into focus.

"I last saw you at the fund raiser. You were standing behind me, telling me who was next in line. I appreciated your help, especially that tidbit about how Ray Wood has a charity for animals in war zones."

Marcus brightened. He opened his mouth to say something, but nothing came out.

Why wasn't he talking? Kimberly had never shut up, always criticizing her driving. Maybe he had brain damage and he couldn't think straight. Could a ghost have brain damage?

"And that tech woman who cheats in online gambling?" Dana made it a question to draw Marcus in. "I had to bite my lip to keep from giggling." She flinched. Could this be the reason he'd been shot? That he'd revealed Marsha Ferguson's secret vice?

"You don't think it was her, do you?"

Marcus shook his head.

She waited a moment, then gently asked, "What's the last thing you remember, Marcus?"

His eyes flew wide. He put his hands up in front of him.

"Who are you talking to, Mom?" Hoa's voice reached her from the stairs.

"Shit, another ghost?"

"Watch your language, Minh." Dana whirled around to find her two teenage children watching her, Minh with his hands on his hips, a sardonic expression on his face. Hoa looked around the living room as if she might see who was haunting them this time.

Dana turned back to the chair and found it empty. "Marcus?" she whispered.

"Marcus? That new guy Dad hired?" Minh asked.

"But I liked him," Hoa said.

"Me, too." Dana surveyed the kids. "Why are you up so early?"

Lele rushed in and twined around Hoa's ankles as if to comfort her, but Dana suspected she wanted chicken sausage. She'd developed a taste for it lately. Hoa leaned down and picked her up.

"I heard a lot of noise outside." One set of windows in Hoa's bedroom looked out onto the street.

"Yeah, there's a bunch of news vans out there. We came down to see what was happening," Minh said.

"Is Dad all right?" Hoa asked in a timid voice.

"He's fine. At least he's not on the news."

"So, they're here because of Marcus?"

"Yes, one of them knocked on the door and started to ask what I knew about his—" Dana didn't want to say murder "—death. I told them to get off our property."

"But why would they think—" Hoa began.

"Did you tell them you'd just ask him?" Minh snickered.

Dana frowned at him. Minh had matured after the events in the spring. When they'd gone out on John Newman's boat to rescue Laurie who'd been kidnapped by the two people who murdered Kimberly, Minh had gotten on his computer and helped identify all the boats out on the Sound. He took care of his younger sister when the adults had gone to rescue Laurie. After everything had been settled, John took Minh under his wing, giving him a summer job, teaching him more about the Puget Sound ecosystem and their Orca pods. Dana had relaxed, thinking Minh was well on his way to adulthood. But since Kevin's campaign, he'd regressed back to being a sarcastic teen partying with his friends.

Minh turned on his heel and ran back up the stairs. She heard the shower turn on. Hoa sat on the sofa petting Lele.

"Want breakfast?" Dana asked.

"Eww. I haven't even brushed my teeth."

"Well then, get up there and do it. Any requests?"

"Blueberry pancakes."

"I think I can manage that."

Hoa put Lele down. The cat protested, then climbed up on the back of the sofa and made herself comfortable. Hoa ran upstairs just as Dana got a call. It was Kevin's ring tone. She answered immediately. "What happened?"

"You left," he said.

"That's what you lead with? I told you I didn't want to do the breakfast. What about Marcus?"

"If you'd been here, you'd know."

"For heaven's sake, what happened? Were you close when he was shot? When did you find out? What do the police say?"

"Which question do you want me to answer first?"

"Kevin, a man is dead and you want to pick a fight with me?" She could hear him take a deep breath.

"I was in my hotel room. Alone." He said this last as if she'd accused him of something.

"And?" she prompted, not taking the bait.

"I got to sleep late. My phone started blowing up around four o'clock maybe, so I put it on 'do not disturb.' About ten minutes later, somebody started pounding on my door. It was the police. They told me they'd found Marcus's body in some bushes near Capitol Lake."

"Oh, my God," she whispered. "When did you last see him?"

"Maybe two o'clock. He walked me up to my suite while we talked about the schedule for the next day and plans for future ad campaigns. What am I going to do, Dana? This will sink me."

Dana felt a stab of rage. She took a deep breath to keep herself from screaming at him. "I think the death of this young man is more important than your campaign."

"Can't I feel sad and worried about my future at the same time?"

Before she could answer, Minh and Hoa ran down the steps and headed out the front door. "Going for a run," Minh called over his shoulder.

"Wait," she shouted after them, then dashed to the front window and flicked open the curtains. As soon as the kids reached to the sidewalk, they were mobbed by the press. She could hear the shouted questions from inside.

"Why do you think Marcus Robertson was murdered?"

"Did you know him well?"

"How do you feel about your dad losing his campaign manager?"

Dana stuffed her feet into a pair of shoes next to the door, which unfortunately were the high heels she'd worn last night, and flew out the front door and down the steps, ignoring the pain from the blisters on her heels. She pointed at Minh when he opened his mouth to answer and he snaped it shut, then she directed her attention to the group of reporters. "These two are minors. I am their mother. You do not have permission to speak to them."

Microphones appeared in front of her face, which she ignored. "Now, you have violated the law by accosting these children on the street."

"Accosted? Lady—"said a round-face man with an unfortunate porcine-like nose, but Dana marched right over his objection.

"You will leave immediately or I'll call the police."

"Aw, come on. It's just a few harmless questions," the same man said.

"I am an attorney. I will not hesitate to prosecute your companies." She stood straight, willing her five-four frame to stretch as tall as possible.

A young blonde stepped forward and asked, her voice snarky, "It seems murders follow you, Mrs. Preston. Any idea why that might be?"

Dana stared at the impertinent upstart, pulling what the kids called her court room face. She tried to keep her expression deadpan, but she felt one eyebrow creeping up toward her hairline. She turned to the teens. "Inside, now."

Hoa took off. But Minh followed a little slower, looking over his shoulder. She hoped he wasn't making faces at the reporters. They'd get that on camera for sure.

She pulled out her phone and started taking pictures of their vans, all the while counting down. "Ten, nine, eight."

The crews started packing up, but the insolent blonde remained where she was.

She heard a faint, "What is going on?" and realized Kevin was still on the line. She ignored him. "Seven, six, five."

"I can't believe this," the woman mumbled and headed for her van. She was a local KROL reporter.

Dana would look her up later. She held her ground until the last news van pulled away. She put the phone back up to her ear. "Kevin, you still there?"

"Yes, what happened."

"Reporters camped outside the house and they had the temerity to ask the kids about Marcus."

"The kids know about it already?"

"Uh, yeah." Dana hoped he wouldn't ask how, so she didn't give him a chance. "I think we'll need some security here. Let me know when you learn more." She ended the call and went back inside. She kicked off the shoes and considered throwing them away.

The kids were huddled around the windows. "You're so badass, Mom," Minh said, his eyes shining.

Dana didn't bother to scold him for his language. She needed to change their focus. "I think somebody asked for blueberry pancakes."

"Yes," Hoa said.

"I need help. Everyone to the kitchen."

They trooped in to find Lele waiting on the counter. She meowed. "She wants chicken sausage," Dana said.

"How do you know?" Hoa asked.

"She's taking lessons from Laurie," Minh chortled.

Her friend Laurie Olson had been in a plane that almost crashed on her way to their high school reunion last spring. Same one where Dana had dangled from a vine over a three-story drop. Laurie had passed out when the plane went into an uncontrolled dive and when she woke up, the dog her seat mate had brought on board started talking to her. Ever since, she could communicate with animals. High school reunions were to be avoided at all costs.

"Just for that, you can cook one up for Lele." Dana tossed her son the package of sausages, then pulled eggs, blueberries, and oat milk out of the fridge.

"Eww, can't we have real milk?" Hoa asked.

"They take the babies away from the cows, you know," Minh said. "It's animal cruelty."

"That's not true." Hoa grabbed her phone and started googling what her brother had said.

Dana let them squabble. She soon had batter ready and dripped water on the griddle to see if it was hot enough. The water beaded up and danced around on the surface. She took comfort in ladling out the batter and watching the cakes until little bubbles formed on the surface. She'd call a meeting of the posse so they could figure out Marcus's death. Meanwhile, she hoped Kevin would take her request for security seriously.

Minh cut up a chicken sausage for Lele, who supervised closely, then he put the rest on a plate. "Hoa, please get out the maple syrup and butter," Dana said once she had a stack ready to serve.

"Butter, but no milk? Isn't that hypocritical?" her sarcastic son asked.

"And you." She pointed at him with her spatula. "Wash off more blueberries and some raspberries if you want them."

Hoa looked up from her phone. "Mom, is Dad going to keep the government from banning Zing?"

"What are you talking about?"

"Zing."

"It's a place to post videos and stuff," Minh said, then looked at his sister. "She doesn't even know what it is."

"Right?" Hoa rolled her eyes. "Everybody's on it, but they say China uses it to spy on us or something. Congress is going to ban it. That is so lame."

Dana snorted. There were so many things wrong with that statement, she didn't know where to begin. "Do you want to eat? Get out the syrup and butter. But wash your hands first. Both of you."

CHAPTER

FOUR

A s soon as Dana pulled into Fox Fire Farm, Skye's family compound in Duvall, the kids flew out the door in search of their friends and she breathed a sigh of relief. They'd be occupied for hours. She parked next to Laurie's brand new Leaf and felt a rush of warmth. Her friends would help figure this mess out. She locked up, although that seemed unnecessary here, and walked down a narrow, winding path lined with lavender and thyme to a wide, welcoming front porch. Bundles of dried herbs hung from the beams alongside wind chimes made of shells, bones, and bits of colored glass to catch the morning sun.

Skye and Jade had built their cottage slightly away from the big family house where Skye grew up, wanting privacy for their new relationship. Her other family members sometimes did the same when they paired up. Several homes dotted the property, each built with rustic charm—weathered cedar siding, stone hearths, and stained-glass windows. Skye and Jade's was made from hand-hewn timber and river stone, with a cedar shake roof and nestled at the edge of the orchard. The scent of ripe apples and wild herbs drifted through the air. The trees wore their fall plumage in the bright

October sun. The rain had not set in yet, but it would come. No doubt of that. Two farm dogs of indeterminant breed lazed on their cushions and greeted Dana with a thump of their tails, not bothering to get up.

Dana felt her blood pressure drop at least ten points when Laurie opened the door. "Oh, my God. I can't believe this happened," Laurie said, pulling her into a hug.

A sob rose from Dana's throat, taking her by surprise. "It's not fair."

"I know." Laurie patted her back.

Skye stood beside them. "I'm so sorry. Did you know him well?"

"No. He just started maybe a month ago." Dana stood straighter, trying to push back the flood of emotions, but safe with her friends, they rose to the surface. "He was too young." She shook her head, tears leaking from the corners of her eyes.

Laurie stroked her arm, making comforting tuts.

Dana fished for a tissue in her purse and wiped her eyes. "And brilliant. He came up with such great ideas. Had good connections."

"Tragic." Skye shook her head.

"He was so nice to me at the fund raiser. Told me everybody's name and little tidbits about them so I didn't look like arm candy."

"You're too smart for arm candy, girlfriend." Laurie scoffed. "Don't get me wrong. You're gorgeous, but..."

Dana waved her hand. "I know what you mean, but that's how Kevin treats me. Bastard."

"Go get comfortable." Skye gestured toward the well-worn furniture centered around a stone hearth. Gandalf, a gray tom cat, snoozed on his cushion nearby. Skye said he'd moved into their cottage since he'd gotten old.

Jade looked up from the large, overstuffed sofa and waved her over. Dana kicked off her clogs by the door and settled at the end. Two mismatched armchairs sat across from the sofa. Laurie took the high-backed worn leather chair, knowing Skye favored the deep, plush armchair with faded floral fabric next to it. Laurie's little

Havanese jumped up beside Dana and put her paw on her chest, staring into her eyes. She wondered what Rosa was saying.

"She's worried about you. Says we'll find the bad guys." Laurie filled her in.

"Thank you, Rosa." Dana stroked her side and the little Havanese settled between her and Jade.

Skye disappeared into the kitchen and came back with a cup of steaming tea. "Chamomile and lavender for your nerves. I know you've already had too much coffee already."

Dana sputtered a laugh. "Thanks." She put the mug on a stone coaster on the massive wooden coffee table, slightly uneven and deeply scarred from years of use. She pulled a forest green and purple woven throw around herself, more for comfort than warmth. "It was just awful."

"You witnessed the murder?" Laurie asked, alarmed.

Jade studied her with professional interest.

"No, I saw him the next morning just sitting in my living room still wearing his tux. It was really early. I thought he'd let himself in. Wanted to talk about something. Then I saw the red dots." She shuddered.

Laurie's frowned. "Red dots?"

"Some guns shot wounds leave little red dots where the bullet enters the body," Jade explained.

"Three of them. Two in his chest and one in his head." Dana's throat tightened, her voice raspy.

"A professional hit," Jade said in a low voice.

Dana nodded. "I guessed that might be the case."

"Did he say who killed him?"

She shook her head. "Poor guy. He's so confused. When I asked him what he remembered, he just disappeared."

"Kind of like Kimberly," Laurie said.

"Way sadder."

Laurie reached for her mug. "Kimberly remembered more as time went by, though. Maybe he will, too."

"If he keeps showing up," Dana said.

"Have you seen him again?" Skye asked.

"Twice this morning. Then again just before we left. He kept trying to pick up my coffee cup, so I just poured one for him. He seemed to take some comfort in the smell."

"Fresh coffee smells so good," Laurie said. "Did he say anything?"

Dana shook her head. "Just watched me with those sad eyes. I asked him how I could help him a few times, but he doesn't seem to be able to talk yet."

"He needs something," Jade said. "Once we figure it out, we can give him a sendoff like we did with Kimberly."

"And after that? Do I ever get to stop being the ghost whisperer?"

"You could quit your job. Become a medium," Laurie quipped.

Dana snorted, then looked at from Skye to Jade. "You guys know any ways to stop seeing ghosts?"

Skye gave her a sympathetic smile. "We can check the family grimoire, but—"

"Grimoire, what's that?"

"It's a journal where witches record their spells and healing recipes. That kind of thing," Skye said.

"They're usually passed down through families," Jade explained. "My grandmother still grieves for the one we lost during the slave times."

"A big loss. My family's is ancient. When you go back a couple hundred years, it switches from English to Gaelic, both Scottish and Irish, depending on who wrote the spell. Momma made me learn both." Skye sounded aggrieved.

Jade chuckled.

"It was hard work," Skye objected.

Dana and Laurie stared at them, eyes wide.

"Anyway, there might be a spell or two in ours that would help, and Jade's family specializes in spirits. I'll ask my cousin Iona if I can show you sometime. She's our official keeper these days."

"Uh, thanks," Dana said, flummoxed.

27

Jade sat up straighter. "Did you see anything suspicious at the fund raiser? A starting point for us to investigate?"

"The whole thing was suspicious." Dana waved her hand in the air. "They had me all dolled up in a tight skirt. Five-inch heels. I mean you should see my blisters." She stuck her foot out, now clad in wool hiking socks.

"Five inches?" Skye's eyebrows rose

"And you wore them?" Jade sounded skeptical.

"How's your back?" Laurie asked.

"I had to stand in this line forever making small talk with billionaires and athletes. What do I know about sports? Minh would have been in heaven."

"That's for sure," Laurie said. She'd spent a lot of time with him during the summer.

"I wanted to leave as soon as I shook the last hand—"

"Did you take your rings off?"

Dana frowned at Laurie. "What?"

"The queen used to take off her rings so her hands wouldn't get hurt."

"Okay, Ms. Anglophile."

"It's true. I saw it on a documentary."

Dana picked up her tea and took a sip. "Hum, this is good. Anyway, I just wanted to go home. Leave Kevin high and dry at his breakfast meeting."

"Good for you."

She nodded. "But I was starving, so I grabbed some food and a glass of wine."

"Ooh, good stuff."

"Passable, but the smoked salmon and spinach swirls—" Dana gasped.

"What?"

"Marcus told me they were to die for."

There was a respectful silence.

Dana recovered. "The point is I wandered around snacking so I

28

wouldn't be hungry on the drive home. I mean, I turned invisible once I wasn't next to Kevin and you wouldn't believe what I heard. The waiters thought they'd spotted a spy. Some rich folks were wondering what Winton Foster and Baldwin Cress were plotting."

"He was there?"

"Asshole. That new woman he's with has had too much plastic surgery."

Jade and Skye looked at each other and shook their heads.

"What?"

"Different world," Skye said.

"That's for sure. I think Kevin is in over his head. Senator Langton think's some contracts Kevin's negotiating are suspicious and, good Lord, two people were talking about the president as if they owned him."

"You think all this has something to do with what got Marcus killed?" Laurie asked.

"There was so much intrigue there I don't know where to start."

"Sounds like we need to do some research," Jade said.

A laptop sat open on the coffee table among the clutter of crystals, small bowls of dried herbs, and three pillar candles. A small carved fox figurine was almost lost among the clutter, a protective totem from the first years of the farm. The red wood matched the gleam of Skye's hair when she leaned forward to set her own teacup down. "What's going to happen now? I mean with Kevin's campaign?" she asked.

"You going to divorce him if he wins?" Laurie dove straight to the point, as usual.

"Don't think I'll need to. He'll be in D.C. I'll be here. Nary the twain shall meet." Dana finished off her tea and burrowed into the cushions. "Besides, it would create political waves. I don't want to be in the press."

"Goddess forbid," Jade said.

"Do you know a bunch of them swarmed the kids when they

went out for a run this morning? Trying to get information about the . . ." she hesitated, then whispered, "murder."

"The press was at your house?"

"Yes, at the crack of dawn. Several vans and that perky know-it-all from KROL. Suggested that I attract murders."

"No way," Skye said.

"The nerve." Jade's mouth pressed into a thin line.

"Anybody need anything before we get started?" Skye asked, getting them back on track.

Laurie lifted her coffee cup as answer and Jade shook her head no. Skye went to get Laurie a refill.

"Where should we begin?" Dana asked. "I remember some of the names of the suspicious people at the event."

"Let's find out everything we can about Marcus first," Jade suggested.

She was the pro, so they agreed. Skye returned with fresh coffee and a plate full of chocolate chip cookies fresh from the oven. They all reached for one at the same time.

Jade nudged the computer awake and started typing. A few windows opened. As a police officer, she had access to several protected data bases, but Dana was an attorney and knew Jade would be cautious about which ones she used.

She echoed Dana's thought. "Since this will be a sensitive case, I'll have to stay off some sites."

"Yes, do keep your job, dear." Skye smiled at her.

Jade looked up from the screen, her silver reading glasses picking up new gray in her hair. "For you, anything. Now, do you know his full name?"

Laurie got out an iPad and Dana poked her phone to life. Laurie answered before Dana could even type anything on the tiny screen. "The Seattle Times reports it as Marcus Alexander Robertson."

Jade clicked away, then sat back. "Hmm."

Dana adjusted herself on the couch so she could see Jade's

computer screen, but only columns of names were visible. Rosa objected when she tried to move closer.

"Huh." Jade opened a search window and typed some more. She squinted at the screen, then after another minute, started clicking on names.

Dana could see that much at least. More tabs opened.

Jade inhaled sharply.

"What?" Laurie asked.

Jade shook her head. Clicked each tab and read quickly.

Faster than Dana could follow.

"Oh, my," Jade said, but just kept reading.

"What? You're killing us," Dana finally said.

"Aren't you reading over my shoulder?"

"I can't keep up with you. Gary usually does my cyber snooping. And Maxwell when we need extra help."

Jade sat back and propped her ankle on her opposite knee. "Our Marcus came from a very interesting family."

"Interesting how?" Laurie asked.

Jade picked up her cup and frowned. Skye reached over and poured more hot coffee for her. "Thanks, sweetie." She took a sip and then sat back. "This is going to get deep. He was born in D.C. in 1996, went to private schools, was on the debate team, summer camps in New England. Attended Georgetown University, majoring in political science and international relations. yadda, yadda, yadda." She waved her hand in the air, then took a sip of coffee.

Laurie wrinkled her forehead. "That all sounds pretty normal."

"Yes, on the surface. Master's in public administration from Harvard's Kennedy School of Public Policy."

"Yeah, Kevin was impressed with that," Dana said. "And I know he worked for the Seattle mayor's campaign."

"Right, and before that was a congressional fellow, and then a consultant at Polaris Strategies."

Dana frowned. "I'm not familiar with them."

Jade clicked to another tab and read, "*A top political consulting firm specializing in crisis management and grassroots mobilization.* Looks like they help underdog candidates develop a great public image. Focus on improving liberal candidates' chances in swing districts."

"I wouldn't call Kevin liberal," Dana scoffed. "Not really."

Laurie laughed. "He seems liberal to the public. You have an insider's perspective."

Dana gave her a wry look. "That I do."

"So, where's the intrigue?" Skye asked.

"Well, his family." Jade snagged a cookie and held up a finger while she chewed quickly. "His father was a former CIA analyst turned private security consultant. The mother is a corporate attorney who works in contracts and lobbies for major tech firms with ties to government regulations."

"So, his parents are power brokers," Laurie summed up.

"The CIA makes me wonder," Dana said, "especially after some of the things I heard at the fund raiser."

"That's not all," Jade said. "I've heard of his older brother, Derek, at work. He has a reputation as a fixer for high-level financial crimes. Let's say he knows how to make problems disappear, legally or otherwise. He's never been formally charged, but he's been a suspect in other states for insider trading. Got a ton of offshore accounts. Derek followed his brother to Seattle and got involved with local organized crime connections."

"Geez." Dana fell back on the cushions. "Something could have gone wrong from any of these connections. The suspect pool is getting bigger and we haven't even looked at Kevin's activities."

"There's more." Jade opened another tab. "His fiancée works as a media consultant for prominent candidates. Her resume says she specializes in damage control, political messaging, and voter outreach strategies."

Laurie frowned. "Damage control doesn't sound entirely above board."

"Depends," Dana said.

Jade pressed on. "Name's Madeline Carrington."

"Carrington?" Laurie mumbled. "Wonder if she's related to Dora Carrington."

"Who?" Skye asked. "What do you know about her?"

"Oh, never mind." Laurie waved her hand. "Dora Carrington was a painter during the modernist period."

"Modernist?" Jade asked, her forehead wrinkling.

"You know, like Virginia Woolf and James Joyce."

The other three looked at each other baffled. "What does this have to do with—" Jade started to ask.

"Nothing. Sorry." Laurie blushed. "I just—"

Dana felt a rush of warmth for her friend. "Laurie might be out talking to whales these days, but she'll always be an English professor."

Jade shook her head and looked back at her screen. "Our Carrington"—she emphasized the first word—"studied political science at Yale before earning a master's in political communications at Columbia. Based on her social media activity, looks like she met Marcus in D.C. and followed him out here once they got engaged. That was less than a year ago."

"This is so sad," Dana said. "He was such a good guy."

"Which is remarkable given his family background." Jade gave a disbelieving chuckle.

"He treated me well." Dana felt defensive on Marcus's behalf.

"Yes, so we want to help him settle his earthly business and move on." Skye gave Dana a sympathetic smile, then asked Jade, "Where should we start?"

Jade closed the laptop with a snap. "I say with the fiancée."

CHAPTER
FIVE

"I've spoken with the police already." Maddie didn't look anything like the polished profile picture on her website. Her long, chestnut brown hair, styled in soft waves in the photo, was now pulled back in a messy ponytail. She studied Dana and Laurie with red-rimmed eyes.

"We're sorry to bother you in this time of grief." Dana winced inwardly. She sounded like some mortician trolling for business. "I'm Kevin Preston's wife—"

"I know who you are, Mrs. Preston." She looked at Skye and Laurie expectantly.

"I'm Skye Yarrow, Dana's friend."

"Laurie Olson." She stuck out her hand and Maddie shook it reluctantly. "We came to support Dana."

"I see." She focused back on Dana. "I hadn't realized you knew him so well." Maddie's tone suggested she knew the opposite was true.

Dana didn't quite know how to proceed. She couldn't exactly say Marcus was hanging around her and his ghost was unlikely to leave until she solved his murder. Or at least figured out what he wanted.

And he wasn't talking yet. "Marcus was so helpful to me that night. He helped Kevin enormously in the short time he was with him. Things were really taking off."

"I'm not interested in working for Kevin." Maddie said, her gaze assessing. She did not invite them in.

A door down the hall opened and a woman with a standard poodle walked out, giving them a curious glance. The woman's silver raincoat matched the bling on the dog's collar. Rosa took a step toward the dog, but the woman hauled the poodle away. Laurie looked down at the two and gave a little snort of surprise.

Maddie nodded at her neighbor as she walked to the elevator bank, then turned to Dana. "You'd better come inside." She looked down at Rosa who sat and wagged her tail, looking up with brown eyes that were pools of doggie love. Maddie bent down and stroked Rosa's head. "Such a good puppy."

Rosa licked her hand and gave a whine that sounded sympathetic.

"Thank you." Maddie straightened.

Dana wondered for a wild second if Maddie could hear Rosa, too, but she gestured for them to walk into the living room. Marcus and Maddie's apartment perched on the fifteenth floor of a sleek high-rise in Belltown. Floor-to-ceiling glass windows framing a panoramic view of Elliott Bay drew the three friends over. Gray and cobalt blue clouds shrouded what would have been a spectacular view of the Olympic Mountains.

"You get used to it. Make yourselves comfortable," Maddie said, but they continued to take in the view. "It's too easy to forget how beautiful it is. That things are fleeting." She gestured toward a low-profile, charcoal gray sectional.

Dana, Laurie, and Skye arranged themselves on the sofa, leaving room for Maddie at the end. Rosa sat on Laurie's foot. Maddie grabbed up a stack of folders from a glass coffee table with brass legs. "I'll just get this mess out of the way." Maddie ducked into the back of the apartment, to hide her fresh tears Dana guessed.

She scanned the newspapers on the table, the local Seattle newspaper vied with the New York Times, Washington Post, London Times, the Süddeutsche Zeitung, in German no less, and political journals Dana was less familiar with.

Laurie picked up an old copy of *The Art of War* with a dozen dog-eared pages. "An old favorite, I guess." She replaced it quickly when Maddie came back and hovered near the kitchen door.

"Please don't go to any trouble," Dana said. "We won't take much of your time."

Maddie walked to the other side of the sofa and stood, arms crossed in front of her. "I don't mean to be rude, but three of you seems a bit like overkill."

Dana winced at the word, then tried to suppress her reaction when Marcus appeared beside his fiancée, more solid than ever. Rosa gave a little woof. Skye shot Dana a knowing look, then explained to Maddie, "We're concerned about Dana's safety."

"You're her security detail?" Maddie gave her a skeptical look.

Laurie let out an easy laugh. "I know we might not look like much, but last spring, I was kidnapped by a murderer—"

"You?" Maddie interrupted. Then she pointed her index finger at Laurie. "I remember something about this in the deep background check we ran. Was it that crazy writer Baldwin was so excited about?"

She's on a first name basis with the owner of Galactic. Interesting, Dana thought.

"That's the one," Laurie continued. "Since then, we've trained in self-defense. Skye was a pretty good shot already. Her family has a farm out near Duvall." She said this as if it explained Skye's use of firearms.

"My family used to hunt and my father wants us all to be safe since our land is a bit isolated," Skye added.

"I see." Maddie settled on the end of the sofa and faced Dana. "Why are you worried about your safety?"

Marcus sat on the arm of the couch, his arms around his fiancée.

Dana tried to keep her attention on Maddie and not the ghost. "We've been mobbed by the press at my house."

Maddie snorted as if the press was as common as house flies, but Dana pushed on. "And I don't know why Marcus was—" she hesitated, searching for a softer word.

"Assassinated?" Maddie supplied with an arched brow. Her eyes might be red from crying, but she was as fierce as a lioness.

"Well, yes. Could Kevin be a target? Are you?"

Maddie looked them over for a full minute during which Marcus walked around his old home looking at his former possessions. He tried to pull some books off the bookshelf but frowned when his fingers went right through them. Rosa got up to follow him, but Laurie called her to come back.

Finally Maddie said, "Why don't you trust the police with this? Do you seriously think three, pardon me, middle-aged women are better detectives than they are?"

"My wife is on the police force. She thinks the detectives aren't always as thorough as they should be." Skye held her palms up. "You never heard that from me, of course."

Maddie's mouth crooked up. "Of course not. We're both political consultants. As you can imagine, we're privy to quite a few secrets, both political and personal, but I can't think of anything that would have gotten Marcus killed."

Skye's nod was almost imperceptible, but Dana knew what it meant. When Laurie had been arrested for killing Kimberly and they'd tried to figure out who'd really done it, Skye had told Dana and Laurie that she was an empath. She could tell what people were feeling—their moods, read the atmosphere of a room, and best of all, she knew when people were lying. Maddie was telling the truth.

Dana hunched her shoulders. "I can't tell you how sorry I am. He really was a rare one. Kind, smart—"

A sob shook Maddie and she leaned over, clutching her sides. Dana wanted to hug her, to offer some comfort, but she didn't think Maddie would welcome that. Besides, Marcus had wrapped his arms around her, his face full of love. Dana realized with a start that she could see him quite clearly now. Maybe he'd be able to remember more soon.

"Oh, sweetie." Skye made little comforting sounds. Rosa ran over and leaned against her legs.

Maddie rocked back and forth. "I'm sorry," she gasped out between sobs. Rosa put her front paws on Maddie's leg and tried to lick her face. She hugged the dog to her.

"It's all right. We understand." Dana fished in her purse and pulled out a clean tissue, offering it to the grieving fiancée. She pulled one out for herself and dabbed her eyes. It would be unseemly for her to break down in front of this woman who'd just lost the man she was going to marry. An equal partner by the looks of things.

The storm of tears passed and Maddie sat up, wiping her face and blowing her nose. She fanned her face with her hand. "Whew. It just sneaks up on me sometimes."

Dana reached over and patted her shoulder. Maddie surprised her by leaning into the touch. "Thank you for understanding," she said.

"Of course," Skye said.

Rosa sat and wagged her tail at Marcus.

Good Lord, Dana thought. She hoped Maddie wouldn't notice the little Havanese staring at thin air, but she only looked at each of them, her face serious. "You three should be careful if you're going to be poking into this."

"I hope you'll be careful as well." Dana looked at the built-in bookcase along the wall. She'd spotted several cardboard boxes stacked next to it while Marcus had been back there. "You look like you're busy. It's really not my place to ask, but are you packing Marcus's things or..." She left the rest of the question hanging.

"I'm going back home. I moved to Seattle to be with Marcus, but now..." Maddie lifted her shoulder, still elegant even in her disheveled grief.

Dana stood. "Please let us know if we can help in any way. I think Kevin is planning a memorial."

"Yes, his staff has been in touch. The funeral will be in D.C. Just family and friends. They have a plot." She bit her lip, holding back more tears.

"May I use your restroom?" Laurie interrupted.

"Sure. Second door on the right."

Dana gave Laurie a questioning look, then spoke to Maddie before the woman noticed. "I'll insist Kevin offer you security if you feel that you need it. In fact, even if you don't, maybe it's a good idea anyway."

Maddie's smile held genuine warmth. "My father has set something up, but you are kind to offer."

"Please let us know if you remember anything that might make sense of this," Dana said.

Maddie walked them to the door as soon as Laurie returned. "I will. Take care." She opened the door and Dana was startled to see a man in a black suit standing in the hallway.

A low growl rumbled in Rosa's throat.

"It's okay, girl. Looks like my security has arrived," Maddie said.

Dana gave the man an appraising glance. He stood like a soldier and she noticed a slight bulge on his right hip. "Good."

The three left the apartment building and stepped into the chilly fall rain that had finally decided to make an appearance. They put up their hoods and umbrellas and dashed down the street to a coffeeshop. Inside, Rosa shook thoroughly, much to the chagrin of a nearby customer. They ordered. Hot coffee drove off the chill.

"Well, she let her guard down a lot," Skye said after they settled at a table. "She was telling the truth."

"Good to know." Laurie wrapped her hands around her mug. "And you, Ghost Whisperer. I saw you watching something at that bookcase none of the rest of us could see. Except for Rosa. Spill it."

Dana took another sip, letting the warmth of the latte seep into her. "Marcus showed up almost immediately. He was looking at his books while we talked, surprised he couldn't pick one up."

"Think he's getting over the shock yet?" Laurie asked.

"Maddie's grief seemed to pull him in more. He's getting more solid. I hope his memory starts to come back."

"That would make things a lot easier." Laurie looked over at Skye, who'd opted for green tea.

She swallowed quickly. "What was that little trip to the bathroom about?"

Laurie pulled the edge of some blue fabric up from her purse. "A man's t-shirt. Rosa might need Marcus's scent. She caught his scent in the apartment, but I wanted to get something just in case, so I found the laundry basket."

Dana frowned. "I hope she doesn't miss that shirt."

"He traveled a lot, so she'll probably think he left it somewhere if she even notices," Laurie reasoned.

"Hope so." Dana felt a bit disgruntled.

Laurie looked at Skye. "What's next?"

Skye and dabbed her mouth with a paper napkin. "Getting background on who was at the fundraiser. Have you gotten a list yet, Dana?"

"It's on my computer. I'll send it to Jade and you two."

"We should know as much as possible before we go to the memorial. Unless our ghost tells us who shot him before that." Skye's phone played some New Orleans jazz and she answered. "Hey, sweetie. What's up?" After a few uh, huhs and then an ooh, Skye ended the call. "Jade's got hotel footage."

"Let's get over there." Laurie jumped to her feet and Rosa let out an excited bark. The barista frowned and Laurie mouthed, "Sorry."

"The list of people who attended the fundraiser—" Skye pointed at Dana "—it's not on your phone, right?"

"I think it's on my laptop."

"Let's swing by so you get it, then head out to Fox Fire."

"THIS IS A WORK COMPUTER." Jade patted a tactical case. "The Olympia police force reached out for help and my unit got assigned."

"Lucky break," Dana said.

Skye chuckled. "We made a magical request."

Dana caught Laurie's attention and raised her eyebrows. "Right?" Laurie whispered.

Jade opened the case and hooked up the computer while the rest of them jostled for space so they could see the screen. She turned it on and it fired up almost immediately. She handed Dana a thumb drive. "Download the list of guests for the event."

"Just send an attachment," Laurie said.

"Not secure," Dana and Jade said at the same time, then looked at each other and laughed.

"We need the names of the staff and security who attended as well." Dana got out her laptop.

Jade clicked on a folder labeled 'Budd Bay Inn' and a bunch of video files popped up. "What floor was Kevin on?"

"Uh, I don't remember," Dana said.

Jade gestured to the list. "I don't want to check them all. Each floor has several cameras."

Laurie poked her phone. "I'll see where the suites are located."

"Good idea," Skye said.

"Wait, I think it was the ninth. I remember him complaining he didn't get the top floor with the best view."

"We can cross-check that list with the hotel registration when it's ready," Jade said.

Dana finished copying the guest names and handed the thumb drive over to Jade. It took her only a minute to come up with a list of who'd stayed in the hotel. She clicked on that folder and dates appeared. She picked the day of the fundraiser and studied the options.

"The good views are on the west side. Starting with room 919."
Laurie turned her phone around to show them the hotel map.

Jade opened the list of guests and cross-checked it with the hotel
register. Dana didn't ask how she had access. "Yep, Kevin was in
919," Jade said.

She went back to the list of video feeds and clicked two cameras.
Each end of the ninth-floor hallway appeared. She sped up the feed
and they watched until people appeared, then slowed to normal
speed. The suites took up a lot of space, so there were only two on
the west side. They watched Senator Langston's group check in, the
security guys going in first, then his staff swarming in carrying
luggage and computer bags.

"Any cameras inside the rooms?" Dana asked.

"If there are, the hotel hasn't admitted it," Jade said.

Jade sped up the video and about an hour later, Kevin's group
arrived. Marcus waited for the security check, then he went in and
out, directing the team to bring in their equipment and boxes. Once
they were inside, Jade fast-forwarded through the hours, slowing
down to watch Kevin and Dana arrive, then the senator. People came
and went from the two suites. In the evening, Dana walked toward
the elevators, her face crunched up.

"God, I can't believe I wore those shoes," she said.

A few minutes later, Senator Langston went down with his aides.
The tape showed an empty hallway until it ran out. "Let's check the
next day, starting right after midnight," Jade said.

"Kevin told me that Marcus escorted him up around two o'clock
and he started getting texts about his death around four."

"That window is helpful. Still, we need to see if anybody suspicious is hanging around or gets a room earlier in the day. They could
even have set up a couple days before."

Skye let out a long sigh.

"Babe, you don't have to sit here. It gets tedious going through
these videos."

Skye leaned forward. "I want to see what happens after Marcus leaves Kevin."

Jade found the time stamp and went back about half an hour, then put it in fast forward. The hall remained empty until the two men appeared, their heads together in conversation. Jade slowed it down and moved back to when they first showed up. The talked, then Marcus pulled out his phone and showed it to Kevin.

"Kevin said they talked about his schedule. That's probably what he's showing him," Dana said.

The two talked a couple more minutes, then Kevin went inside and a bodyguard took up his post outside the door. Marcus walked a few steps toward the elevator, then took out his phone and squinted at the screen. He looked around, searching for something, then hurried toward the exit sign at the end of the corridor. He pushed open the door and went through.

"Stairways, stairways," Jade murmured, searching for the right folder. "Shit, no cameras for the stairways. That's a big oversight."

"What room was Marcus in?" Laurie asked.

Jade switched tabs. "Room 502. Not the best view." But Marcus did not appear on the video feed. They ran it back and forth, extending the time window.

"Looks like he didn't go to his room," Skye said. "Whoever called him might have asked to meet him somewhere. It could be the murderer."

"Let's check the public areas." Jade squinted at the list. "Probably not the gym." The bar of the hotel appeared on the screen. No Marcus. Jade switched to the lobby. A few people left, but Marcus was not among them. She ran it three times to be sure.

"Are there any exterior cameras?" Laurie asked.

They studied the files and opened one covering the front. Marcus never appeared there. Jade searched for more external cameras, Dana leaning close to help, but they came up with nothing.

Jade sat up and rubbed her neck. "He could have gone to another person's room. It will take hours to search for him, but we've already got two uniformed officers scouring every video."

"Any security cameras around Capitol Lake?" Laurie asked.

Jade shook her head. "Nothing."

"He just disappeared," Dana said.

Skye walked over and squeezed Dana's shoulder. "We'll find out who did this. Don't despair."

"I have an idea," Laurie said. "I'll take the nose down there. Maybe she can sniff out his trail. Get the scent of the killer even."

"You're calling Rosa the nose now?" Dana asked.

"Honestly, I think she's got some bloodhound in her mix," Laurie said.

"Psh." Jade shook her head. "All dogs have a fantastic sense of smell. We use German Shepards at work. I think it's a great idea, but don't go alone."

"I'm free tomorrow," Skye said. "We can drive down. Most of our dogs have some hound in them. I'll bring a dog or two."

"And some discreet protection," Jade said. At Skye's skeptical look, she added, "Please."

"Oh, all right."

CHAPTER

SIX

Skye and Laurie pulled into the parking lot of the Budd Bay Inn in Olympia and found a spot between several cars. They'd taken her old Subaru because three dogs didn't fit in Laurie's new Leaf. "Best they don't see my beat up car when we go inside asking for a favor."

"Good plan," Laurie said. She snapped a leash onto Rosa's collar and waited while Skye grabbed the harnesses and leashes for her two dogs. "Ashe, come here girl." The huge, mostly gray and white husky who looked suspiciously like a wolf acquiesced, but the brown and black farm dog seemed less inclined. "Taran, we need to go inside and you have to be on the leash."

"Taran?" Laurie asked.

"Means 'thunder' in Welsh. He's mostly hound, but his head is wide and all black. We think one of the neighbors had a Rottweiler."

"And the wolf?"

Skye shrugged. "We've been on the farm a long time. The wolves must have paid a few visits over the years."

Laurie put her hand under Taran's chin and lifted his head to meet her gaze. After a few seconds, the dog leaned against Skye. Laurie chuckled. "He says just this once."

Inside, Laurie approached the front desk. "We're with Kevin Preston's campaign and he asked us to check for an external hard drive that was lost during the unfortunate events last weekend."

"Such a tragedy." The slender man at the desk slumped his shoulders. "We're very sorry for your loss."

"Thank you," Skye said, giving Taran a nudge to sit. The clerk eyed their dogs.

"Mr. Preston couldn't spare any security personnel—" Laurie made up the story as she went along "—so we brought some four-legged protection."

"They're good dogs. Well trained. Won't hurt anyone unless somebody tries to hurt us," Skye reassured the man.

It was complete bull.

Rosa perched on her hind quarters and stretched out her paw. The man smiled. "She's a cutie. I'll check lost and found."

"Maybe we should have snuck in," Skye said after he ducked into the back office.

He returned, shaking his head. "Nothing there."

"Can we look in the suite?" Laurie asked.

The man checked the computer. "Looks like nobody's been in it since the event. The hard drive could still be there, although the police were quite thorough. They just took the crime tape down, so I suppose you can take a look around." He handed them a keycard.

"Thank you so much," Laurie said.

They headed for the elevator. Taran balked, but Rosa bumped against him and the big hound followed her inside. Upstairs, the maid's cleaning cart was parked on another hallway. "Do we need to go in the room?" Skye whispered.

"I don't think so."

"I'll open the door just in case they have some way of tracking it." Skye stuck the plastic card into the slot and the light turned green. She opened the door and waited a few seconds, then closed it again.

The dogs sat watching, wondering what the humans were up to. Laurie pulled out the old t-shirt she'd nicked from Maddie's apartment and held it out to the three canines. They gathered round and sniffed, nostrils flaring, their heads moving from side to side.

"Follow this scent," Laurie whispered to the dogs.

The three canines fanned out in the hallway, noses to the ground. They milled around the door of the suite, then tracked back toward the elevator and stopped. Rosa turned back and the other dogs followed, noses to the ground, retracing his steps. Ashe gave a low woof and started toward the stairway door. The others shadowed her.

It was as if they'd watched the video, Laurie thought.

The pack stopped at the door and Rosa trotted back to get Laurie. *Please open the door*, Rosa said.

Laurie happily obliged.

Thank you, came the gruff voice of Taran in her mind.

Such a good boy, Laurie said mentally to him.

Humans, Ash grumbled. *Always with the baby talk.*

With that comment, the canines ran down the stairs, the humans in their wake. The dogs stopped a few floors down, milling around the landing.

"It's the fifth floor. Didn't Marcus have a room down here?" Skye asked.

"I think so. Seems to be a lot of his scent here. Maybe he usually took the stairs instead of the elevator. He seemed fit."

Rosa scratched at the door and Laurie opened it. The dogs surged through, noses to the ground like an army of vacuum cleaners sucking up any lingering smell. They reached the end of the hall and rounded the corner, leaving Laurie and Skye in their wake. A woman screeched and a man's voice said, "It's okay, Rachel. Where did you come from?" He seemed to be addressing the dogs.

Laurie and Skye ran to catch up. "They're with us. Sorry for the surprise," Skye said.

"Is this animal part wolf?" the man asked, clearly fascinated by Ashe who watched him with her eerily intelligent eyes.

"Maybe. We're not sure."

"I didn't know this hotel allowed pets." The woman pulled her jacket tighter around her.

"We're just visiting," Laurie said over her shoulder, following the dogs who had already taken off down the next hall. They stopped near the end in front of a door and sniffed around, Ashe whining.

Laurie checked the room number. "502. Wasn't this his room?"

Of course, you think we'd make a mistake? Rosa asked.

"Sorry to doubt you." Laurie said this out loud and Skye snorted a laugh.

All three dogs sat and stared at Laurie.

"What?" Skye asked.

"They're telling me the trail ends here, but that the scent in the stair was a little bit fresher." Laurie looked down at the canines. "Should we go back to the other stairs?"

They took off again.

"Wait," Skye huffed.

The two humans ran after them, hoping they wouldn't run into any more humans. Turning the corner, they almost collided into the maid, who pointed behind her. "Perros."

"Sí, son nuestras," Laurie answered without stopping. "Gracias."

Rosa sat watching Laurie catch up while the other two dogs had decided to lay down and take a rest. Skye pushed the door open. Taran heaved himself to his feet and the dogs poured through, noses to the steps.

The smell is stronger, Rosa sent, and Laurie relayed the message to Skye. They reached the bottom of the stairs and the dogs milled around, waiting for the laggard humans to arrive and open the door.

Skye hesitated. "Should we put them on leashes?"

"I don't think so, but"—Laurie looked down at the eager faces—"let me check for cars and people."

We already did. There's nobody out there, Rosa replied.

48

"Still, be careful. No squished dogs," Laurie said out loud to include Skye in the conversation.

"Yes, please. Be careful," Skye said. She pushed the door open and held the dogs back. She stuck her head out and looked around. "Clear."

The dogs surged out. They emerged at the side of the hotel near Capitol Lake. A narrow black-top road separated the brick hotel from a riot of green with some orange and yellow mixed in. Rosa ran across and disappeared into the bushes. The other two followed.

Laurie looked over at Skye, her mouth crooked. "Guess we're going bushwacking."

"Let's hope there's a path."

The humans pushed through a cluster of Oregon grape and found a faint trail leading down the hill. A riot of ocean spray, spirea, and red elderberry bushes covered the hillside. Rhododendrons and azaleas dotted the path with red-osier dogwood and shore pine trees offering handy branches to hang onto when the trail got steep. The humans kept their eyes to the ground, looking for anything that might have been left from Marcus's trip down the hill. After a few minutes of scrambling, they emerged onto the packed gravel loop that surrounded the lake. The dogs had not waited. The two looked around for them and were answered by barks.

"Rosa says they've found him," Laurie said.

They broke into a jog and found the dogs clustered close to the water in the middle of thimbleberry bushes. Rosa trotted up to Laurie and sat in front of her. *This is where his trail ends. There's blood.*

Laurie translated for Skye, then address all three dogs. "Did you find another strong scent here?"

Ashe glanced at her companions. Noses to the ground once more, then checked the area. After a few minutes, the three sat and stared at them. "What?"

Many humans have been here and two German Shepherds, Rosa reported.

"Right." Laurie spoke out loud once again. "A lot of cops searched this area. Is there a smell that is as old as Marcus's?"

Ashe gave Laurie an approving look.

"You can tell?" Laurie asked Ashe.

You seem surprised, came the smooth voice of the wolf.

"You have quite superior senses." Laurie was still speaking out loud so Skye could keep up.

Ashe looked pleased, then all three dogs put their noses to the ground. While they waited, Laurie picked a few bright red caps from the thimbleberry bushes and popped them into her mouth. "I missed this fruit in Boston."

"You're having a snack at the murder scene?"

Laurie paled. "Sorry, Marcus."

Skye picked a few herself. Rosa trotted up to them and reported that there was another older smell belonging to a man.

"Do you get a picture of what he looked like?"

Humans and their eyes, Ashe scoffed.

Laurie felt a stab of annoyance, which the dogs picked up immediately.

We've helped you, Taran objected.

Yes, you have. I appreciate all you've done. Laurie kept this to herself. No use telling Skye she'd insulted her dog.

Taran sneezed, his way of accepting her apology or dislodging the intense sweetness of the fall fruit, she couldn't say. "Could you recognize this person if you smelled him again?" she asked.

Ashe regarded her askance.

"I'll take that as a yes."

Of course, my rescuer, Rosa said. She put her paws on Laurie's thigh and waged her tail. Laurie had taken Rosa away from a woman on the airplane who'd stuffed the little dog into a cage under the seat and ignored her wails of fear when the plane almost crashed.

Laurie scratched behind her ears. "Thank you."

We like the lake, Rosa said, and all three waded in. Taran swam after a flotilla of ducks. The other two stuck to the shoreline.

"Oh, Lord. This is why I keep my old car," Skye said. "Taran, come out of there. This water is polluted."

The hound kept swimming toward the ducks who watched him, not overly alarmed. When he got close, they flew to another spot in the lake.

Laurie laughed.

"What did he say?" Skye asked.

"That it seems fine to him."

Skye shook her head. "Maybe they have a hose at the hotel so I can spray him off before we drive back."

Laurie looked around at the tangle of bushes. "Let's check around and see if the police missed anything. Looks like there's an open area over there."

They divided the general area between them and started poking around, pulling stems gently aside, looking through the leaves. Laurie felt around on the ground and under each bush. Rosa joined her. Ashe lay near the jogging path keeping a protective eye out.

After about ten minutes, Skye called, "Found something."

Laurie joined her and Skye pointed to something leather almost hidden beneath old leaves. Laurie picked it up and brushed off the moist dirt. It was a wallet. She opened it and found a driver's license. Marcus stared out from the photo. "Handsome. I always look awful in these pictures," she said, a tug pulling at her heart.

Skye patted her shoulder, feeling Laurie's sadness. "We lost a good person."

Laurie handed the wallet over to Skye. "Do you feel anything?"

Skye closed her eyes for a moment, then shook her head. "Nothing. I don't always get impressions for objects." She opened the wallet and checked the contents. "Looks like all his money and credit cards are still here."

Taran arrived, tongue lolling in his happy face. He shook himself and water flew everywhere.

Skye yelped. "Now we all need baths."

I don't, Rosa said. She sat far enough away from the large hound.

Laurie didn't share this little piece of information.

"At least I've got towels in the car," Skye said.

Taran sat on his haunches and regarded his mistress with adoring eyes, entirely unrepentant. They climbed the hill but found no water hose behind the hotel, so they headed for the car. Skye retrieved two beach towels from the back of the Outback and dried Taran off, then wiped the paws of the other two dogs before letting them jump in the back.

She pointed at Taran. "Mister, you're getting a bath when we get home."

The dog didn't seem to care. He curled up and went to sleep, exhausted from his swim.

CHAPTER
SEVEN

"I will not dress like a porn star at Marcus Robertson's memorial," Dana said, holding the sheer tulle strip of fabric with dangling straps out to Nicolette.

"But it's so chic. Garter belts are so much nicer than nylon panty hose." The campaign stylist curled her lip with distaste as she said those last words. "I only have these black, silk stockings and just look at the lace detailing on the belt."

Dana stared at the young woman in disbelief. "A man has died, Nicolette. A man you worked with and liked as far as I could tell."

"Yes, and you and Kevin should honor him by being the best dressed couple there. Next to his parents, of course. Mrs. Robertson always wears Virginie Viard."

Dana blinked, for a wild second imagining Mrs. Robertson wearing a person. "Oh, Virginie Viard." Dana repeated the name but had no idea who she was. Probably some fashion designer. And Nicolette was calling her husband by his first name? That didn't bode well. Then again, maybe she could send Kevin off to live with the stylist and Dana could appear only at official events.

Nicolette nodded, her kohl rimmed eyes wide. "Marcus had an impeccable sense of fashion. He always knew what to wear for every occasion,"

"Nobody will see the lace."

"But you'll know it's there and that will make you feel beautiful." The young woman's hand with perfectly shaped opalescent nails flew to her mouth, "Not that you aren't already."

Dana stepped around Nicolette and pawed through the top drawer of her dresser. No black pantyhose. Blast it. She'd have to wear this device. With a sigh, she reached out her hand and the vindicated stylist put the lacy garter belt in it. It looked downright medieval. "Thank you, Nicolette. I can get dressed by myself."

"I'll be happy to do your hair and make-up, Mrs. Preston," she said.

God, give me strength, Dana thought. "I think simple is respectful. I'll go with a chignon."

"Yes, ma'am." Nicolette was trying not to sound victorious but failing. She flitted off to the guest room where Kevin had opted to dress. Apparently, their bedroom had grown too small for his majesty. He'd moved back in part time since the campaign had started. "We don't want our marital problems to become fodder for the media," he'd said. Actually, she was glad he kept mostly to the guest room.

She turned her thoughts to Marcus and the case, but the stylist soon returned, flitting around, doing her hair, fussing and carrying on, making it impossible to focus. The drive to Saint Mark's Episcopal Cathedral was short, too short to warrant the limousine Kevin insisted on. Kevin talked nonstop on the way, asking her opinion on possible replacements for his campaign manager.

She interrupted him. "Aren't you sad?"

Kevin blinked like a deer in headlights. "Uh, yeah. Of course. But November is only two months away."

"What have you done about security? Do the police think you could be a target?"

"The police," he scoffed, running his hand through his already neatly trimmed hair. "The FBI is looking into the murder. Haven't you noticed the extra security in my retinue?"

Retinue. He'd called them his retinue. She had to get out of this situation. Other politicians' wives were invisible, weren't they?

They pulled into St. Mark's drive. "Get ready. There will be press," he said.

And indeed there was. A whole bevy of them. The photographers crowded close and Dana tried not to squint at the flash of cameras as they walked inside. Why did they still use flashbulbs, she wondered. Must be the overcast sky, which suited the occasion in her opinion. Kevin crooked his arm and she took it. She was thankful for the low heels she'd insisted on. This was the last time she would suffer the ministrations of Nicolette Voss.

Inside, the glass wall at the far end of the chapel caught the sun and lit the space in golden light. Dana took a deep breath. She was thankful no one stopped them to talk politics. They just received nods and sympathetic tilts of heads, but Kevin stopped to speak with the Robertsons and Maddie, who gave her a knowing look while Kevin expressed his profuse condolences and told the Robertsons what a gifted campaign manager Marcus had been. Once they settled into the row behind the family, Dana's gaze went to the gleaming mahogany coffin and the ghost standing beside it.

As soon as Marcus noticed her, his voice sounded clearly in her mind. *I'd never seen him before.*

Never seen who? Dana asked. Or was it whom? She shook off this thought.

The man who met me by the lake.

So, you remember getting—Dana stopped herself from saying 'shot' and, stumbling, substituted it for—*the phone call.*

Marcus looked surprised. *How did you know about that?*

We watched the hotel surveillance video.

Smart.

The bishop's voice interrupted them. "Mr. and Mrs. Robertson,

Derek, Madeline." He nodded to each as he named them, then looked out at the congregation. "Family and friends. We are gathered today to lay to rest Marcus Alexander Robertson, a brilliant and kind man, gone from us too soon."

Marcus laughed, a reaction that startled Dana. *They think I'm dead, but I'm right here.*

That's true. Relieved she could see Marcus clearly now and that his memory was returning, she started to ask more about the night he was killed, but the ghost's attention was fixed on his fiancée. *Poor Maddie. We're such a perfect match. What will she do now?* He looked back to Dana for an answer.

What was she, a spiritual guru? But he looked desolate, so Dana tried her best. *She will mourn for you, Marcus, even though you're right here and will be beside her often in the next few months.*

At least, Dana hoped so.

I will?

If you wish. But she will heal. She'll start to remember the happy times more that the loss. She'll always feel the love you shared.

We were such a great team, he said, his eyes shining.

The bishop raised his arms, the sleeves of his cassock spreading like wings. "Let us read from the Book of Common Prayer."

There was a stir as the congregation reached for the hymnals in the racks on the pews in front of them and opened to the Burial Rite. People murmured, a few asking about the page number. A woman on the aisle across from them reached for her reading glasses hanging from a gold chain and perched them on her nose.

The bishop began his recitation. "I am the resurrection and the life, saith the Lord; he that believeth in me, though he were dead, yet shall he live; and whosoever liveth and believeth in me shall never die."

Dana's attention went to the circle in the middle of the rose window above the altar. It soothed her heart, speaking to her somehow of light. The rays extending from the center echoed the bishop's assurance that the spirit continued. Dana smiled. The evidence was right in front of her.

I guess it's true that I haven't stopped existing, Marcus said, *although I wasn't much of a believer.*

The bishop continued, oblivious to Marcus's commentary. "I know that my Redeemer liveth, and that he shall stand at the latter day upon the earth; and though this body be destroyed, yet shall I see God; whom I shall see for myself and mine eyes shall behold, and not as a stranger."

I haven't seen God, though. Marcus looked disappointed.

You have unfinished business, Dana said. *Have you seen anyone else who's passed over?*

I think so. I remember a whole crowd welcoming me. His eyes lit again. *Yeah, but my grandfather told me I couldn't stay yet. He said I had a job to do before I could come back home. Like you just said. What do you think it is?*

The bishop continued. "For none of us liveth to himself, and no man dieth to himself. For if we live, we live unto the Lord. and if we die, we die unto the Lord. Whether we live, therefore, or die, we are the Lord's. Blessed are the dead who die in the Lord; even so saith the Spirit, for they rest from their labors."

I guess I can't rest from my labors yet. But all this Lord business. I do remember seeing one of my old professors who was a professed atheist and he was over there with everyone else. No hell fire that I could spot.

Dana ducked her head so the people around her couldn't see her smile.

The bishop looked up at the congregation and said, "The Lord be with you."

Half the congregation responded, "And with thy spirit." The other half looked around, surprised.

The bishop bowed his head, "Let us have a moment of silent prayer."

Grateful, Dana closed her eyes and continued her mental conversation with Marcus. *Maybe you're supposed to solve your murder. Find out why it happened.*

I think so, Marcus said.

The man you met by the lake. Can you describe him?

He was dressed in a dark jogging outfit. Hat with a brim. He had something over his eyes. I wondered why he was wearing sunglasses at night, but then realized they were something else. He reached into his pocket and—Marcus spread his hands as if in a plea to her—*that's all I remember.*

I'm so sorry. Dana opened her eyes to watch Marcus. After a moment, she asked as gently as she could, *Do you think he was special forces?*

You mean like a spy?

Something like that.

Marcus's form wavered with the shock, then disappeared. She wanted to reach out to him, to comfort him.

"We will sing Hymn 493, 'All is Well with my Soul,'" the bishop announced.

Dana didn't know this one. She stood holding the hymnal in her hands, staring at space where Marcus had stood. She felt terrible. Had she retraumatized this nice young man by pushing too hard? The bishop, unbeknownst to him, rescued the ghost. Just a few lines into the hymn, Marcus popped back clear as day and began to sing, giving a full-throated rendition of the hymn. Dana sagged in relief.

Kevin gave her a quizzical look and she just patted his arm. The service had softened her. She used to be in love with him. He'd always be a part of her life. A father to the kids. Funerals tended to remind people of what was important and to let go of the trivial. If Kevin died, she'd be sad.

If he didn't haunt her.

The service ended and the bishop announced a reception in Loyola Hall. They waited for the family to be escorted out first, then joined the line behind them. The Robertsons had helped Kevin with the catering expense. Black clad waiters circled the crowd serving hors d'oeuvres from the Pacific Northwest and offering glasses of white wine or grape juice.

Dana approached Marcus's mother. "I can't tell you how sorry I am. Your son was always kind to me. At the fundraiser he helped me remember all the names of donors and told me little details so I could greet them properly."

Mrs. Robertson sniffed. "He knew his way around politics."

"Kevin's campaign took off once he joined."

"That was partly Maddie. The two of them were quite a team."

Dana looked around for his fiancée but didn't see her. The brother was surrounded by a cluster of guys who'd been friends with Marcus. She'd heard them telling stories about their college days when she walked by. Mr Robertson stood in a separate group of people offering their condolences. At least that's what she hoped was going on with the tight circle. She recognized a man standing slightly behind him keeping a watchful eye on the crowd, the very one the waiters had branded a spy at the fundraiser.

Before she could think about what that could mean, Marcus appeared at her side. She tried not to react, but he noticed and moved behind her. Just as he had that fateful night, he whispered to her, *Tell Mom how much I liked the pony she gave me when I was six. Tubby was his name.*

"He mentioned how much he loved Tubby, his pony. Was that his name?" Dana repeated.

His mother's head jerked up in surprise. "He told you about that?"

"Yes, he must have had a wonderful childhood."

Marcus snorted behind her, but she ignored him.

"Please, call me Alexandra." She dabbed her eyes with a tissue.

Surprised, Dana said, "You gave Marcus your name."

Alexandra smiled, her watery blue eyes softening. "I did. He was such a bright child. Loved the outdoors. Adored that pony."

Another person hovered nearby wanting to speak with Alexandra, so Dana took her leave. "Marcus was a special person. He left us too soon. Please let us know if there's anything we can do."

"Thank you," she said and Dana stepped away. She found Kevin in conversation with Senator Evelyn Whitmore. She'd always liked this woman. Whitmore was in her early sixties, her mostly silver hair swept back into a low twist. The senator had been a formidable force in American politics for over two decades, known for her unwavering commitment to healthcare reform, workers' rights, and educational equity.

Kevin noticed Dana standing just out of earshot and motioned for her to join them. "You know my wife," he said. "She's an attorney at Wyndham, Cole & Ashcroft."

"Dana." She supplied her name rather than the label 'wife' and shook hands.

Senator Whitmore leaned toward her, and Dana caught a whiff of rose and vanilla. Whitmore studied her with steel-gray eyes that locked onto her with an intensity that was famous for making lobbyists squirm and interns sit up straighter. "Didn't you work on that class action suit representing the families of the women who died because they were refused abortions in emergency rooms?"

"I did for a while," Dana said, then shot Kevin a look. "But I was pulled off because Kevin was working on the State House of Health Care and Wellness."

"Ah, possible conflict of interest." Whitmore squared her shoulders. "That seems like a stretch considering it was a national case."

"I agree. It's still working its way through the system. I wish I could have stayed with it."

Whitmore studied her for a minute. "I'm chairing the Senate Committee on Health, Education, Labor, and Pensions."

Dana waited for the senator to say more, but she just stood there, letting the implications hang in the air, so Dana took a risk. "That case challenges the national abortion ban the new administration has declared. It has a chance to go to the Supreme Court, although..." Dana lifted a shoulder to suggest her critique of that legal body.

"There's a lot of work to do with healthcare nationally."

"I've always admired your efforts in this area. It takes courage."

Senator Whitmore gave a crisp nod. Then she smiled at Kevin. "I see you married up."

Dana almost spit out the wine she'd just sipped.

Kevin's mouth tightened, then he forced a jovial laugh. "Gotta stay surrounded by smart women."

"Indeed." Senator Whitmore's tone was dry. She looked over at Alexandra Robertson as if taking note of another smart woman. "You know, Marcus consulted with me a few years ago. A rising star. It's a tragedy to lose a man with such talent."

"I couldn't agree more," Kevin said, trying to recover from his faux pas.

Whitmore's aide appeared at her side and whispered something in her ear. She nodded, then said, "Apparently, I have another engagement. We'll be in touch." They shook hands and she walked away.

Kevin looked around the room. The crowd had thinned considerably. "She likes you. That's a feather in my cap."

Dana felt a rush of anger. "Your cap?"

"United front. Remember?" Kevin whispered.

Dana fumed but kept her thoughts to herself. People were watching. They always were.

The Robertsons were heading toward the exit. "I think we can leave soon," he said and fell in behind the family. Dana tugged on his arm so they kept a respectful distance. She noticed the same man from earlier walking near Marcus's father. He had a square jaw, a high-and-tight haircut just starting to gray at the temples, and impeccable posture that gave away his military background. He scanned the crowd with cool detachment. No wonder the waiters had thought he was a spy.

Outside, the chauffeurs lounged under the towering Douglas firs.

Senator Whitmore's aide got their driver's attention and he jumped up. He hurried across 10th street to where the police had cordoned off parking for the service. He pointed his fob at the gleaming black Lincoln Town Car when he got to the sidewalk, and Dana was surprised when the engine purred to life. She'd expected it to just unlock.

Then the car exploded into a fire ball.

CHAPTER

EIGHT

S kye watched the chauffeur fly through the air from the force
of the explosion and land in a crumpled heap. Several drivers
ran toward him. The crowd that had been wending out of
Loyola Hall rushed onto the pavement, blocking her view. Panic,
shock, horror—the crowd's reactions flooded Skye. Her empathic
sense shut down with a snap. Thank the goddess she had an auto-
matic overload switch.

"Somebody call 911," several people in front shouted at the same
time.

Skye already had her phone out. "There's been an explosion at St.
Mark's Episcopal Cathedral—"

"We've had multiple reports. Emergency vehicles are on the
way."

"There is one injury."

"That's been reported. Thank you, ma'am."

Skye ended the call. When the crowd in front of her thinned, she
saw two people supporting the driver who hung limp between them.
They walked him over to the grass and laid him down away from the
burning car. The fire had spread to the trees above, but thankfully

the rains had come and they hadn't lit up like torches. The lower limbs burned and the ones above smoked ominously.

Skye heard sirens in the distance. The fire trucks should arrive before the blaze got out of control. Her phone buzzed and she saw Dana's name on the screen. She answered. "You okay?"

"I'm not hurt. Are you?" Dana said.

"No, you were closer than me."

Kevin's head swiveled toward his wife, frowning.

"Let's hang up before your companion asks who you're talking to," Skye said. Best not to say names out loud.

Yesterday, the three friends had decided a second person should attend the memorial to observe. And to watch out for Dana. Skye had been the logical choice. Her empathic skills helped her notice unusual reactions from people. These could be good clues. She'd grabbed a brown wig off a manikin in Star, Stone & Flower and dressed in an old black dress handing in the back of her mother's closet. She borrowed her grandmother's fancy wool coat from who knew what decade and perched a veiled black hat on her head. Dana had looked straight at her and not recognized her. Skye was confident of her disguise.

She noticed quite a bit at the service and reception. Marcus's mother was filled with contradictory emotions. Grief predominated, but she also radiated guilt. Skye knew those who survived the death of someone close often forgave everything the person who'd passed had done wrong and blamed themselves double for all their own misdeeds, but this felt different. It was guilt over something sneaky. The woman somehow blamed herself for her son's death. Or wondered if something she'd done had contributed to it. And what surprised Skye the most was she felt relief at times. Skye tried to figure out if there was a pattern to this. Was it associated with a certain person who talked to her or was she genuinely relieved her son was gone? The relief was always followed by shame. What a rollercoaster.

Smoldering anger lay beneath the father's heartache and it flared up when a couple of people approached him. One man in particular incited a big spike. Mid-fifties, graying temples, a permanent smirk. Skye positioned herself so she could get a few pictures of him for later research.

The second person who provoked William Robertson's anger was a hapless woman who seemed jovial at this somber event. The two resembled each other. Maybe a sister or cousin. The same dark brown hair Marcus had, only the elders' hair had grayed. Straight nose. Tall. Skye snapped a picture of the woman when she walked away. Jade could track her down. Or Minh for that matter. They had so much research to do that Dana had agreed to let her teenage son pitch in. Probably hoping it would keep him out of trouble.

Skye watched people's reaction to the car explosion. The place swirled with intrigue. Not everyone was horrified. One group passed her in a bubble of prurient interest, even glee. She snapped a picture of them, pretending to aim at the fire. One woman stared at her in outright shock. Skye shrugged and the woman huffed at her, then walked away. Skye got as close to the group as she could, listening to their whispered conversation.

"Whose car was it?"

"The senator's."

"Whitmore?"

"Yes, I thought it was—"

A man's bullhorn voice sounded in her ear, cutting the group off. "Mr. Robertson. Is everyone all right?" He pushed people aside getting to the family.

Skye didn't recognize him, so she hurried around the group and snapped a photo of his bellowing red face. Someone jostled against her and her wig went askew. She tried to right it but based on the alarmed and amused faces of the younger crowd she'd been following, her efforts had not been successful.

"Chemo," she said, hoping her full head of red hair wasn't peeping out from beneath the brown wig.

The group turned around, a couple of them embarrassed. One

young woman grabbed her friend's arm and pulled her away as if cancer were contagious.

Skye decided it was time to go. She made her way around the back of the reception hall and walked a few blocks down 10th Avenue to where she'd parked her Outback. Shedding the wool coat, she got behind the wheel and headed south. The police had already blocked the street off to the north, so she'd have to double back to get home. She'd show Jade the photos tonight.

But the moment Skye turned onto the drive of Fox Fire Farm, she knew something was wrong. Her old green Subaru rattled to a halt outside the main farmhouse, and she noticed the odd cluster of parked vehicles—her cousin's aging Prius, Eamon's work truck, Jade's cruiser, and even Aunt Siobhán's powder-blue Volvo.

Why was Jade home in the middle of the day? She stepped out of the car, the gravel sharp under the thin soles of the ballet flats she'd worn to the memorial. The weight of something unspoken pressed down on the familiar scent of lavender, rosemary, and sun-warmed cedar.

Inside, the Yarrow family kitchen was bursting at the seams. Fíona stood at the head of the long pine table, her silver-streaked hair loose for once, eyes fierce. Cormac was perched on the windowsill, arms crossed. A storm brewed in his expression. Cousins, aunts, and even Great Aunt Luna—who rarely left her meditation loft—had shown up.

"What happened?" Skye asked, hanging her grandmother's wool coat by the door.

Grandmother Moira pointed. "Aye, so it's you who's a borrowin' my clothes without askin' leave."

"Sorry, Grandma."

Jade looked up from her seat at the table, her expression taut with worry. "You'd better sit down."

"You're home early," Skye said, pulling out a chair.

Aunt Siobhán didn't waste time. "We received a cease-and-desist letter from the state medical board this morning. Accusations of practicing medicine without a license. They're targeting the apothecary."

The words landed like stones in Skye's chest. "That's absurd. We've followed every herbal regulation, every product labeled properly, every—"

"They're not coming after the shop," Aunt Aoife said sharply. "They're coming after us. After *our kind.*"

There was a murmur of agreement around the table. Skye's cousin Brenna, newly apprenticed and still wearing her herb-stained apron, looked pale.

"Someone reported the tinctures we gave to that cancer patient a few weeks ago," Aunt Siobhán explained. "Said we made medical claims."

"Those were Aunt Crofa's formulas," Brenna added in a trembling voice. "From the family book."

Cormac thumped the end of his staff against the floor. "Fear tactics."

Skye reached for the mug that appeared in front of her— steaming with tulsi and rose hips. Her mother had made it. She always knew what Skye needed.

"I've warned you all before," Fíona said, voice low and tight. "We walk a line. We *always* have. Our tradition is older than their rules, but that doesn't make us untouchable."

"We've been healing people for generations," Grandfather Angus said tightly. "Never claimed to be doctors. Never needed to. Our remedies come from the land, the stars, the bones of our bloodline."

Cormac glanced at his father. "We could go underground again. Like Nana did back in the fifties."

"Do you want to go back to only helping neighbors under cover of night?" Aunt Aoife snapped. "Do you want to stop teaching the apprentices? Close the community kitchen?"

"We need a lawyer," Jade said.

"Vivienne Grant handles our legal business. She's in the know."

Aunt Aoife laid her finger against her nose, meaning Vivienne followed a pagan path.

Jade looked confused by the gesture but continued. "We'll need public support. Testimonials. People trust this place."

Fíona's eyes settled on Skye. "We need you."

"But we're helping Dana with this young man's ghost. He was murdered and based on what I saw this morning," Skye looked over at Jade, "more people could be in danger."

"Ack." Grandmother Moira waved her hand in dismissal. "That'll sort itself, won't it?"

Her mother's voice softened but didn't lose its strength. "You've got the balance. The right blend of old ways and modern savvy. You're our voice to the outside world."

"And the strongest empath among us," her father added.

Skye felt the weight of it settle over her. Family. History. Tradition. Heavier than the death of the young campaign manager. A closer danger than the senator's car exploding. And now—this threat to their livelihood.

"I'll help," she said. "We're not going back into the shadows."

The kitchen fell silent, but the fire in the hearth flared, unbidden.

Somewhere deep in the house, the ancestral bells chimed once—soft and solemn.

Even the spirits were listening.

Great Aunt Luna opened her eyes at last. "A shadow's falling across our home, child. But we've walked in darker places before."

Fíona rose. "With so many of us here, this would be a good time for a protection spell."

"Let's go upstairs to the ritual room," Great Aunt Luna said.

The attic had been turned into a place for magic, especially during the cold months. It stretched the length of the large farmhouse, accommodating the whole extended family if they squeezed in. This afternoon, some were still at their various jobs, but a large group had responded to the emergency. Shelves ran along the whole back wall of the cavernous space, accommodating a plethora of books, crystals and stones, wands, bowls of different sizes, incense, matches, bundles of sage, jars of herbs, feathers, a bird's nest. Whatever someone came across they needed in their personal practice or thought would be useful.

The family grimoire held pride of place on an altar in front of a round stained-glass window featuring a rose. A few small tables sat against the wall opposite the bookcase for individual practice, some cluttered with that person's project, others empty. But the middle of the room was always kept clear. Two cousins, Connor and Eamon, moved a three-legged black caldron into the center and tossed a bundle of dried rowan twigs, oak, and dried hawthorn leaves tied with red thread into it. Connor murmured a prayer, lit a match, and held it to the braid. Smoke curled up and Eamon opened a vent in the ceiling.

Fíona nodded her approval, then lifted the ceremonial bell wrought with triskele and ash leaves, the bronze smoothed by countless rituals. "Let's begin the warding," she said, her voice suggesting distant thunder. "We call on Brigid for protection and clarity. We defend not only our name—but the work of our forebearers."

The room fell into stillness—deep and sacred.

One by one, the Yarrow clan formed a wide circle. Smoke from the caldron curled toward the rafters like a rising spirit. Skye slipped into place between Jade and her cousin Brenna, their hands linking, forming an unbroken chain.

Aunt Maeve, a dream walker, stepped to the east window, holding a beeswax candle carved with knotwork. "I call Air to bring wisdom and shield our words. Let every whisper spoken against us be carried away like chaff on wind." She struck a match from her belt pouch and lit the wick. The flame flickered but held, casting strange shadows against the worn floorboards. She held a stick of incense to the fire, the flicked it through the air, dowsing the flame. Fragrant smoke billowed out.

"In the South I call Fire, sacred forge of Brigid," retired blacksmith Grandfather Declan intoned, his voice deep and weathered. "Burn away false accusations. Kindle courage in our hearts." He dropped dried yarrow blossoms and cinnamon bark into the central cauldron. The scent spread immediately.

Cousin Isla, a water witch, stepped to the western archway, holding a bowl of spring water from the old well. "Water, great tide of knowing, wash away lies. Carry our truth like a current that cannot be stopped." She sprinkled the water in an arc across the floor, then anointed the brows of each family member, murmuring old words in a mix of Gaelic and whispers only the spirits remembered.

In the North, Fíona—matriarch and root—took her place. She held a bowl of salt and black soil from the family's oldest garden. "Earth, bone of our bloodline, shield this house. Ground us in legacy, nourish our strength." She poured the mixture in a circle at her feet, then traced a sigil in it with the tip of her finger—an old protection rune passed down mother to daughter for over a century.

The circle pulsed.

Fíona stepped into the center, her bell now silent. She raised both hands. "Brigid, Lady of the Hearth and the Forge, Healer and Poet, we call to you. Stand with us now. We are your children."

The bell rang once.

The sound shimmered through the air, dissonant and resonant all at once, rippling through every bone in Skye's body. She silently pulled in Marcus, Dana, and her children. Then Laurie, John, and Rosa. *Protect them, too.*

Cousin Jamie, the musician, began to chant under his breath, calling up the old family blessing. Others joined, layering harmony and rhythm—voice, breath, will. Skye added her own verse, improvising the way she'd learned as a child when spirit and spell intertwined.

From root to bloom, from blood to flame,
Protect this hearth, defend our name.

No shadow cross this sacred space,
No ill befall our kin or place.

A flicker of movement drew Skye's eye upward. Hanging above them, the ancestral bells—dozens of them, each for a mother of the line—swayed on their cords. One by one, they began to ring, a silver chime like starlight against stone.

Aunt Maeve's eyes glistened. "They're with us," she whispered.

Outside, wind picked up through the orchard, rustling the apples heavy on the limbs and carrying the scent of sage from the apothecary garden. A streak of foxfire lanced across the field—bright, green, and utterly unnatural.

The circle spread outward. The energy surged—gentle but unyielding—like a rising tide or the slow pressure of spring breaking through frost.

Fíona gave the bell a final ring. The sound echoed, then faded.

"So it is sealed," she said. "By herb and bone, by oath and stone. The circle is open but unbroken."

No one moved.

Skye stood rooted to the floor, her pulse thrumming with ancient power. She looked at her mother, who gave her a proud, quiet nod.

"We'll fight," Skye said, her voice firm. "But we're not fighting alone."

Jade slid her hand into hers.

"No," Fíona said, smiling for the first time that evening. "We've never been alone."

CHAPTER

NINE

The lawyer's office smelled like lemon polish and nerves.

Skye Yarrow sat stiff-backed in a chair upholstered in something aggressively tweedy, her fingers curled around a travel mug of lavender and oat straw tea she'd brought from home. Across from her, Laurie Olson sipped from a to-go cup that smelled suspiciously like peppermint mocha, while Rosa, her Havanese sidekick, sniffed around the floor with investigative purpose.

Vivienne Grant, Esq. nodded to them both and leaned back in her ergonomic throne, a woman built of chic jackets, black-rimmed glasses, and not a shred of visible patience for nonsense. Her long fingers drummed on a manila folder marked Foxfire Farm / Kearney-MacAllister v. State Licensing Board.

Skye introduced Laurie to the family attorney. "She's a bit new to everything. Started hearing animals' thoughts after a near plane crash. That's Rosa."

Laurie leaned forward and shook her hand. Rosa sat at attention, clearly expecting a treat, but the lawyer was all business. "This isn't a garden-variety regulatory complaint," she said. "I've seen this before. And it's getting worse."

Skye exchanged a glance with Laurie. "Define worse."

Vivienne flipped open the folder. "The apothecary—Old World, correct?"

Skye nodded. "Run by my Aunt Siobhán and her apprentice Brenna, my cousin."

Vivienne adjusted her glasses. "You're being accused of practicing medicine without a license because someone claims a tincture was 'marketed as a treatment.' The language is vague on purpose. But it's not isolated. Wellspring University's legal team is scrambling —naturopaths, herbalists, acupuncturists, even reiki practitioners are being slapped with cease-and-desists or investigations."

"That's ridiculous," Skye said, heat rising in her voice. "Some of those people *are* licensed. Wellspring gives actual degrees. What are they trying to do? Shut down alternative healing altogether?"

Vivienne nodded slowly. "That's what I'm trying to figure out. Something big is happening. And it's not just here. We've got reports coming in from Colorado, New York, Oregon—even Arizona. And not all of these are about legality. Some of them are just...weird."

Laurie's brow furrowed. "Weird how?"

"There's been harassment. Break-ins. Mysterious inspections that don't result in paperwork. One Reiki practitioner in Sedona said her crystals all shattered overnight."

"Maybe her cat knocked them off their shelves," Laurie offered.

Rosa let out a single yip, clearly agreeing with this idea.

"She says it's the cat," Laurie translated.

Skye pinched the bridge of her nose. "Okay, so...this is more than just a bureaucratic coincidence. What do we do?"

"We fight it on both levels," Vivienne said. "Legal and magical. I've already filed a preliminary injunction to stop the order from being enforced until we have a hearing. We'll gather community testimony, customer statements, and historic context."

"You want to use history to defend us?"

"Foxfire Farm has been operating as a community healer's site for over one hundred and fifty years. Your family's been here since before statehood. There are precedents for traditional medicine—especially if it's cultural."

"We're not exactly indigenous. At least to Washington State."

"But your family brought an old tradition over when they immigrated."

"How do we prove that?"

"You could call your great-great-grandmother as a character witness," Laurie teased.

Skye smiled for the first time that day. "She'd be terrible under cross-examination. All riddles and threats."

"We need to prove ancestral lines back at least three hundred years. You can do that, right?" Vivienne asked.

"Iona MacAllister keeps the family records," Skye said.

"The grimoires?" Vivienne asked.

"Which cannot be taken into court for obvious reasons."

"Of course not. Those can never be taken into evidence. Kept in some vault." Vivienne's tone suggested what a sacrilege this would be.

"Iona is quite the scholar. She joined that site to trace your family roots." Skye relaxed telling the story. "Traced us back to some king. Cormac something. She got all excited."

Laurie sat forward. "Cormac mac Airt?"

"Yeah, I think that's it." Skye gestured toward Laurie. "English professor."

"Retired. Now I work with Living Earth Designs."

Vivienne perked up. "John Newman's firm?"

"Yes, you know him?"

"He's done great work with environmental protection. I love the whales."

"Me, too." Laurie's eyes shone. "It's great that you know his work."

"Tell me." Vivienne leaned forward, her hard-edge softening into fascination. "Can you talk to them?"

"Talk to—oh, you mean the whales?"

Vivienne nodded.

"Sometimes."

Rosa nudged Laurie. *I can always hear them.*

Laurie looked down at the proud Havanese. *Yes, and I'm jealous.*

"What did she say?" Vivienne asked, clearly fascinated.

Laurie repeated what Rosa had claimed.

"That would be wonderful," Vivienne said, a dreamy look on her face. Where had the hard-edged attorney disappeared to?

Skye cleared her throat. "So, our time's almost up. Who's this Cormac guy? It's a family name."

"Right." Laurie focused. "High King of Ireland way back. Best guess is second to the fourth century. He's famous for restoring Tara."

Skye's eyebrows shot up. "Wow. Amazing."

"Tara as in the ancient seat of the Irish high king? Site of the Stone of Destiny? That should do it," Vivienne said. She put her hands flat on the desk. "I plan to liaise with the attorneys working on these other cases. I'll try not to let the fees get out of hand."

A silence settled. Rosa trotted over and jumped into Skye's lap to offer her support. "Maybe there'll be some rich clients who'll help fund a group case," Skye said, stroking Rosa's ears.

"Yes, but these come under state laws, so—"

Rosa barked.

"She says we need to follow the trail," Laurie said. "That this is bigger than we realize."

Skye's jaw tightened. "This is clearly not just about a few disgruntled customers."

Vivienne closed the folder with a crisp snap. "No. It's about control. And someone is trying to wipe out every trace of what doesn't fit in their box."

Skye stood. "Then they've clearly never been to Star, Stone & Flower. Nothing there fits in a damn box."

Vivienne grinned. "Good. Because we're going to need a hell of a lot of magic, and maybe even a few theatrics, to win this one. I'll be in touch."

～

"MOM." Hoa slammed the door of Dana's new SUV.

Dana winced at the loud sound. "Not so hard." She'd tried to calm down after the explosion, but she was still jumping at loud noises a day later.

"Some weird guy was hanging around today."

"Another student was bothering you?" Hoa was a freshman and pretty enough to attract the attention of older boys.

"No boys have noticed me." She sounded a bit put out.

Dana flicked on her turn signal and looked for other cars pulling out from Hoa's high school, half listening to her daughter. "Who then?"

"Some ninja guy. I saw him three times."

This got her attention. "Ninja? Why do you call him that?"

"He was dressed in black. Looked shady as hell."

"Language."

Why did she bother?

"Where did you see him?"

"At the Northbean we all go to before class."

"Hoa, I've told you no caffeine."

Hoa let out a dramatic huff. "Would you listen? Anyway, I get green tea."

"I guess that's better than coffee."

"Do you even care that I'm being stalked by a murderer?"

"What?" Dana shot a glance over at her daughter. "Don't be dramatic."

"Tell that to Marcus. And that lady whose car blew up."

Dana stopped at a red light and turned to her daughter. "You know about that already?"

"Mom, it's all over Zing. Were you there?" Hoa's brown eyes swam with tears.

"Sweetie, I'm sorry. Yes, but we were far away from the explosion. Not in danger."

Hoa nodded, somewhat appeased.

"Now, tell me everything about this man you keep seeing."

"After Northbean, he was on the bike path that runs by the soccer field when I was in PE. I think I saw him yesterday, too. Then just now while I was waiting for you."

"Now?" Dana looked in the rear-view mirror, then the side mirror. "What was he driving?"

"A car this size. Minh would know what kind."

"What color?"

"Ninja colored." A timid smile broke out on Hoa's face.

"This is not a joke."

"Right? Like I've been telling you." She crossed her arms in front of her chest. "Black. Don't they all drive black cars?"

"Do you see the car now? Don't be obvious."

Hoa unclicked her seatbelt, turned around, and got on her knees, craning her head around.

"For heaven's sake. I said don't be obvious." The car behind Dana honked and she realized the light had been green for a while. Seattle drivers were so polite. Sometimes. She moved forward slowly so Hoa wouldn't get thrown around.

"Sit back down and just notice if he's following us." Dana fished for her phone and hit Kevin's speed dial number. It went to voice mail. She left a message telling him about Hoa's stalker. "We need security," she said and ended the call.

"Can you describe this man?" Dana asked.

"Better than that," her daughter said with an impish smile. "I got his picture."

Dana felt a flash of triumph. "That's my girl."

At home, Dana fished out her keys and opened the front door. Minh glanced up from his laptop on the dining room table, Lele lounging beside him. He nodded, then turned his attention back to his screen. Lele flipped her tail. That was all the greeting she got. She was glad Minh was keeping the door locked even while he was here. He had opted to stay home while he did his freshman year at the University of Washington. At first, she'd worried he would miss out on important parts of college life, but he'd made friends and gotten quite independent.

"Up for some online snooping?" she asked.

"That's what I'm doing now," Minh said. "Checking backgrounds of people who went to both the fundraiser and memorial."

"While you stream a Seahawks game?"

"I'm running a comparison program. It dings me when it gets results." Minh's attention strayed to the game.

"Great. I hope you're being careful," Dana said.

Hoa ran to her brother before he could answer, holding out her phone. "This guy's been stalking me."

"No way." He grabbed it and stared at the picture. "Don't know him. Send it to me."

Hoa's fingers flew over her phone, doing something in five seconds it usually took Dana a full minute to figure out. She sent the photo and Minh switched off the football game and started a facial recognition program he'd downloaded from who knew where. Dana didn't want to ask. She stood behind him and watched the faces flash by. He switched to another database. This might take more than five seconds, so she climbed up the stairs to her bedroom and changed out of her work clothes. She pulled on sweats, stretched out on the bed, and stared at the ceiling.

What was going on? A murder. A car bomb. And now somebody stalking her baby girl? She sat up and checked her phone. No answer from Kevin. What about Minh? He was less protected. The UW campus was big and he was taking the bus to class. Probably wandering up and down The Ave, sticking his head into shops. She felt some comfort knowing Skye's store was nearby. Frustrated, she started to call Kevin again just as the doorbell rang.

"I'll get it," Hoa shouted.

"Wait, you don't know who it is." Dana was already halfway down the stairs. She opened the peephole in the front door and saw a young man with a buzz cut and a crisp uniform standing almost at attention. Curious, Dana opened the door. "Can I help you?"

"Yes, ma'am. I'm Chris Devon. I was assigned to guard Mrs. Dana Preston and her two children" —he glanced at a piece of paper "— Hoa and Minh." His voice lifted up in a question. He had no idea how to pronounce these names.

Dana said the kid's names for him as she looked him up and down. His olive-green jacket had a logo in letters almost too small to read, at least for Dana's eyes. She squinted and made out 'Sentinel Protective Services.' His matching pants had a crease sharp enough to cut flesh and his black boots gleamed.

Freshly minted, Dana thought.

"The Preston campaign sent me."

"Great," Dana said. "Can I see some identification?"

"Yes, ma'am. Boss said it was urgent." He held out an ID from the company and his driver's license.

Dana looked between the photos and his face. She noticed his birthday was just a few years before Minh's. They'd sent a baby. Or was her age showing? "New to the job, Chris?"

He shuffled his feet. "I've been on for six months, but our training is extensive." He sounded like he was quoting from the company brochure.

"This is a serious situation. A man has been murdered and another attempt was made on a senator's life."

Chris nodded. "I was briefed."

Dana opened the door. "Come meet the kids." Chris followed her through the living room where Dana caught a glimpse of the man's face on Minh's computer. He slammed the lid shut. Her son had already checked out their new guard. She realized she was relieved.

Hoa held out her phone. "This guy is following me. Think you can take him?"

Chris studied his face. "Can you send me this picture?"

"Just snap a shot of it," Minh said.

Chris pointed his finger at the teen. "Good idea."

Dana felt like an antique rotary dial phone watching these youngsters navigate tech.

Laurie and Skye were coming over and with the new security guy here, Dana decided not to cook. It would be rude not to feed him and she didn't feel like doing that much work in the kitchen. "I'm ordering from the Asian fusion restaurant for dinner. What would you like?"

The kids shouted their favorites before their new security guard had a chance. Chris looked out of his element. Must be new to Seattle. "I'll get you something good," Dana said.

"Thank you, ma'am." With a nod, Chris headed back outside and started patrolling the perimeter of the house.

Dana turned to Minh and asked in a low voice, "What did you find out about him? Think he's up to the job?"

"Took the state championship in wrestling when he was in high school. Majored in criminal justice." Minh shrugged. "I guess he's better than nothing."

Dana blew out a breath, then pointed at his computer. "Find anything suspicious on your previous search?"

"Nothing on Hoa's stalker."

"How about the ones at both the fundraiser and memorial?"

Minh sat back. "Mom, these people are squeaky clean online, but they make big donations to—" he squinted at his screen "—501(c)(4) groups with names like Americans for Progress and Stability or The Heritage Horizons Project. I mean, what does any of this even mean?"

"When they passed that bill that let dark money into politics, I knew this was the end of—" Dana stopped herself from finishing that sentence when she saw Hoa's sweet face.

But Minh had no such compulsion. He finished it for her. "Democracy? They've even got a group called Voices of the Heartland. I mean, that sounds like a bunch of farmers, right? I kinda doubt that's who it is, though."

"What's dark money?" Hoa asked.

If some nutjob was stalking her, Hoa was old enough to know. Dana explained, "It's about politics. When the name of a donor to a candidate is hidden. It makes it so rich people and corporations can pour millions of dollars into campaigns without disclosing it."

"They buy the government," Minh summed up in his direct style.

"That's not fair," Hoa said.

"Exactly. These 501 groups. I could check on which candidates they support, but there's so much." He threw his hands up.

"Laurie and Skye are coming to help."

"Jade's better," he mumbled.

"She's on swing shift. I think. Anyway, I need to order dinner. And you need to do your homework."

Minh perked up. "One of my professors is studying how to restore coral beds. You wouldn't believe how many species depend on them." Minh started talking about fish and how smart octopuses were. She noticed he didn't say octopi and smiled. Dana preferred that pronunciation.

She walked into the kitchen to order their food, mumbling "uh huh" and "wow" until it was just the kids talking. Better not order any calamari. Was squid the same as octopus? She couldn't remember and she wasn't going to ask Minh. That was for sure.

After she got dinner taken care of, she went out to the back patio to enjoy some quiet before the next storm. She was glad Minh's studies excited him, although she worried he'd fly off to the Great Barrier Reef sooner rather than later. Maybe John could keep him local. Puget Sound needed plenty of help. And Hoa. Her daughter was a bookworm. Gobbled up Japanese anime and fantasy. Laurie had expanded her reading to some contemporary women writers and even a few classics. Hoa also loved history and archaeological shows on PBS. Who knew where she'd land.

Half an hour later, Laurie texted that they were on their way.

Dana went in to find Minh finishing up a paper on endangered fish species in Puget Sound. Good, that was local. Hoa sprawled on the sofa, her face in a book. Lele snoozed on her stomach. "Did you finish your homework?"

"Uh, yeah."

Dana recognized a fib when she heard one. "You better get it done if you want to hang out with Laurie and Skye."

"It's just math. I can do it in five minutes."

"That's about as long as you have."

With a dramatic sigh, Hoa put down her book and nudged Lele to get up. The cat let out a protesting squeak and jumped to the back of the couch. Dana didn't know which was more of a diva. "Math before pad thai," she told Hoa.

Her teen ran up to her room and Dana headed for the kitchen to put out plates and glasses. One her third trip, she heard a car door slam and looked out the front. The new security guard was headed toward Skye and Laurie, his hands out to stop them. She rushed out onto the porch. "They're my friends. They can come in."

Chris looked back over his shoulder, his eyes invisible behind his dark sunglasses. What was with these security people and their Ray Bans, anyway? This was Seattle, not LA.

"I'm supposed to check everyone for weapons, ma'am."

Dana'd had just about enough of being called 'ma'am,' but really. He was only seven years older than Minh. She supposed she'd better get used to it.

Skye pulled out her pistol and Chris reached for his sidearm. She dangled it from her fingers. "Easy. I've only got this Sig. Good to have protection for my friend."

Chris held out his hand. "I'll have to take that."

Skye snorted and blew past him.

"Ma'am, stop." He made a feeble effort to get in front of her.

Laurie followed Skye, holding both palms out. "I've only got a Swiss Army knife. And my dog."

"But—" Chris turned around to watch them climb the stairs.

"They're fine," Dana said.

"I don't know how I'm supposed to do my job..." he mumbled, his words trailing off as he walked toward the sidewalk.

Dana waved her friends into the house, then remembered. "I got you orange chicken," she shouted to Chris.

He just shook his head.

"You can inspect the bags."

"This is serious, ma'am."

"It is and we appreciate all you're doing for us." Dana closed the door.

Minh looked up from where he sat at the dining room table his lap top open. "Orange chicken? I should have ordered that."

Dana ignored him. Rosa ran around to say hello, then went in search of Lele. Or food maybe. Skye flopped onto the couch in the living room. "You won't believe what's happened."

"There's more?" Dana sat in one of the chairs across from her.

Skye told Dana about the charge against the apothecary and the plethora of cases and harassment against alternative health practitioners.

"That's serious. I know a great attorney who deals in that area."

"I can pass the name onto Vivienne. She could use the help."

"Vivienne Grant? She's solid."

"And a witch," Skye whispered, "but don't tell anybody."

"I found a lot of money going to members of a health committee in Congress." Minh's voice surprised them. Dana looked up to see him leaning against the doorframe of the dining room.

"Minh's been checking out the people who attended the fundraiser and the memorial," Dana explained.

"Interesting," Laurie said. "Find any connections?"

"I took some photos while I was at the memorial this morning," Skye pulled up an image. "When this guy spoke to William Robertson—"

"Which one is he now?" Laurie asked.

"The father," Skye said. "Robertson got really angry when this guy walked up to him."

Minh held out his hand for Skye's phone. He took it into the dining room and transferred the photo to his laptop that still sat open on the table. The posse gathered round to watch the facial identification program at work.

"Whew, that's fast," Laurie said. "Almost like looking at those old microfilm files. You'd have to blur your eyes or you'd get dizzy. Remember?"

Hoa and Minh both looked up at her, confused. "What's micro-film?" Hoa asked.

Laurie chuckled. "That's how libraries stored records. On film stock, only not—" She waved her hands, trying to find a way to explain this apparently ancient technology. "They photographed documents at a greatly reduced size on film. Then you'd put the roll in a special viewer and move it through real fast until to you got to the page you wanted to read. Then you'd make it bigger."

Minh shook his head and went back to his computer.

"You'd have to see it," she said.

Hoa wrinkled her nose. "No thanks."

"Found him," Minh read from his screen. "Thomas Ellsworth. Recently engineered a hostile takeover of Primewell Health Insurance and pushed out the CEO, Ethan Caldwell. Caldwell, a former surgeon turned healthcare executive, said in his corporate bio that he'd seen too many patients suffer due to lack of coverage and was working to reform the system. This blog says Ellsworth replaced him with a slick, media-savvy executive—"

"Wait, it says slick?" Dana asked.

"Yes, it does. Right here." He resumed reading, his tone a touch smug. "A slick, media-savvy executive who previously led a PR firm, now using his influence to shift public perception of health insurance."

"Wow. More health connections," Skye said.

Dana got out her own laptop and Laurie pulled out her iPad. Skye and Hoa got their phones ready. The food arrived and they dove into their research fueled by pad thai, three-flavored tofu, fried rice, stir-fried vegetables, and lots of rice. Dana gave Chris his meal in a big bowl and he sat on the porch, wolfing it down. Inside, the posse and kids munched and read on their devices, trying not to smear them with hoisin sauce.

After a few minutes, Dana pointed her chopsticks at her laptop. "Listen to this. Ethan Caldwell threatened a lawsuit citing illegal termination. Weeks later he was shot on the streets of Chicago in a move the press termed 'gangland style.'"

Skye let out a low whistle. "So, Marcus's father might have known Ethan Caldwell. Maybe that's why he was so pissed when Ellsworth approached him at his son's memorial. Maybe he suspects Ellsworth's involved in both murders."

Minh's sudden laugh startled Dana. She frowned at him. "What?"

"One employee said Ellsworth is never seen without his Rolex," Minh said.

"Probably an ex-employee now," Laurie muttered. "I've been looking at who backed Kevin's campaign and this Ellsworth is one of the biggest contributors."

Skye sat back and folded her arms across her chest. "Prime suspect."

"And that senator whose car blew up. What does she do in the Senate?" Laurie asked.

Minh typed quickly, then sat back. "Okay, Senator Whitmore chairs the Committee on Health, Education, Labor, and Pensions."

"Check your list for Damien somebody. He was with an older woman. Did they attend the memorial? They stuck in my head from a brief conversation at the fundraiser," Dana said.

Minh did a quick check. "There's no Damien. And I can't check for 'older woman'."

Dana huffed out a breath.

"Why?" he asked.

"Just a feeling," Dana said.

"Never ignore those." Skye pushed her chair back on two legs and Dana bit back the admonition she'd give the kids not to do that. She realized Hoa was half asleep.

Laurie noticed and said, "We'll check them tomorrow. It's late,"

"Agreed. We've got our work cut out for us, but I think it's safe to say Marcus's murder is connected to the health care industry or legislation in some way." Dana looked around the table at the nods of agreement and was surprised to find Marcus standing in the same place Minh had stood earlier, a look of satisfaction on his pale face.

Laurie put her hand up to cover a big yawn.

Dana checked the time. "Wow, it's close to eleven o'clock. Hoa has school tomorrow."

"I guess we'll call it a night, but there's so much more to check out," Skye said. Her two friends trailed out to their car, Dana watching from the porch steps. Halfway down, they found a new security guard. He gave Dana a two fingered salute. "José. I'm on night shift."

"Thank you, José. Don't hesitate to wake me up if there's a problem."

He patted his side. "Got your number here, ma'am."

Jose looked a bit more solid than Chris had. Plus, he was older. Was she getting ageist in reverse? Maybe so, but she felt more secure with this new guy. She waved goodnight to her friends as they pulled away, Rosa's head hanging out the back window taking in the night breeze. It all looked so ordinary. Except for the armed security guard.

CHAPTER
TEN

Dana walked down Marion Street toward the Federal Building. The clouds had parted and the sun lit a path across Puget Sound, gleaming off the highest points of the Olympic Mountains. Seattle at her finest. She'd decided not to take the car. It wasn't worth the time to find a place to park, even though Gary, her legal assistant, had objected. "It's not safe. Kevin's campaign manager was shot, and now Hoa has some pervert stalking her."

"He's not a pervert," Dana objected. "Just a—"

"Yeah, a murderer? And you're going to traipse down to Pioneer Square to meet with the woman whose car got blown up the other day?" He stared at her, widening his eyes as if to ask if she was hearing him.

"I'll be fine." Dana would be damned if she'd let these people intimidate her. And she wasn't alone. Marcus had stuck with her all morning, sitting in the client chair across from her desk, watching everything she did.

Don't you have somewhere else to be? she'd asked him when nobody else was around.

Things are heating up. I can't let you get hurt.
Any idea who hired your killer?
Too many options.

Great, that was just great. And here he was walking beside her to the Federal Building where Senator Whitmore had her local office. Dana didn't know how a ghost was going to protect her. If somebody grabbed her, would he rush through them and give them a chill? He couldn't tell anybody if she got kidnapped. None of her group could talk to ghosts. Still, she had to admit he was good company, enjoying the city and making little witty quips from time to time.

Yesterday, Whitmore had sent her an email asking for a meeting. Something about an excellent opportunity for them both. Nothing more specific. Dana wasn't sure she needed an opportunity, whatever it was, but she did want to learn what the senator knew about who had blown up her Lincoln Town Car and if it was related to Marcus's death. It had to be.

The Art Deco brick building rose up in front of her, not intimidated by the gleaming glass high rises of Seattle's downtown, but holding its own with a stepped façade and central tower. She went through security and walked past the postal service lobby with its original windows and terra-cotta tile floors. The cast-bronze moldings and bronze-and-glass doors of the interior continued the Art Deco theme.

She took the elevator up and found Senator Whitmore's office, frosted glass doors bearing her name in understated brass lettering. Dana pushed them open and found a discrete security desk just inside, where a stone-faced man greeted her with practiced politeness. An assistant ushered her into the senator's private office that smelled faintly of eucalyptus and jasmine. A bank of windows overlooked the busy ferry terminal and offered a commanding view of Elliott Bay. The senator glanced up from her desk as her assistant showed Dana in—Dana and Marcus if they only knew.

"Thank you, Mary."

"Senator Whitmore." Dana stepped forward and held out her hand.

"Please, call me Evelyn," the senator said as she rose to take Dana's hand.

The Bainbridge ferry blasted out its deep, low arrival horn. Evelyn jumped at the sound. "I spend most of my time in D.C., so I forget how loud it is."

Dana smiled. "I used to live at the top of Capitol Hill. The horn was reassuring to me for some reason."

"A true Seattleite."

Dana chuckled. "I suppose." Marcus hovered by the windows perhaps taking in the view. She wondered if spirits saw the same things humans did or if they saw deeper colors, more detail. She'd done some reading about near-death experiences after her experience with Kimberly and that's what they claimed. Maybe she'd ask him. He'd been alive recently enough to remember.

"Thank you for coming." The senator waved her hand indicating for her to take a seat.

Dana lowered herself into one of the chairs in front of a maple desk. Behind it stood bookshelves lined with policy tomes, law journals, and a few strategically placed photos—Whitmore with the president, Whitmore with local tribal leaders, and one of her planting a sapling in a school garden. Dana stopped herself gawking at the photos and said, "Thank you for the invitation. How are you doing? That was a close call the other day."

Evelyn lifted a shoulder in dismissal. "I'm fine. The FBI is looking into it."

"Do you think it's related to Marcus's murder?"

Marcus turned around to listen.

"I'm sure they'll let us know what they find out." She put one hand on top of the other, as if closing this line of discussion. "I wanted to talk to you about some legislation I've been working on with several people on the Hill. I think it might interest you."

This surprised Dana and she sat a little straighter. "Oh, I see."

"This all must remain between us. I've discussed only the surface layer with Kevin. I'd like it to stay that way. Does this suit you?"

Dana smiled. It suited her just fine and she said so.

"Good." The senator's face lit with enthusiasm, erasing ten years in a flash. "We're going to be able to bring the U.S. health care system into the twenty-first century."

Dana had heard about this legislation. Whitmore had been working on it for years, but Dana had always imagined it was more a pipe dream than a reality. She leaned forward. "Do you mean we're getting free health care? You've got the votes."

"Universal, free health care for everyone. And control over drug prices."

"Oh, my God. Senator Whit—Evelyn. This is outstanding. How can I help?"

"You can join my team."

Dana sat back, deflated. "Move to D.C.? I'd love to help, but my youngest just started high school and—"

"You can stay right here. Don't have to change a thing. In fact, it's best you stay clandestine at the moment."

"You mean work in secret?" Dana knew what 'clandestine' meant, but she was so surprised, she asked anyway. Marcus came to stand beside her, both of them intrigued.

"That's right." The senator glanced at her computer screen. "You're not a full partner yet. I've already spoken with Bill to see if he can spare you. He said it would be a fine opportunity for you and the firm."

No pressure there, Dana thought. She felt both excited and annoyed that Evelyn had gone above her head to one of the firm's founders before asking if she was interested. Then she remembered their conversation at the memorial, how the senator had asked about her work on women's health care. Maybe she had asked her in a roundabout way.

Evelyn's smile was conspiratorial. "Bill will keep your involvement on the down low."

"What about my staff?"

Whitmore raised an eyebrow. "Surely they're used to keeping cases confidential."

"Certainly." Dana gave herself a shake. She was acting like an amateur.

"I need help in several areas, but as a litigator, you'll be anticipating arguments against the bill in the Senate and drafting rebuttals. We've done a lot of this already. The vote is scheduled soon, so I want a final edit from you."

Dana nodded, thinking this was right up her alley.

After the bill passes, there's more. It's a prodigious effort."

"I'd love to see us catch up with the rest of the developed world when it comes to health care."

"You just need to sign this NDA and we can get started." Whitmore pushed the piece of paper over to her and offered her a pen.

Dana scanned the document. It was standard language, so she signed.

"Now, let's sit over here and I'll catch you up." Evelyn moved to a comfortable seating area where a loveseat—could you call a piece of furniture in a senator's office a loveseat, Dana wondered. It sounded slightly scandalous. A small sofa then and soft-backed chairs surrounding a round table. A stack of briefing folders sat to one side, along with a carafe of still water and glasses arranged neatly on a slate tray.

"We're closing in on a final draft of the legislation and my working group's finalizing the votes." Evelyn spent the next half hour diving into the legal details of the bill. Dana's enthusiasm grew as the senator laid it out. "Sounds like you're close to finished."

"First, I'd like you to review the bill with an eye toward the work you did on women's health care. You've had experience there. Then compare it with the French, British, German, and Canadian systems. What are the pitfalls they've run into? Have they fixed these problems? What can we learn from their experience? You know how the right-wing likes to claim nobody can get appointments for months or seen for emergencies. All this with an eye to rebuttals to their objections, press releases, publicity campaigns."

"Just me and my staff?"

Evelyn's laugh filled the room. "I've got other people working on this. I'll connect you with them."

A rush of relief filled Dana. And excitement. This was one of her dreams. To break through the barriers put up by the health care companies buying up the hospitals, the accountants deciding how doctors could run their appointments and what tests they could order. Not to mention denial of care. Dana realized Evelyn was talking.

"...the transition. How long do we need to implement this new plan? What kind of staff is required? Should we do this in stages or all at once?"

Dana tried not to panic, but Evelyn must have seen it on her face. She chuckled. "Don't worry. We'll have a group focused on this aspect as well. I'll keep each group connected."

"Before we get to that phase, though," Evelyn dropped her voice as if she didn't want to be overheard, "try to suss out what the insurance and pharmaceutical people who are donating to Kevin's campaign are up to."

Dana's stomach dropped. Was this the real reason Evelyn had asked her to join in this effort? Because of Kevin? How much should she tell her about their relationship?

Once again, Evelyn sensed her hesitation. She reached over and touched Dana's hand. "You are brilliant. You've been on my radar for a while. Before his campaign. I want you for your mind, not your husband."

This pulled a laugh out of Dana.

"Honestly. It's just that we have big corporations up against us and we need to use every weapon in our arsenal to discover their plans."

Marcus stood behind Evelyn, nodding his head as if to confirm the senator was telling the truth.

Dana felt a rush of anger. Kevin used her without a second thought. Go to this fund raiser. Talk to that person. Smile. And his style consultant. Wear this dress. These shoes. This ridiculous garter belt with these silk stockings. Why shouldn't she turn the tables and use him to do some good? Then doubt ceased her. Kevin's campaign supported better health care and expanding access to good insurance. But as the senator pointed out, they were dropping some big bucks to support his election. She'd have to see.

Dana stuffed the thick folder into her leather messenger bag and stood. "I can do that. Those companies have done enough damage."

A big smile spread across Evelyn's face, softening her features and crinkling the corners of her steel-gray eyes, like a sudden break in the clouds revealing the sun. "That's the spirit."

Dana headed for the door, but Evelyn stopped her. She handed her a small, black phone. "Please use this for all communication with me. There's a number in it. Don't upload anything on it or use it to phone anyone else."

"You're giving me a burner," Dana asked, realizing she was shocked. But she remembered Marcus sitting in her living room with two red bullet holes in his chest and one in his head, the town car exploding in a ball of fire, and the seriousness of the situation finally sank home.

"Oh," she said, then looked up at the senator who nodded, a look of satisfaction on her face.

"Yes, what I'm asking for is dangerous."

Dana pocketed the small phone.

Evelyn asked, "Did you walk? It started raining again."

Dana chuckled. "Big surprise there."

"Best not take any chances with that packet. It's heavy and I'd rather you not be out on the street alone with it." Evelyn went to her desk and pushed a button. "Mary, we'll need the car for Mrs. Preston."

"Thank you." Dana had a flash of the senator's Lincoln exploding and pulled the messenger bag tight.

"Don't worry. The cars are under tight security here."

Dana flushed. "I forgot to ask. How is your driver?"

"He's fine. Just a few cuts and scrapes. And he's sore from that hard landing."

"That's good. It could have been so much worse."

The senator's assistant opened the door. The security guard Dana had seen coming in loomed behind her. "The car is ready. Carl will escort you."

Dana started to object that she didn't need extra protection but then realized that maybe she did. The documents she was carrying definitely needed it. She said her goodbyes to the senator and followed Carl's broad shoulders down the hall.

Carl didn't get into another black Lincoln Town car with Dana and she was grateful because Marcus appeared as soon as they left the garage. *I realized something.*

Dana nodded for him to continue.

Before I accepted the job as Kevin's campaign manager, I was approached by Florence Hospital Conglomerate. They wanted me to work to gain support in Congress for some type of shift in health care delivery. It seemed like they supported Americare for all with certain changes.

That's surprising, Dana thought loudly.

Marcus's form wavered. *You don't have to yell.*

Sorry. Dana whispered the thought.

Marcus chuckled. *I was surprised, too, so I delved into it. They weren't entirely on the up and up. Shocking.* He put his hand to his chest, pretending.

What surprised Dana even more than this information was how Marcus had suddenly remembered so much. After a mostly quiet morning, he was a flood of information. Maybe he could remember who had killed him and move on with his life—afterlife. Existence? At leave move out of her house and office.

The car stopped and Dana realized they were inside the parking garage of the Columbia Center. Marcus snapped out of sight. She gathered her brief case and reached for the door handle, but it

94

opened before she grabbed it. The driver offered his hand for her to take. She wasn't used to such treatment and thought to ignore it but then realized her mother could consider this rude. Why was getting out of a car so complicated? Would he have offered Kevin help getting out?

She blew out a breath and grasped the driver's hand. "Thank you."

"My pleasure. Here's a card with my number. Senator Whitmore says I'll be your driver from now on."

Dana just stood there staring at him. "She said what?"

"I'll be your driver. It's safer that way."

"Uh, I have my SUV here now. I'll have to drive myself home. And, I'm sorry to be indelicate, but didn't one of her cars blow up the other day?"

"Well, yes ma'am, but we've implemented more safety precautions. I'm confident you'll be safer with me."

"But I'm supposed to be clandestine. I'll discuss my concerns with Evel—Senatore Whitmore."

"As you wish, Mrs. Preston. Just give me a call if you need anything. I can drive your family, too." He pushed the card closer to her.

Dana had a sudden image of Hoa arriving at her new school in a Lincoln Town Car to the tune of Beethoven's 5th symphony, her hair floating behind her, all her classmates agog. Until she realized more than half of them arrived in fancy cars with their own private drivers. How had they afforded this school, anyway?

Dana plucked the card out of his hand without looking at it and thanked him. "I'll let you know if we need you." She made her way back up to her office on the 20th floor and placed the messenger bag in the center of her desk. She didn't open it but instead walked to the windows and looked out at her view of Elliott Bay and the Seattle Wheel visible between the downtown skyscrapers. Gray clouds obscured the mountains.

She was waiting for Marcus to reappear and fill her in on this new part of the growing conspiracy, but he never showed up. Dana sat at her desk and dove into the file she'd received. She needed to know as much as possible before she told her staff. And probably go see the head of the firm, Mr. Wyndam—Bill as the senator called him —to tell him she'd accepted the new assignment. Lordy, the air she was breathing was getting more and more rarified. And increasingly dangerous.

CHAPTER
ELEVEN

The walls of the conference room in Grant, Everhart & Vale were paneled in warm alderwood, the table long and polished to a shine. A jug of lemon water sat in the center, untouched. Outside, rain slicked the windows. Inside, tension was thick. Vivienne Grant, tall and composed, adjusted her glasses and spoke in her low, calm voice. A court reporter sat off to the side, fingers poised over a stenographic keyboard.

Skye's aunt, Siobhán Kearney-MacAllister, sat beside her attorney with a stone-faced glare. Beside Siobhán was her daughter and apprentice, Brenna, her gaze sharp as a hawk. Skye watched from a row of chairs behind the table, hands folded, trying to keep her expression neutral. Laurie observed silently, Rosa curled up at her feet. A bunch of Skye's family members wanted to come, but Vivienne said it would look like overkill to have so many extra people attending the deposition.

At the end of the table, Deborah Johnson nervously twisted her beaded necklace, her short blond hair slightly frizzy from the rain. Her lawyer, a thin young man in a blue suit, sat next to her, his briefcase leaning against the side of his chair.

Vivienne had sidelined Skye on the way in. "I already cleared this with your aunt. I'm going in a different direction. New evidence. Just a heads up."

"Not tradition then?"

"It'll be a surprise." Vivienne squeezed her arm, clearly excited.

But now the no nonsense, slightly terrifying warrior was back. Vivienne cleared her throat and spoke to Deborah. "Please raise your right hand. Do you solemnly swear or affirm that the testimony you are about to give is the truth, the whole truth, and nothing but the truth?"

"I—I do."

"Please state your name for the record."

"Deborah Johnson."

"And do you reside at 52670 20th Avenue NE in Seattle?"

"Yes."

"Represented by Brian Welch," interjected the young man.

Vivienne gave him a nod, then turned her attention to his client. "Ms. Johnson, did you file a complaint against Old World Apothecary, owned and operated by Siobhán Kearney-MacAllister?"

"I guess. Is that your name?" The round woman glanced toward Siobhán, eyes round, and shrank under her glare. Her hands rubbed together, her voice uncertain.

"The witness will refrain from addressing the defendant directly," Vivienne said in an even tone. "You did file a complaint, is that correct?"

"Uh, yes."

"On what grounds?"

"Practicing medicine without a license," Deborah's attorney interjected.

"Yes, we are aware of that, but what specifically made you file this complaint."

"Unsafe herbal mixtures. I said the teas made me dizzy."

Vivienne nodded. "I see. Did you consume more than the recommended dose?"

Deborah squirmed in her chair. "Maybe? I mean, it was just tea. I didn't think it could actually..." She stared at her hands.

"Could actually what?" Vivienne coaxed.

Deborah looked up but kept her gaze away from Siobhán. "Well, do anything."

"So, you didn't believe the herbs could have any medical effect," Vivienne stated, "Is that correct?"

Deborah stared at her like a small rabbit sensing a trap. Her attorney leaned over and whispered in her ear. Everyone waited for her to answer, but neither Deborah or her attorney said anything.

Vivienne asked her next question. "Did you visit an emergency room?"

"No. I just called my doctor."

Vivienne looked down at her notepad. "And what did your doctor say?"

Deborah answered quickly, on more sure footing now. "That I probably shouldn't mix herbs with my chemo treatments."

There was a pause. Vivienne leaned forward slightly. "We're all very sorry about your diagnosis. Did you come to our clients seeking treatment?"

"Not really. A friend recommended the shop. Said it helped her with hot flashes."

The young man held up his index finger. "My client assumed the proprietors of this shop would know if their plant mixtures—' he said this a curl of his lip "—were contraindicated for cancer patients."

"But you stated, Ms. Johnson, you were not seeking treatment."

Laurie whispered to the little Havanese, "Do you smell a lie?"

She reeked of guilt before she opened her mouth, Rosa replied softly.

Deborah looked flustered. "Just some relief. I was so tired after four weeks of chemo."

"So, you weren't seeking treatment, but relief?" Vivienne once again didn't give her a chance to explain this contradiction. She

99

leaned forward and asked in a gentle tone, "Who paid you to file the complaint?"

The room stilled. Laurie leaned forward slightly and Rosa lifted her head. Skye gripped the arms of her wooden chair.

Deborah blinked rapidly. "I—I didn't say anyone paid me."

Vivienne smiled softly. "That wasn't my question, Ms. Johnson."

Deborah's eyes dart to her attorney, to Vivienne, and finally to the window, where rain trailed down in silver threads. Her mouth opened and closed like a fish yearning to be in the water outside.

"Objection," her attorney shouted somewhat belatedly. "There is no evidence my client was paid to report what is clearly malpractice."

"Objection," Vivienne countered. "Counsel states this charge as if it is a fact. It has not been proven by the court."

The reporter acknowledged that she had noted both objections.

Vivienne continued her questioning. "Ms. Johnson, can you explain this deposit into your account of $5,000 the day after you testified to the state medical board about this allegation?"

"Objection," Brian shouted.

Deborah whispered, "It's not a lot. They just...suggested it. Said they'd cover my time and give me a stipend for the inconvenience."

"Who, exactly?"

Deborah hesitated.

Siobhán sat motionless, her energy collected like a storm.

Finally, Deborah muttered, "BioCure Pharmaceuticals. They said they were compiling reports on herbal malpractice."

"Oh, my God," Laurie whispered.

Skye leaned over and said in a low voice, "Vivienne said she had a surprise."

"And they encouraged you to file a complaint against Old World Apothecary?" Vivienne asked, ignoring the muttering around the room.

"Objection," Brian shouted, but once again Deborah didn't listen to him.

"They gave me a list of questions to ask. I thought it was just a survey thing. But then I got a letter from the board—" She broke off, face flushed.

Vivienne's look was triumphant. "Did they promise you anything else?

"No, but the money helped. Cancer treatment is expensive," Deborah whined.

"I'm sure it is," Vivienne said sympathetically and repeated the question.

Deborah folded. "They said they'd take it from there."

Skye's aunt let out a low snort of disgust. Rosa tried to muffle her growl with her paw and Laurie bit her lip to keep from laughing.

Vivienne straightened in her chair and looked over at Brian, whose shoulders drooped. "No further questions at this time. Let the record show the witness has admitted to being compensated by a pharmaceutical corporation to file a complaint of dubious merit against my client."

The court reporter nodded, confirming the record. Brian ushered his client out of the room, muttering in her ear. The reporter packed up, then said, "The transcript will be available tomorrow morning."

"Thank you," Vivienne said.

Everyone gathered at the table and pulled the chairs close together. Vivienne stood at the head and took off her blazer, rolling her sleeves up to her elbows. "That, ladies and gentlemen, was the soft sound of a complaint collapsing under its own fraud."

She looks like a panther after a successful hunt, Laurie sent to Rosa.

Rosa ran a lap around the room, celebrating, then paused to sniff Vivienne's sleek leather briefcase, her tail giving one decisive flick. *Panther's not bad,* she said with a little huff. *But she's more like a jaguar.*

Laurie blinked. *A jaguar?*

Yes. Shinier. More dramatic. And she keeps her claws sharp. She's got that 'I-could-eat-you-but-I-won't-because-I-have-court' energy. Rosa hopped up on the chair Vivienne had just vacated and circled twice before settling in.

Laurie stifled a grin. *So, you approve?*

I'd let her represent me. If I ever got arrested for chasing a squirrel into a museum.

"Rosa thinks you're like a jaguar," Laurie told Vivienne.

"That's nice. I guess she can have my chair, then."

"Deborah looked like she was going to melt into the upholstery," Laurie added.

Skye agreed. "She won't be the last. If BioCure's coming after herbalists, they'll be doing it with deeper pockets and dirtier hands than Deborah Johnson's. And with this information, they'll fall like dominos."

Brenna spoke up for the first time. "We need to know how far this goes. Who else they've surveyed." She put air quotes around this word. "Mom wasn't the only one."

"I could have told you they'd start with me. I'm loud about our practice. Proud of it. That makes us a target," Siobhán said.

Vivienne told them about the multiple complaints. "They've targeted practitioners in other states. Even come after Wellspring University. With your permission, I'll get in touch with those other attorneys."

"Yes, of course," Siobhán said. "Let's take these jerks down."

"Good." Vivienne gave a decisive nod. "We don't let them control the narrative. We'll file a motion to dismiss the complaint and submit a countersuit—wrongful accusation, reputational harm, and malicious prosecution, depending on what we dig up. I'll need all correspondence Deborah received from BioCure. We subpoena that next."

"And we make it public?" Skye asked.

Vivienne tilted her head. "Eventually. But carefully. First, we shore up the legal angle. Then we let the media chew on how a billion-dollar company is paying cancer patients to destroy small family businesses under the guise of health advocacy."

Laurie scratched behind her dog's ears. "Rosa says it's all very cloak-and-dagger. She wants a biscuit and a press release."

Vivienne chuckled. "I like her style, but I'm fresh out of dog treats. Sorry, girl."

Fíona spoke for the first time. Skye had almost forgotten her mother was there. "What about protection for the other shops? I don't want our other businesses to come under fire."

"If we can prove a pattern—multiple complaints filed under similar terms—we can file an injunction. Maybe even take it federal under RICO statutes. That kind of corporate interference crosses a line." Vivienne's look was as ferocious as the jaguar Rosa had named her.

"We'll talk to the Circle. The other witches need to know what's coming," Siobhán said.

"And we enchant the shop wards. Stronger this time. Something layered, something sticky. If they send anyone else in, they'll leave marked," Skye added.

Brenna grinned. "I've been working on a tincture that reveals corporate malice. Smells like burnt plastic and avocado toast."

Laurie chortled. "Perfect for a wellness line. 'Unmask Corporate Sharks—Now in a spray!'"

General hilarity broke the tension for a moment.

When things quieted down, Vivienne said, "All jokes aside, this is bigger than Old World Apothecary. We're looking at a campaign to discredit alternative medicine while consolidating pharma profits. If we want to win, we need evidence, allies, and attention. And a lot more lawyers."

Skye pushed back her chair and said in a steady voice, "Then we fight back—with roots deep and fire ready."

Laurie's phone dinged and she glanced at the message. "Dana says she has news and Minh has done some digging, too. Should we meet tonight at the farm?"

"Yes," Skye said.

"I'll cook something to celebrate," Fíona said.

Laurie texted Dana and the group gathered their belongings. "We'll keep you informed," Skye told Vivienne as they walked out of the conference room.

"I have a good feeling about this," the jaguar replied.

CHAPTER
TWELVE

"Marcus gave me some new information," Dana told her friends. They were gathered around the long table in the large family farmhouse laden with salads, roasted vegetables, fried trout, and casseroles.

Skye's Aunt Aoife pushed a cheesy vegetable casserole closer to her. Dana put her palm up. "No thank you. I'm about to go into a food coma as it is."

Minh took a second, no third helping.

"Don't eat them out of house and home," Dana half-joked.

"He's a growing boy and we have plenty," said Uncle Rowan, the creator of the magical combination, pride evident on his face.

Minh gave her a triumphant smile. Unfortunately, he had something stuck in his teeth which ruined the effect he was going for. She gestured toward her mouth, but he just took another forkful. Hoa had gone off with some of the other younger teens and would be engrossed for the rest of the evening doing who knew what. Dana wasn't worried.

She'd driven them out to Red Fox Farm, not wanting to take Evelyn's offer of a driver and let her in on this part of her life. Dana's friends were too dear to her to bring them to the attention of such high rollers and she wasn't ready to be chauffeured around just yet.

"Marcus has been around more lately," Dana said, then laughed when Laurie started looking around the room. "Not now, but this afternoon he listened in on a meeting I had with a new client and his memory is better" She was struggling with how much she could reveal. Attorney/client privilege and all that. If anything seemed relevant, she had figured out ways over the years to share information without divulging too much context.

Rowan and Aoife started cleaning up around them. Apparently, all of the Yarrow family was in the know. Given the legal action against the apothecary, she figured they were entitled to listen.

"We have news, too." Skye sat back with her mug of tea. "You first."

"It's touchy. I can't reveal too much about the meeting. Let's just say it has to do with health care in the country." Dana explained that Marcus had been offered a job with Florence Hospitals to lobby in favor of Americare for All legislation with certain changes. "He turned it down. Took Kevin's offer instead, but he thought it might be connected to his—"

"Death?" Laurie asked.

Dana nodded, surprised her eyes filled up with tears. Laurie patted her arm.

"Florence Hospitals," Skye repeated. "I'm not familiar with that name."

Siobhán filled her in. "They're an up-and-coming conglomerate. Been snapping up hospitals right and left. Just made an offer for Bayview."

"How do you know that?" Skye asked.

"One of our consultants is a nurse there. Lots of controversy. The staff is afraid new ownership would impose restrictions on how they treat patients."

"Would that happen?"

"Oh, yes. They let the accountants decide how much time

doctors can spend with patients. Push less risky procedures. They even make certain hospitals go-to places for prevalent surgeries, cutting back on other operations."

Skye turned back to Dana. "Why would a hospital group support Americare for All? Wouldn't that cut into their profits?"

"Worse than that. It would put national health care under public control. Maybe cut out private corporations altogether. Marcus said they were pushing for changes, though."

Laurie shook her head, picking tiny bones out of her last bite of trout. A gray stripped cat waited patiently, eyeing the morsel. "Seems to be a lot of action from companies involved in health care."

"Right," Minh said. "I found out that guy at the memorial who pissed off—"

"Language," Dana muttered.

Minh huffed. "Mom. I'm in college now."

Dana couldn't think of a rejoinder to that.

"As I was saying, the man Mr. Robertson got upset over"—Minh gave his mother the side eye—"bought that health insurance company."

"Thomas Ellsworth," Skye said.

"Took over Primewell Health Insurance," Minh reminded them. "And the former owner was murdered after he threatened a lawsuit."

"We thought he might have had something to do with Marcus's death," Dana said.

Skye raised her finger. "Here's another connection. We discovered that BioCure Pharmaceuticals paid that woman to file the complaint against the family apothecary."

"That's fraud," Dana said.

"There are complaints against Wellspring University and tons of other small herbalist and alternative practitioners in several states," Siobhán said as she placed a large piece of apple pie hiding under a huge scoop of vanilla ice cream in front of Minh.

Dana opened her mouth to object that her son was going to

explode, but Laurie pressed on. "Vivienne is checking to see if they're behind any of the other complaints."

"So, one company is supporting free health care for the country under Americare with some caveats while another is attacking alternative practitioners," Skye mused.

"Florence Hospital and now BioCare," Jade said.

"BioCare, BioCare." Dana got out her phone and searched the name. "Largest pharmaceutical company in the world."

Minh turned his laptop around. A row of pictures displayed the CEO and his top staff. "Damien Blackwood. Mom, didn't you say the other night that you met a Damien at the fundraiser. Is this him?"

"I'll be damned," Dana said.

"Language," Minh mouthed, but his mother didn't notice.

"That's him. They were talking about the president. Said that he was 'their idiot'. They clammed up as soon as they saw me."

"This is some serious shit," Skye said.

Minh snorted.

"Let me see the rest of the staff pictures." Dana crouched down beside her son and scanned the screen. "Hmm, I don't see the woman he was with."

Minh clicked on a link that read 'Board of Trustees.'

Dana pointed. "That's her. Right there."

Minh enlarged her picture and read, "Olivia Mercer, Chair of the Board."

"This company has donated a lot of money to Kevin's campaign," Dana said. "And the President of the United States is their idiot," Jade said.

They all sat in silence for a minute, absorbing this information.

"Three big corporations, all involved in a different aspect of health care, all connected to us in some way," Jade said.

"Conspiring to do what exactly?" Skye asked.

Three dogs burst into the kitchen covered in some foul smelling something. Laurie shouted, "Rosa, what have you—"

"Taran, not again." Jade stood and pointed to the dog flap in the kitchen door. "Out."

We went hunting and Taran said we had to mask our scent, Rosa explained, tail wagging, tongue hanging out.

"You call that masking?" Laurie asked out loud. "I could smell you a mile away. You're getting a bath before you get in my new car."

Can't she stay here? Taran asked. *She's in our pack now.*

Hoa ran into the kitchen, then stopped, hand to her nose. "Eww. What's that stink?"

"The dogs rolled in something." Jade opened the door. "Come on, outside. You all get hosed off. Good thing it's still warm."

Not me, Taran said. He took off for the woods, a streak of black under the moonlight. Ashe sat in the grass off to the side of the house and let Jade wash her down.

Do I have to? Rosa whined.

Yes, Laurie said.

Uncle Rowan stood on the porch chuckling. "Here's a dog towel. They get into things pretty regular."

Dana watched from her seat at the kitchen table, Siobhán by her side. "Seems like we've got ourselves into some stinky mess, too."

Siobhán nodded. "I'll think on what kind of magic will help us out. Can you come by tomorrow night for a spell?"

Dana blinked, realizing she didn't mean come by for a while, but for a magic spell. "You think that will help?"

"No doubt about it. Bring these two." Siobhán pointed to Dana's two teens who were watching with eager faces.

"Mom, Cillian asked me to stay. Can I? Pleeeaase," Hoa asked, dancing in place.

"Malcolm promised to show me the salmon run in the morning," Minh said. "If I'm here, we can go out early. Then we're watching the Huskies game."

"We'd be glad to have them." Siobhán said. "There's so many of us, we'll hardly notice another two kids."

Dana agreed to letting the kids stay over. She'd known Skye all her life and loved being connected to this great big Scots Irish clan. It was good to see the kids being a part of it. She was only now realizing how deep their magical roots were and finding herself grateful for that as well.

She enjoyed the quiet on the ride home, turning everything she'd learned today over in her mind. There was a lot of work to be done. Should she text Evelyn what she'd learned about Florence Hospitals? It was late. Maybe in the morning. The nerve of those people naming themselves after one of the most compassionate nurses in history. Dana parked, gave the security guard who stood on the sidewalk a nod, and climbed the steps.

She slipped her key into the front door, the old Victorian sighing around her like a tired dowager. The hall was dark, just a crack of warm light spilling from the kitchen. Skye's farm still clung to her skin—the scent of sage, the warmth of her friend's kitchen. She set her purse down and toed off her shoes, ready to pour a glass of wine and watch the late news on the living room TV. But then she heard it —Kevin's voice. Low. Firm. On the phone.

"No, I'm telling you—it's going to pass," he was saying. "I think that's what they want."

She stopped mid-step.

Kevin's voice grew sharper, his footsteps audible across the tile. "Yes. Americare for All. I think they want to let Whitmore take her victory lap."

A silence. Then, "I agree. It seems like they'd be against it."

Dana took a step closer. What was this?

"BioCure, Primewell, and Florence Hospitals. They're already drafting some plan."

Dana's stomach flipped. The same three companies they'd identified at the farm tonight.

In the corner of the dining room, something shifted. The faint outline of a man emerged beside the sideboard—faded jeans, blazer, no shoes. Marcus Robertson, still looking twenty-eight, clean-shaven, and with a little frown. He gave her a sympathetic raise of the eyebrow.

Kevin again. "The big meeting is tomorrow afternoon. They'll try to get my support."

Dana blinked. Did they want Kevin to get involved in shutting down alternative health care around the country? How was that connected to Senator Whitmore's legislation?

"The money is more than I could ever have imagined. And it's more than the money."

Marcus snorted, if a ghost could do such a thing. She looked over at him, but he was staring at the floor, shaking his head. Sadness stabbed her.

Kevin's voice was quieter now. "Dana doesn't know and I don't want her involved."

"Jesus," Dana whispered. She reached for the doorframe, steadying herself.

Behind her, Lele the tortoiseshell cat padded silently into the room, tail flicking. She rubbed against Dana, maybe sensing her distress.

Marcus stood with his arms crossed, eyes fixed on the kitchen. *He's been taking calls like this for weeks.*

Dana turned her head toward him. *Why didn't you say something?*

I only put it together right before—

Before you were killed. Dana's pulse thrummed in her neck. The health care industry wasn't fighting the bill. And Kevin was being courted. Helping Whitmore push it through so his allies could—do what? Had Marcus gotten in the way?

She stepped back from the doorway. Lele trotted off since Dana didn't sit down.

Kevin's voice came once more, firm and smooth. "Marcus warned me about the plans before my meeting with the primaries. I asked Ellsworth about it, but he said they'd lay it all out at the meeting."

Silence, then. "Do you think it was really a robbery?"

Dana's thoughts tangled. Could he be that naïve? Then snapped into a sharp line. No, he wasn't just hiding something from her. He was hiding something from everyone. And thought he was smart enough to get away with whatever game he was playing. The man she thought she separate from amicably? He was in deeper than she'd imagined.

She turned to ask Marcus a question, but he'd disappeared. Dana climbed the steps to the bedroom, quiet as the cat. Kevin had taken to sleeping in the guest room when he was home, which was less and less often. Frankly, it was a relief. Now that she knew, she couldn't stand to be close to him. The man she'd slept next to, loved, whose children she had borne, had revealed things that helped snuff out the life of a vibrant, kind, and promising young man. Accidentally or not.

THIRTEEN

The morning light spilled into the kitchen falling on Dana like a soft, comforting touch. She stood motionless by the coffee pot, her mug cooling beside her. Kevin had left early, claiming a breakfast with donors, but she knew now he wasn't being truthful. Later today, he was going to this mysterious meeting to hear more about whatever these CEOs were plotting.

She glanced toward the hallway, then up at the ceiling, where the air felt subtly...off. A shimmer. A presence.

"You've been lurking since last night," she said aloud. "Come on out."

From the edge of the dining room, Marcus appeared—his form half-substantial, a worn blazer over jeans, dark hair unruffled by any living breeze.

I wasn't lurking, he said. *I was waiting for you to get over the shock of what Kevin said.*

Dana turned, folding her arms and said out loud. "Tell me what you've remembered."

Marcus approached slowly, his face solemn. *I can't give you every-*

thing. Not yet. Some of it has only recently came clear. And even now, it's like I'm chasing smoke.

She said nothing, just waited.

Before I was killed, he began, *I'd started putting together a pattern. Kevin was having off-the-record meetings—after hours, no notes, no phones. Some of the people were from BioCure Pharmaceuticals. Others from Primewell Health and Florence Hospitals. I assumed it was about donations at first. Backroom deals. Shady, but normal politics.*

But it wasn't, Dana said.

Marcus shook his head. *They weren't talking about messaging or campaign strategy. They were talking about data. Medical trials. Something about immune response modulation to some studies they were conducting. Whatever they were doing, it wasn't public. And it wasn't legal.*

Dana's mouth tightened. *Human subjects?*

I think so. I heard the phrase 'non-consensual data harvesting.' And 'offsite facility.' They were playing with something they couldn't control.

She pressed her fingers to her temples. *And Kevin?*

He was careful. Never directly involved. But he wasn't ignorant, Dana. He knew enough to stay close but keep his hands clean.

Dana's voice was a whisper. "And this is why they killed you."

Marcus looked down. *I got too close. I had documents—meeting minutes, internal memos, encrypted drafts of something called* The Lazarus Directive. *That's when I started pulling together a dossier.*

He looked up, meeting her eyes. *I called it 'Fallback.' I hid the drive inside a carved wooden puzzle box I gave Minh. Thought no one would look twice at a gift from me. It's probably still in his room.*

Dana's heart pounded. *You think what's on it could stop this?*

I think it's a start, Marcus said.

Then we dig, Dana finally said. *And we bring it all into the light.*

Marcus nodded. *I knew you would.*

He faded slowly, leaving the faintest scent of rain and cedarwood behind.

She took a sip of her coffee, but it had gone cold. Time to find that drive. It turned out to be a good thing that Minh had stayed over at Red Fox Farm. Dana paused at the door to his room, bracing herself. She'd raised this boy for seventeen years, but nothing prepared her for the level of entropy he called "organized." She took one step inside and was immediately assaulted by the pungent aroma of gym socks, leftover pizza, and teenage musk. Clothes blanketed the floor, covering every inch of the carpet. Somewhere, probably, there was a desk. Maybe even a chair.

"Minh!" she shouted. Maybe she shouldn't have told him it was his job to clean his room now that he was in college. She sighed and stepped gingerly inside, trying to avoid stepping on anything squishy.

A blue hoodie was draped over what must be a gaming chair that swiveled on its own as she passed. The surface of the desk was clear as only an altar to the internet could be. A pile of comic books had been arranged into a teetering tower next to the bed, and under the bed—Dana squatted—she found a veritable junkyard of crumpled energy drink cans and granola bar wrappers.

Lele padded into the room with the regal disdain only a tortoise-shell cat could manage. The feline sneezed delicately, then launched herself onto the windowsill, curling her tail around her feet.

Dana yanked open the closet door and was hit with a second wall of smells: a heady mix of Axe body spray, old sneakers, and...was that a pepperoni stick? Clothes spilled out in a slow-motion avalanche. She caught a glimpse of tangled charging cords, a skateboard, and three mismatched shoes.

The cat stretched, yawned, and then, in one graceful leap, landed on a shelf halfway up. She pawed at a shoebox tucked behind a stack of manga volumes. Lele seemed to be directing the search. Dana fervently hoped she would not start hearing Lele's thoughts like her friend Laurie. Ghosts were enough to deal with.

Dana pulled the shoebox down, dust flying everywhere. She coughed and opened the lid. Inside was a tangle of cords, a pocketknife, a half-melted chocolate bar, and—there it was.

The wooden puzzle box.

Now to open it.

Turning it over in her hands, she studied at all six sides. The smooth wood, worn from handling by some previous owner, gave off a faint scent of cedar, reminding her of her current ghost. She checked for seams, panels, tiny gaps, or oddly placed inlays. Running her fingers gently along the edges, she felt a piece give slightly. It slid horizontally, then stopped. She pushed along the edge of the box and felt something shift. She tilted the box over and the other end popped open revealing a small cavity.

Inside was the thumb drive. Blue plastic.

"Thank God."

That was fast, came a voice near her elbow.

Dana yelped and spun. Marcus leaned against the doorframe, arms crossed. He was looking more like the snappy, erudite guy he'd been when he was alive.

"Don't sneak up on me!" she snapped, clutching the drive like it was a lifeline.

Thought you might need help with that. He pointed toward the blue drive.

Lele leapt down and rubbed against Marcus's leg. Dana narrowed her eyes. How she managed to touch an incorporeal being was beyond her. *She likes you. She didn't like Kimberly as much.*

The cheerleader sends her regards, Marcus teased.

Dana opened her mouth to ask but then decided she didn't want to know. She grabbed her messenger bag from the bedroom, went into the home office, and pulled her computer out. She stared at the thumb drive in her hand, the label catching the desk lamp's glow —'Fallback' scrawled in blocky, all-caps handwriting.

She plugged it into her laptop, her fingers trembling just slightly. The screen flickered, then opened to a single encrypted folder. She entered the password Marcus whispered to her—*persephone13*—and the files bloomed open like toxic flowers.

Lele, ever the curious sentinel, hopped up beside her and stared at the screen, tail flicking.

The folder was packed. Emails. Meeting minutes. Draft contracts. Names of donors. Line after line implicating corporations and political operatives. BioCure Pharmaceuticals, Primewell Health Insurance, and Florence Hospital Conglomerate dominated the list.

She clicked into a document titled "Q3-Shadow_Meeting_Notes" and began to read: Ellsworth confirmed Representative P. will introduce language that appears public-friendly. Once passed, Primewell initiates Step Two. Florence to handle media rollout. Mercer agreed to quiet opposition via H.A.C. contributions.

Dana's mouth went dry. H.A.C.—Health Advancement Coalition. A 501(c)(4) she'd heard mentioned at the last fundraising gala, supposedly advocating for "affordable access."

She clicked another file: "donor_matrix.xlsx." Rows of names. Amounts. Meeting dates. Side notes. And beside Kevin's name was a short annotation: Gatekeeper. Keep clean on paper.

"This seems to be about Senator Whitmore's bill. You mentioned clandestine research," she whispered. "How is this connected to the injunction against Old World Apothecary?"

Marcus appeared beside her, his features dim in the screen's glow. *What's this about the apothecary?*

Dana explained to him that BioCure was bribing people to submit false claims against herbalists and other alternative health practitioners.

First I've heard about that. It's all connected somehow. We just need to figure out the whole picture. A few days before the fundraiser in Olympia, somebody searched my office at the campaign headquarters. The place was trashed. I was afraid they'd break into our apartment. That Maddie was at risk.

Dana turned to him, jaw tight. *So, you made this backup.*

I didn't want my research disappearing.

And gave it to Minh?

He's smart. And most importantly, nobody was watching him.

And you didn't think this would put him in danger? her teeth clenched.

No, I spread it around that I'd put some sensitive information in a safe deposit box. Said it to a few people who couldn't keep a secret if their life depended on it. Marcus flinched, realizing what he'd said.

I'm sorry, Marcus.

He squared his shoulders. *I apologize if I made a mistake.*

Dana exhaled sharply, bracing herself on the desk. *If anyone finds out Minh has this—*

They won't, Marcus said. *Not unless we screw up.*

Can we trust what's here? Dana asked.

Marcus gave a grim nod. *I cross-referenced every file I could.*

Does Senator Whitmore know about any of this?

I didn't get a chance to tell her. She has an excellent network, though. She might have figured out some of it.

I need to warn her.

Marcus's form glowed. *She's such a bright light. You should see her from this side.*

Dana's gaze locked on a folder near the bottom of the file list. Unlike the others with sterile, businesslike names, this one stood out: "Threats."

She hesitated for just a second, then double-clicked. The folder opened slowly, revealing a sparse collection of files—only four. But each name felt weighted, as if the folder itself were holding its breath.

The first document was titled "Dickinson_Report_1.docx."

She clicked.

Subject: Frederick A. Dickinson – BioCure Internal Audit Division

   Date: February 12, 2025

   Summary: F.A. Dickinson has flagged multiple irregularities in the allocation of funds for Project PHOENIX and associated subcontracts. Believed to have made contact with outside parties, including media.

   Risk Level: HIGH.

Status: Under surveillance. Do not approach directly.
Potential leak target identified: NYT contact "Janus."

Dana sat up straighter. "Fred Dickinson," she murmured. "He's a whistleblower."

Marcus's expression darkened. *He reached out to me a few days before I died. His thoughts were quiet. Said he couldn't sit with what they were doing anymore. I told him to be careful. They already suspected. We planned to meet.*

The second file was a surveillance photo—grainy, black and white—of a man in his fifties with thinning gray hair and a worn briefcase, stepping into a Link station.

Caption: *DICKINSON. MARCH 2025.*

The third contained a partial email chain, flagged with the subject line: "RE: Containment options." In it, Damien Blackwood casually discussed "legal redirection" strategies—planting evidence of workplace misconduct, leaking tax documents to suggest fraud, and initiating a "security breach audit" to justify termination and public discrediting.

Dana opened the last file: "Transcript_Call_O.M.–D.B." She scrolled, her stomach tightening as she read:

> Olivia Mercer (OM): We don't have time to play gentle. If he's talking to Janus, we take the gloves off.
>
> Damien Blackwood (DB): Agreed.
>
> OM: Dickinson goes dark. You understand?
>
> DB: Understood. I'll activate the Vancouver team.
>
> OM: No trails. No ghosts. Just like last time.

"No ghosts," Dana repeated, a chill running through her. "Too late for that."

Marcus's form wavered.

Dana leaned back, absorbing the depth of it. She closed the folder, her resolve hardening. She turned to Marcus and said out loud, "We need to find out if Dickinson's still alive. If he is—he needs protection."

Marcus faded slightly, voice echoing just above a whisper. *Then we'd better move fast. Because Olivia and Damien? They don't wait for second chances.*

CHAPTER

FOURTEEN

D ana pulled out the burner phone Senator Whitmore had given her in their meeting. She found only one number preprogrammed and she pressed it.

Whitmore answered immediately. "What's happened?"

"I've discovered why Marcus was murdered." She told her about the thumb drive, the information he'd collected. "They want to sabotage your legislation. I don't know how. And they're doing illegal research. Hiding the results."

There was a loaded silence. "And Marcus had proof of this?"

"Yes, I'm looking at it right now."

"Send it," Witmore demanded.

"I can't. I'm on my home network. I don't want to put my family in any more danger."

"What then?"

"I'll make a copy and bring it to you."

"Too risky. I'll send a car."

This time, Dana had no objection to being chauffeured around. She even hoped Carl would be there. Then she realized Whitmore had ended the call before she had a chance to tell her about Fred

Dickinson. She put the burner back in her bag, made a duplicate of the thumb drive, and slipped it in next to the little black phone. Next, she texted Laurie and Skye on her own phone, asking if they could free themselves up for the afternoon.

Skye: Working at the store. Can do tonight.

Laurie: I can help.

Dana: I'll pick you up. Bring Rosa.

Laurie: Of course. What's this about?

Dana: Have to tell you in person.

Dana wrote down Fred's address from the information on the thumb drive, then considered where to hide it. Probably back in the puzzle box. She opened the cedar rectangle and replaced the drive, then took a deep breath before daring Minh's closet again. She was going to have to have a serious talk with that boy.

Dana stopped as she was settling the puzzle box back in its original hiding place. She couldn't put her son at risk. She headed to her own closet and scanned for a good spot. A wicked thought came to her. The five-inch heels. The stylist had told her to keep them. "You wore them. I can't return them."

She opened the shoe box, slipped the small puzzle box in with the torture devices, closed the lid, and stuffed them behind all her other shoes, some still in their own boxes. Then grabbed a jacket and her computer, ran downstairs, and poured extra kibble into Lele's dish. The cat sniffed it, then sat beside it and gave her a disapproving look.

"Geez." Cats were more demanding than ghosts. "I'll give you chicken sausage, but don't let it sit long. I might be late."

Dana could swear the cat lifted her eyebrow in disdain at such a ridiculous comment. She refused to start hearing Lele's thoughts, too. Ghosts were enough. Wait, had she accepted this spirit-seeing situation was permanent? That she'd become—what had Laurie called it? A medium? No way. Maybe she could help the occasional stuck soul, but that was it. Dana grabbed everything, then remembered her Ruger. She had no idea what they'd find when they arrived at Fred's house. Carl better be there.

And he was. The Lincoln Town Car idled at the curb. He opened the door as soon as she walked out onto the porch. The security guy Kevin had sent was still on duty. She wondered for the first time if she could trust them. Kevin was turning out to be more shady than she imagined. She wondered how he'd react when he learned what these corporations had in mind.

The young Chris moved in front of her to inspect the car, startling her out of her thoughts. "It's all right. I've got security," she pointed to Carl.

Chris eyed the bulky man with maybe some professional jealousy, then moved to the side, standing right next to Dana. "If you say so, ma'am."

"I'll be fine. Nobody's home, so you can take off if you'd like."

Chris gave her a condescending smile. "I'd better stay, ma'am. An empty house is a temptation."

"Good point." Chris moved back and Dana slid into the car. Carl took the front passenger seat and she gave Chris a thumbs up as they pulled away. The side streets made the ride down the hill to Whitmore's office only last about ten minutes. Once they pulled into the garage, Dana started to get out, but Carl stopped her. "Joey can run it up."

She hesitated. "This is highly sensitive."

"We all have top security clearance, plus he's combat trained. He's more equipped to protect the drive than you are. No offense intended."

Dana blinked. This was getting too serious. She handed the copy she'd made over to the driver.

"It's in good hands, Mrs. Preston," Joey said and headed for the stairs.

Not the elevator? Dana wondered. Must be part of his combat

training. In five minutes, he reappeared, not even out of breath—the nerve—and they were off to pick up Laurie and her canine assistant in the Sunset Hill neighborhood.

Her friend had used a chunk of her settlement money from Anthony University to go in with John on a house there, shortening their commute to work on their boats in Shilshole Bay Marina.

If you could call floating around on Puget Sound work.

Laurie sued for wrongful termination and a few other charges after her department chair had fired her, a tenured professor no less, citing bogus claims from students. As it turned out, Dr. Brown, said chair, recruited the students, making promises of grades and recommendations for jobs, graduate school, even money. He'd even written up the complaints himself. Dr. Brown was rightfully terminated, not with extreme prejudice like poor Marcus, and Laurie had retired on a few cool million.

Joey headed north out of downtown, weaving through traffic with a deft hand at the wheel. They arrived in decent time. Laurie and Rosa were waiting outside her small mid-century modern home whose price tag had most decidedly not been small. Dana was glad they'd bought way back before the Seattle real estate market soared higher than Mt. Rainier. She hoped Kevin wouldn't put up a big fight for it.

The little Havanese mix jumped into the car first, and Dana braced herself for traces of what the dog had rolled in at the farm. To her relief, she smelled of lilacs and chamomile. Laurie nudged Rosa over so she could get into the car. "Yeah, she got a bath. Rosa says she doesn't like smelling like flowers."

"How did she know—" Dana shook her head. "Never mind. I have news."

"What's with your entourage? And this car?" Laurie asked.

"Senator Whitmore insisted."

"Senator—"

"It's a long story, but I discovered what got Marcus killed."

Laurie looked around the car, probably for the ghost, then glanced down at Rosa. "Oh," she said, looking sheepish.

"Can Rosa see ghosts? Or the lack thereof?" Dana asked, her mouth twitching into the smile she was trying to suppress.

"Maybe," Laurie answered, then got to the subject at hand. "Okay, spill it. And what's up with all the cloak and dagger?"

Dana filled everyone in on what she'd discovered since last night.

"Wait, Kevin is involved in this debacle?" Laurie asked.

"Up to his cummerbund. Except I don't think he realized he was endangering Marcus's life. He has a meeting soon where they're going to expose their whole plan. Wish I could be a fly—wait."

"Think we can get Kevin to tell us?"

Dana shook her head. "Highly doubtful. Apparently, my husband is being seduced by large sums of money. I was just thinking maybe I could talk Marcus into attending."

Laurie looked around again, then at Rosa. The little dog seemed to shake her head.

"Except Marcus doesn't come when he's called. Unlike your little canine here."

Rosa narrowed her eyes at Dana.

"She says she likes her pack leader," Laurie said, then asked before the two of them—Dana and Rosa—got into a squabble, "Who's this whistleblower?"

"Fred Dickinson."

"All this information is on the thumb drive you sent up to the senator?" Carl interjected.

"Most of it, but I overheard Kevin on the phone last night. I'm not sure Senator Whitmore understands how deeply he's involved."

"Copy that," Carl said, then hesitated. "And am I to understand you see ghosts and your friend here talks to animals?"

Dana studied him, looking for signs he was mocking them, but Carl looked serious. The two friends hesitated, so Rosa stook up and barked in the affirmative. At least it seemed that way to Dana. She raised one shoulder and said sheepishly, "Uh, yeah, but do you mind not sharing that with the senator."

"Why not? They seem like handy skills."

"Uh," Dana didn't know how to respond to Carl being nonplussed by what some would call supernatural abilities. "It's just —I'm not sure the senator would see it like you do."

"Roger that," Carl repeated and took out his own version of the little black phone. "Do you mind if I tell her the other parts of this?" he asked Dana.

"Go ahead." Dana hadn't looked forward to telling Whitmore face to face that her husband was a traitor and had inadvertently contributed to the murder of Marcus Robertson. Carl spoke to his boss and told her what he'd just learned. He ended the call and Dana finished explaining Fred's part in the ever-spreading conspiracy. Or as much as she understood.

Dana looked up, surprised when the car came to a stop and Joey deftly pulled into a tight parking spot. She'd been so absorbed explaining the complicated mess that she hadn't realized they'd arrived.

Joey turned off the engine. "Let me know if you need me."

Carl clapped him on the shoulder. "Best to wait here. Let's hope he's still alive."

Dana's stomach knotted up. What if they found a body? Or worse, no body but blood everywhere? Was that worse? What if he defended himself with deadly force and they had to help him hide his attacker?

Laurie grabbed her hand. "Let me take the lead on this."

Dana nodded, grateful to her friend. They all got out of the car, closing the doors quietly.

Rosa ran up the metal steps of Fred Dickinson's Northgate

apartment and stopped suddenly, drawing back and pawing at her nose. "This place stinks," she told her human.

"Kinda like you did last night?" Laurie asked from the landing right below.

Rosa sat up straighter. "That was hunting camouflage. This is—" She sneezed.

Laurie caught up to Rosa and walked close to the door to read the number. This was it. The odor of stale coffee, sweaty clothes, and something fried long ago and never properly cleaned up came from an open window.

Dana arrived beside them and knocked twice, firm but polite. She waited but got no answer. She knocked again before nudging the door open. Dana seemed to have recovered from her bout of nerves. "Fred?" she called.

Laurie followed close behind, Rosa's tiny nails clicking against the dingy tile as they stepped inside. The place was chaos. Half-packed suitcases lay open on the floor, clothes jammed inside at awkward angles, as if Fred had stuffed them by the handful rather than folding. Papers were everywhere—strewn across the couch, the table, even the floor near the door. It looked like he'd dropped an entire file box in his scramble.

And there he was, thin as a rail, hunched over, yanking a laptop cord from the wall with shaking hands. His glasses slid down his sweaty nose, and his eyes were wide, frantic, flicking toward the door like a cornered rabbit.

"No—no, no, please—don't—" he stammered, hands up as if Dana had come armed, which she probably had if Laurie had to bet on it. His gaze shot to Carl standing behind them with his unruffled, mountain-of-a-man look, arms crossed, wearing his security jacket like a badge of certainty.

Fred's thin lips quivered. "They...they sent him, didn't they?" His voice cracked. "I knew it. I *knew* they wouldn't let me—" He backed toward the window like he was ready to fling himself out of it if Carl so much as blinked.

"Fred," Dana's voice cut in, steady, calm. "Carl's not here to hurt you. He works for Senator Whitmore. He's assigned to me. We're here to help you."

Fred's fingers spasmed where they gripped the laptop bag. "Help me?" His laugh came out high, breathless, wrong. "Sure. Right. That's what they all say until I end up at the bottom of the Sound."

Rosa positioned herself between Fred and Laurie. "This one's about to bolt," she warned. "You're not safe."

"Fred, listen." Laurie kept her voice low, the way she'd talk to frightened dogs at the shelter, the ones who'd flinch at every movement but desperately wanted to believe someone might be kind. "We know about BioCure. We know what you were doing. The file. The donors. We're not here to stop you—we're here because we believe you."

They didn't exactly know, but they understood enough. She wasn't lying. Not exactly.

His eyes flitted between Laurie and Dana, confusion knitting his brow, sweat beading at his temple. "But that guy—" He wave a shaky hand at Carl.

"Carl is not the enemy," Dana repeated firmly. She nodded toward him. "Carl, show him your ID."

Carl reached slowly into his jacket, pulling out his security badge, and held it out for Fred to see.

"I...I don't know..." Fred's voice cracked again. His knees buckled, and he dropped onto the edge of the couch, fingers threading into his hair. "I'm dead either way."

"No, you're not," Dana said, stepping forward. "That's why we're here. You're not running. You're not dying. You're going to tell us everything you know, and we're going to make sure you live to see these bastards go down."

Fred's chest heaved as he tried to catch his breath. Laurie could hear Rosa panting beside her, feel the dog's tense energy. Laurie sent her a calm thought, and she settled, still wary but waiting.

Fred stared at the badge like it might bite him and not the dog watching him closely, then finally dropped his head into his hands. His voice was so small Laurie barely heard him. "They were going to sell out the whole damn trial. The longevity research, the donor lists...all of it. Primewell, Florence, BioCure—they're all in on it."

"Longevity?" Laurie mumbled.

Dana crouched in front of him, steady as a rock. "Start from the beginning."

Fred's hands trembled where they gripped the edge of the sagging couch, knuckles sharp and white against the threadbare fabric.

Laurie stayed still, keeping her voice soft. "It's okay," she said, easing closer. "Take a breath. You're safe right now."

Rosa's dark eyes stayed locked on Fred, ears tipped forward. *He's like a rabbit with a fox at his back,* came the thought from the little dog.

Laurie gave a slight nod, acknowledging the truth of it. Tension rolled off Fred like waves of static. He smelled of panic—acrid sweat clinging like a second skin.

Beside them, Dana waited, steady, patient. "Fred. Tell us what you know."

Fred's lips pressed together hard, as if trying to hold the words in by force. His thin frame shuddered. He looked at Carl again, mistrust flickering in his bloodshot eyes—but Carl didn't move, arms crossed, his weight solid at the door.

Finally, Fred let out a shaky exhale, one hand coming up wipe his brow. "I wasn't supposed to know half of it," he mumbled. "Middle managers don't get brought into the really dirty parts. But I'm in procurement—I see things."

Laurie stayed quiet, listening. She settled on the edge of the sofa next to him, but not too close. She could feel the pull of his fear, but beneath it was something else. Guilt maybe. She wished Skye was here. Ms. Empath would know.

Fred swallowed hard. "There's research—longevity studies, genetic manipulation."

"Wait, genetic manipulation?" Laurie asked. This was beyond what Dana had explained in the car.

"Yes, but that's not the worst of it. BioCure's been funneling trial results through shell companies, hiding the failures. Suppressing reports of side effects, even deaths. The drugs don't work the way they claim."

Dana's face stayed calm, but her eyes hardened.

"They want to make longevity available to those who can afford it." Fred's hands knotted into fists on his knees. "I found the contracts. The emails. There's a donor list, too. Senatorial campaigns, Super PACs, fake charities—all getting payouts and promises."

Laurie felt Rosa stiffen beside her. The dog's thoughts pushed into her mind again, sharper this time. *He's not lying. He's afraid for the right reasons.*

That's what I thought, too, Laurie sent back.

Fred dragged in another breath, fingers flexing uselessly. "I started copying files. Quietly. Stashing them on a drive. Thought maybe if I went to the Times—" His throat worked hard as he swallowed. "But then Damien Blackwood and Olivia Mercer...they found out. They're not just corporate executives, they're predators. They made sure I knew what would happen if I talked."

His gaze shot back to Carl again, a flash of terror. "That's why I thought—I thought you were them. Sent to finish the job."

Laurie leaned forward, resting her elbow on her knee, keeping her tone low. "You've been carrying this alone, haven't you?"

Fred's eyes brimmed, the fight draining out of him. He gave a jerky nod. "I—I don't even know who to trust. The company has friends everywhere."

Dana's voice was steady but iron hard. "You were right to be afraid. But you're not alone anymore."

Laurie caught the quiver in Fred's lower lip, the raw exhaustion behind his panic. She kept her own breathing slow, willing calm into the space between them. Rosa padded closer, sitting down squarely in front of Fred, tail flicking once against the floor. She stared up at him, alert.

Fred stared back, then Rosa jumped into his lap and licked his face. The whistleblower blew out a surprised breath, then gave the little dog a hug. He wiped at his eyes, blinking hard. "I have the drive. I—uh—I hid it. In my sock drawer." His laugh was thin, hollow. "Real high-level spy craft, right?"

Dana stood, her movements slow. "We'll take it, if you'll allow us to. Put it in a safe place. And we'll keep you alive so you can see this through."

Fred flinched at the words, but then sagged, the weight of it all too much to fight anymore. He nodded, defeated. "Yeah. Okay."

Laurie rose and Rosa jumped down. *He wants to believe,* the dog said to her. *Let's make sure he can.*

When Fred went into his bedroom to fetch the external hard drive with all his stolen data, Dana turned to Carl. "Got a safe house? Some place to keep him?"

"We do, but it wouldn't be wise to stash him there. We don't want this coming back on the senator."

"What about Red Fox Farm?" Laurie asked. "They have guest cabins. He could get lost in that big clan."

Dana shook her head. "We can't put them in danger."

"They've already been targeted with the action against the apothecary. By the same companies that are after Fred, by the looks of it."

"True," Dana said.

"If I'm any judge, they're more pissed off than scared. Let me call Skye."

Laurie got Skye quickly and explained the situation as briefly as she could. Fred came out of his bedroom and held out the black box that was the hard drive. Carl took it and slipped it into his jacket pocket. "What were your escape plans?" he asked.

Laurie ended her call with Skye and gave Dana a thumbs up.

"I have a ticket to Mexico City. I've got friends north of there."

Carl nodded, silent for a minute.

"What are you thinking?" Dana asked.

"Think he looks a little like Joey?" Carl asked.

"Oh," Dana straightened in surprise. "That's an idea."

"What?" Fred's eyes went wide and he took a step back.

"We'll let Joey fly to Mexico. They'll think it's you."

"But my passport—" Fred started to object.

Carl dismissed this with a wave of his giant hand. "We can rustle up some fake documents."

Laurie touched his arm. "Fred, we can take you to a safe place. A farm northeast of Seattle. Big extended family who've been affected by another part of this scheme."

"How? Were they part of the study?"

"No, they're herbalists. BioCure is behind legal actions to shut down alternative healthcare."

Fred's face flushed red. "Bastards. So, when they cut off care, patients won't be able to find any help at all."

Cut off care? Another puzzle piece dangled in front of them. Dana and Laurie stared at each other. Now wasn't the time to ask. They'd find out more about this once they got Fred out of here.

Laurie said, "It might be good for you to talk to these people. Your situation seems to be only part of the whole picture."

"Skye agreed to hide him?" Dana asked in a low voice.

"Had to ask her mom." Laurie chuckled. "Says they have a couple of empty cabins and there's room in the big house."

"The Yarrow's place?" Carl asked.

"You know it?" Dana was surprised.

"Their attorney brought this web of lawsuits to the senator's attention just yesterday. We can help defend the place. In fact, maybe you should move your family out there temporarily."

"But we don't want to alert Kevin just yet," Dana said. She turned to Fred. "We've got a great place for you, but I need to ask. How do you feel about magic?"

CHAPTER

FIFTEEN

After settling Fred at Red Fox Farm, Dana spent the night in Skye and Jade's guest bedroom, certain she couldn't hide her confusion and anger if she ran into Kevin at home. The next morning, she stayed until she was sure Fred was fine, which was within five minutes of watching the Yarrow family fuss over him and feed him.

"You've been through a harrowing experience," Uncle Rowan commiserated.

"And just look at you. Thin as a rail," Aunt Aoife said. "Now, you'll be having pancakes with those eggs and sausages."

"Thanks," Minh said.

"She not be a talking to you, laddie," Grandmother Moira chided him, but Aunt Aoife belayed this order with a wink at the two teens.

Dana ate lightly, resisting Rowan and Aoife's protestations that she'd be starving by mid-morning. The kids begged to stay for the day and Dana relented. She had a ton of work to catch up on, handing off cases she was working on and tackling the huge packet about the health care legislation she'd gotten from Whitmore.

She fished for her keys as she walked out the door, only to find her SUV missing. Then remembered she'd been chauffeured to the farm. She reached for her phone to call Joey, but realized he was impersonating Fred on a flight to Mexico City. It would take whoever was on duty too long to come pick her up anyway. How did these politicians and rich people—wait, were they the same? How did they put up with the inconvenience? Or did they force their drivers to hang around for endless hours?

Skye appeared beside her on the porch. "I'm headed to the store. I'll give you a lift to your office."

"But it's out of your way."

"It's just off I-5. I can drop you off quickly, then turn around and head back to the U-District."

"If it's not too much trouble."

Skye made an impatient noise. "You're my best friend. You and Laurie."

They made good time, deciding to leave the mystery alone for the morning and enjoy some music. Skye pulled up to her building and said, "Let's have dinner with Laurie after we're both done for the day. See if we can piece it all together."

"Yes, there are so many moving parts now. Sounds like a plan."

Dana got the cases she was handing over ready for other attorneys, then spent the better part of the day reading through the senator's file. She made a list of research topics in an email for Gary and scheduled it to send at six o'clock Monday morning. Emersed in sketches for speeches and emails to convince conservative legislators it was safe to vote for this packet, she was surprised when her phone buzzed. It was already late afternoon.

> Skye: Meet for dinner in half an hour?
>
> Dana: OK, where?
>
> Skye: At the pub across from Marcus's apartment.
>
> Dana: Interesting choice. Laurie coming?

Skye: Yes, and Rosa. That place allows
dogs.

Dana: See you soon.

As soon as Dana put her phone in her purse, she remembered her car was still at the house. This was getting annoying. Maybe she should turn down this chauffeuring offer. After locking the file in her desk drawer, she called for a ride. It was only when she got in the Honda with a young man that she remembered Carl's warning to be careful. How could she have forgotten Fred's panicked state? But her name hadn't appeared in any threatening texts. As far as she knew. This guy looked harmless enough. Probably a college kid picking up extra change on a Sunday. After he dropped her off in at the corner near the pub, she promised herself not to take any more chances. It would be more inconvenient to get kidnapped or murdered.

Rosa greeted her with enthusiastic tail wags and they settled down at a table next to the front window. They started on drinks. Dana ordered white wine, Skye an amber beer, and Laurie an ale from a local brewery.

"We stalking Maddie now?" Dana asked, half joking.

"I wouldn't call it stalking," Skye said. "Keeping an eye out maybe?"

Laurie shook her head. "Not sure there's a difference."

"We need to keep tabs on everybody involved in this." Skye sounded a bit indignant.

They hadn't ordered yet and that turned out to be a good thing because who should walk out of Maddie's building other than Spy Man. The mysterious lurker at the bar during the fundraiser. The man who seemed to be shadowing Mr. Robertson at the memorial.

Dana almost choked on her wine. "Look, look."

"Stars above, it's the guy from the memorial," Skye said.

"We should follow him," Dana said.

Totally," Laurie said, sounding like one of her former students.

"So, it's a good thing we're stalking Maddie now, right?" Skye quipped.

Rosa yipped in excitement. Dana threw down enough cash for the drinks and a tip and they all ran to the old green Subaru parked on the street.

Spy Man's car pulled out of a parking spot beside Maddie's building. Skye waited until another car got behind him, then started to follow. He wove through Belltown traffic and headed to one of the downtown hotels. He pulled into the porte-cochere and waved off the valet who ran toward him.

Skye hid the Outback behind a bus, but it pulled away leaving them exposed. "Blast it." She put on her signal to get into traffic, but just then William Robertson walked out and got into the back seat of Spy Man's car.

"Well, would you look at that," Laurie said.

The two drove onto the street and Skye followed at a good distance. After a couple of blocks, traffic thinned a bit. "Think he's spotted us?" Dana asked.

"No. I mean, how many green Subarus are there in Seattle?" Skye said.

Laurie looked over at her friend. "No offense, but the real question is how many of them are this old?"

Skye patted the dashboard of her car. "Pay no attention, Ms. Moss. Laurie has no manners."

They had to stop for a red light and the black BMW moved away. Why were these rich people's cars always black? It seemed to take an eternity for the light to turn green.

"We're going to lose them!" Laurie rocked back and forth as if this would make the light change faster.

Finally, it turned green, but the black car was nowhere in sight. "Where did they disappear to?" Skye sped up.

"Just keep going." Laurie watched everything from the passenger's side window. Dana scooted to the left window and Rosa took the right one. Two blocks went by with no sighting. Just as Skye was about to give up, Laurie shouted, "There."

Spy Man had turned into the entryway of a skyscraper. This time he handed his keys off to the valet and the two men entered the building.

"We're going in." Skye pulled in after the revolving door swallowed their prey and stopped her car.

"Wait," Laurie sputtered.

"Is this a good idea?" Dana asked, but Skye was already handing her keys to a valet clad in a black suit and white shirt who looked dubiously at the old Outback. He took the keys between his thumb and index finger, dangling them like they were grimy.

Skye ignored him. "Hurry up. We're late for our appointment." She waved them toward the doors.

Laurie picked up Rosa, who was certain revolving doors would devour her, and the three walked through one at a time, which took too long because the two men were nowhere in sight once they'd all piled into the lobby. They stood in front of the elevator bank and stared at the numbers at the top. "That one?" Dana asked. "It's on the third floor and they just got on. The others are way up there."

Laurie put Rosa down and the little Havanese went to work sniffing the tile. She sat in front of the second to the left and Dana swore the dog smiled.

"It's this one," Laurie said unnecessarily. They watched the numbers until they stopped. But then the car started up again. It stopped on three different floors before coming back down. "Crap, why isn't this easy?"

Skye pushed the up button on the panel. "We'll go to their first stop. I'll check who has offices there. You two check the eleventh and twenty-first."

Everyone got into the elevator when it arrived. They barely had time to get their devices out to check the companies renting in the building before the doors opened on the fifth floor. Stepping out, Skye found a directory on the wall. They clustered around and read over Skye's shoulder. The Citadel Trust had the whole west side and south hallway. Two small legal firms took up the east wall and a tech had a corner on the north side.

"Think he's here to do something with his trust fund?" Dana asked.

"But the family is based in D.C."

Rosa gave a little woof.

Laurie translated. "She says they didn't get off here."

"Thank you, Rosa." Skye called the elevator and they rode to the eleventh floor and emerged into an open area and a young receptionist flashed them a bright smile that belonged in a toothpaste commercial. "May I help you?"

"Bloody broomsticks!" Skye murmured, surprised the place was staffed on a Sunday afternoon.

Dana stepped forward. "We might be lost. Which company is this, now?"

"Primewell Health Insurance," she said with entirely too much enthusiasm. Then she squinched up her face apologetically. "But this is the corporate office. If you're looking to get a policy, we don't do that here."

"Where should we go, then?"

"I think there's an agent a few floors down. Let me look." She ran a crimson tipped nail down a list on her desk. Laurie was surprised she had actual paper. "Yes, ask for Larry Mitchell. He's hot," she confided.

Laurie and Skye exchanged a wry look. Did she think one of them was looking for a boyfriend?

The receptionist wrote down the office number. "Should I call to check if he's in today?"

"That won't be necessary," Dana said.

"Thanks for your help." Laurie turned to leave, but the young woman caught sight of Rosa.

"So cute," she squealed and gestured for the Havanese to come closer.

"Thank you for clarifying this for me." William Robertson's voice boomed out from a back office.

Skye's eyes flew wide.

"I'm glad we've come to an understanding," answered a male voice.

Skye looked back but couldn't see who else Robertson was talking to.

The receptionist picked up the phone and said to whoever answered. "Please tell Mr. Ellsworth his next appointment is here."

"Damn," Dana mouthed.

"Uh, sorry," Laurie said to the young woman "We're in a bit of a hurry." They couldn't let William Robertson see them, much less his security guy. That must be what Spy Man was—security.

They hustled back to the bank of elevators. Laurie spotted a ladies room and they rushed through the door, Dana and Skye trying to go through at the same time. Inside, Skye let out a relieved sigh. "That was close. Who was he talking to?"

"Must be the CEO of Primewell," Dana said. "Thomas Ellsworth."

"Wait, isn't that the same guy who was at the memorial? The one Robertson was angry with?" Skye asked.

"Same one," Dana said.

"Something changed during that meeting," Skye said. "Robertson was furious when Ellsworth spoke to him at the memorial. Now he seems...mollified, I guess you'd say."

They heard voices outside near the elevators. Laurie pointed to Dana and Skye. ""Ellsworth has seen both of you. We're up," she said to Rosa and pushed the door open before the other two could object.

They walked out and stood behind the two men waiting for the elevator. When the car arrived, William and Spy Man moved to the side to let her get in first. At least they were polite, Laurie thought. Spy Man pushed the lobby button, then looked back at her. She nodded, put in her earbuds, and started bobbing her head as if she were listening to music.

Robertson leaned in toward Spy Man and said in a whisper, "What do you think, Gus? He claims not to know anything about Marcus—" Robertson glanced back at Laurie "—but I could have sworn he had something to do with it."

"I agree. We don't have any proof. What would his motive be?"

"I felt certain he was behind that Caldwell business. I should never have backed him when he wanted to take over. Now, I'm not so sure."

But he was, Laurie wanted to scream.

Robertson continued, "Still, let's triple check. I can't live with myself if he's guilty and we let him get away with this."

"Yes, sir."

"It's hard to believe they're supporting—" Gus glanced back at Laurie.

She stared harder at her phone.

"—universal health care. What's their angle?"

Laurie tried not to show the shock on her face. Not that either of them was looking at her, but what had he just said? Supporting universal health care? Primewell Health Insurance? What the hell was going on? And why were they talking so openly in front of another person?

Rosa took a step forward and smelled Gus's leg. *He's not the one who killed Marcus.*

Laurie's shoulders relaxed. She was surprised a small part of her had wondered if he'd done it. After all, he worked for Marcus's father so she'd taken him off the list once she'd realized that.

William Robertson huffed a laugh. "Right? That's always the question with these bastards."

Rosa took a whiff of William Robertson. *He didn't do it either.*

That hadn't even crossed her mind. Still, it was good to know this hadn't been filicide. Was that the right word? It had been years since she'd taken Latin.

Gus nodded his agreement. "Hard to figure."

The door opened and the two walked away. Laurie paused a beat, then followed. She found another women's bathroom and ducked in. Waited a couple of minutes, then went out into the lobby. She found Skye and Dana just coming out of the lift.

"I've got news," Laurie said.

"Let's get the car. Only the Old Ones know how much these people charge for parking."

"I ran back and got a token from the receptionist." Dana waved a small slip of paper.

"Bless you. Let's go to the farm. Jade should be home and we can try to figure all this out."

"Drop me by the house. I'd like to pick up my car."

"I'm still parked in Belltown," Laurie said.

"Now I'm a chauffeur." Skye pretended to be annoyed, but Laurie caught a slight smile on her face.

CHAPTER
SIXTEEN

The posse gathered in the big house at Red Fox Farm in a previously empty back room that now had a collection of mismatched chairs in a semi-circle around two free-standing bulletin boards pushed together. Covered with photos and notes, the boards were divided into four big sections, three for the companies they'd identified and a fourth titled 'Random.' Different colored yarn stretched between items, making it seem that Grandmother Spider had spun down on a thread and created a web.

Dana found it difficult to make sense of who was doing what in the case they were building. There'd been two cases and now Fred's made three. But there was a connection somewhere. One thread would pull it all together. Their job was to find it.

"What do you think, Mom?" Minh asked.

Dana stopped herself from saying he'd been watching too many crime shows. Minh was not fully an adult yet and still needed her parenting skills, questionable as they were. Maybe he'd need them for the rest of her life. But really, the crime board was impressive. "Amazing job. There are so many parts to keep track of. This helps a lot."

"Right?" her son beamed, pleased by her praise.

Laurie had settled into one of the chairs just as Ashe trotted in and sniffed noses with Rosa.

We're going out, Rosa announced to Laurie.

No rolling in...whatever it was you rolled in last time.

But—

No argument.

Rosa huffed and followed Ashe out of the room, tail held straight up in defiance.

"Don't roll in anything," Skye said, not realizing she was repeating what Laurie had told the dogs. Skye shook her head at the uselessness of it, then looked around the room at Dana, Laurie and Jade. Fred sat with them, a little less fidgety now that the Yarrow clan had soothed his nerves. Siobhán represented the apothecary.

Skye gestured at all the yarn. "Let's review. We need to catch Fred up and honestly, this is getting too complicated. This board helps, Minh."

Minh nodded his head, acknowledging the appreciation.

Skye pointed to Dana. "Want to start us off? Catch Fred up on how this all started?"

Dana twisted around so she could see Fred. "My husband is running for the House of Representatives."

"Oh, you're that Preston."

"Yes, so you probably are aware that his campaign manager, Marcus Robertson, was murdered in Olympia a week ago."

"Right, a mugging," Fred said.

Laurie jumped in. "That's the official story, but we found his wallet full of cash and all his credit cards when we went to investigate. We're pretty sure it was murder."

Dana took up the story, gesturing at the board. "Marcus had discovered some of what these companies were up to. He knew a bit about the medical trials. The files he collected mentioned human subjects and non-consensual data harvesting at offsite facilities. Marcus didn't have as much detail as you, Fred."

143

"He was gathering data, too." Fred swallowed hard. "Same thing I started doing. Only he got too close."

Dana nodded. "You were in real danger. I'm glad we found you in time."

"Me, too," Fred whispered.

"What else do we know about the studies BioCare was doing?" Skye asked, keeping them on track.

Fred retold the story of discovering the longevity trials and the genetic manipulation. Everyone knew about it already, but he seemed to get more coherent, more calm, every time he repeated it, so they indulged him.

Dana half raised her hand when he finished as if she were in school. "Marcus confronted Kevin with what he knew about these experiments. He had other information he'd gathered which I'll get into later."

She waved a hand at the other sections of the bulletin boards. "Marcus said these companies were pulling Kevin into something illegal. He thinks revealing this to Kevin is what got him killed."

Fred did a double take. "Wait, thinks? Isn't he dead?"

There was a moment of tense silence while everyone scrambled for a way to explain this to Fred. Dana braced herself and spat it out. "Last fall I had a near death experience that left me with the ability to see ghosts."

Fred started to say something, but Dana held up her hand. "I can communicate with them. This is the second ghost who's come to me for help solving their murder. That's how I found out Marcus was dead. I saw him sitting in my living room before it was on the news."

Fred stared at Dana, blinking slowly, trying to process her confession. Then his eyes darted to the crime board and back again. "You mean like *actually* talk to them? Not in a metaphorical, I-heard-his-voice-in-the-wind kind of way?"

When Dana nodded, his shoulders slumped and he let out a dry laugh. "Well...I thought I was losing my mind, but maybe I'm in the right room after all." He paused, then added, "You don't seem crazy, so I guess I'll go with it. Do the ghosts know anything I should?"

Dana crossed her arms, the corner of her mouth twitching. "Actually, Marcus had proof you were a target. That's how we found you."

Fred let out a low whistle, dragging a hand through his hair. "Right. Of course. Ghost informants. Why not?" He sat back in his chair, muttering, "I thought my panic attack yesterday was the weird part. Turns out that was just the welcome tour."

Skye watched him for a moment. "You all right there, Fred?"

He gave Skye a thumbs up.

"Good. Let's catch everybody up on the case against the apothecary." She nodded for Aunt Siobhán to go ahead.

"Our store, Old World Apothecary, was served a cease-and-desist order," Siobhán explained to Fred. "Claimed we were practicing medicine without a license." She summarized the deposition with Deborah Johnson.

"So, those bastards"—she pointed a finger at the BioCure Pharmaceuticals section of the board—"paid this person to file the claim. Our attorney, Vivienne Grant, discovered there are a least two dozen claims like this, a few against Wellspring University, believe it or not. Vivienne contacted several other firms and in every single one of them, a lump sum was deposited in their accounts around the time they filed their complaints. These were not regular, recurring payments."

"Ah, ha!" Laurie leaned back, satisfaction on her face until her chair started to tip too far. She grabbed the back of Dana's to right herself.

"Easy there," Siobhán said, chuckling. "The evidence is still coming in on who paid those people, but we can prove three more came from BioCure. The legal firm that represents Wellspring University has volunteered to coordinate all this. That's brings us up to date."

"Excellent. I have more to add," Laurie said, then pointed to the big question mark beneath the photo of Spy Man. "I know who he is. His name is Gus and he seems to be working security for William Robertson."

Minh jumped up and removed the paper with the question mark. He grabbed a blank sheet and wrote 'Gus' in large magic marker. "But is he still a suspect if he works for Marcus's father?"

"Definitely not. I rode down the elevator with them and they were wondering if Thomas Ellsworth could have been behind the murder of Marcus. Robertson strongly suspected Ellsworth was behind both murders."

"Both?" Fred asked.

"Ethan Caldwell. He was the owner of Primewell Health Insurance. Ellsworth bought him out, then Caldwell was killed a few weeks later," Laurie explained.

"Another supposed mugging?" Fred asked.

"The press called it a gangland shooting," Laurie said, "but after Robertson met with Ellsworth today, he seemed less convinced Ellsworth ordered the homicides."

Skye snorted. "More fool him."

"They met on a Sunday?" Siobhán asked, as if this was the most important thing Laurie had revealed.

"Yeah, probably wanted to keep it on the down low. I jumped on the elevator with them after their meeting. Gus said something about Primewell supporting universal health care."

"No way," Fred exclaimed.

"What in the name of the gods?" Siobhán exclaimed.

Relief flooded Dana. Now she could reveal what she'd learned about Senator Whitmore's legislation without revealing the connection to the senator. "We have a second source for that. Before Marcus took the job with Kevin, Florence Hospital Conglomerate tried to hire him to lobby in favor of Americare for All with certain changes."

"What?" Laurie asked.

"This is new," Siobhán added.

Dana waggled her head. "Kind of. I couldn't talk about this until somebody else brought it up."

"How do you know about it?" Fred asked.

"That's confidential. Attorney/client privilege."

"You're a lawyer?" Fred asked.

She nodded, then turned to the whole group. "All three of these companies seem to be supporting a new bill that would create free universal healthcare in the U.S."

"Stars above. That makes no sense at all," Siobhán sputtered.

"They'd go out of business," Skye added.

"I overheard Kevin on the phone when I got home Friday night. He was invited to a meeting where all this was supposed to be laid out to him. But I think their 'support'"—she put air quotes around the word—"is a front for something more sinister."

"Like what?" Fred asked.

"That's what we need to find out. It might lead us to the murderer," Dana said. She blinked in surprise when she looked back at the board. Marcus stood there, smiling in approval.

"Mom," Hoa's voice came from the back of the room, taking Dana's surprise up another notch. How much of this had she heard? "Have you guys figured out who's been stalking me?"

Minh pointed to the picture of the stalker in the random section. "Hoa has seen this guy three times."

Dana turned to her daughter, who stood in the doorway, her dark hair falling to her shoulders with—what was that? She stood and picked a few dried leaves from her locks. "Not yet, sweetie. But we will. We've got all these people helping."

Hoa held her arms out to be hugged, something she'd done often when she was younger, but not in quite some time. Dana leaned down to hug her, then realized Hoa was almost as tall as she was. She squeezed her tight and held on until the young teen protested, "All right all ready."

"You folks about done in there?" Fiona stood behind Hoa, her apron splattered with tomato sauce.

"Lasagna?" Skye asked.

"You bet'cha."

During the meeting, Fíona and Siobhán's husband Tadhg had cooked dinner, a big job given the number of people who lived at Red Fox Farm, some of whom might drop by to eat. They all filed out of the kitchen and helped finish up. Dana and Laurie grabbed plates and utensils. Minh put out glasses, making Dana's heart swell. He'd be a better husband than Kevin, helping his partner around the house. Jade arrived home just in time to grab the drinks, pitchers of water, tea, and lemonade. Then they distributed big bowls of salad, steaming vegetables, and baskets of bread. Dana would have to add a mile or two to her jogging route if she kept eating at the farm.

They all sat, a few more of the clan showing up at the last minute. Hoa sat with Caoimhe and Sinead, two opposites if there ever were any, but tight cousins and Hoa's friends since she could walk. Tadhg plopped the last sizzling casserole down on a hot plate and stood at the end of the table, palms out like a priest. He closed his eyes and intoned,

"Blessings on the earth that grows,
On the rain, the wind that blows.
Thanks to flame and flowing sea,
For this food, so mote it be."

Fíona paused a few seconds, then said, "Pass me your salad bowls."

Minh went straight for the lasagna, cutting a huge square and sliding it onto his plate. At least he didn't dump half of it on the table. Then he took a huge mouthful and Dana caught his eye. "Salad."

He frowned, chewing madly.

"And vegetables or no dessert."

Minh picked up his bowl with no good grace and handed it to Fíona. Hoa passed her salad bowl, said thank you, and helped herself to vegetables. At least she raised one child who ate right, Dana thought. But Minh did create that crime board. She relented and smiled at her son, who was too busy forking another huge bite of lasagna into his mouth to notice.

After everyone was served, Fíona filled her own plate and sat. "What's new?" she asked.

The posse took turns between bites telling the rest of the group what they'd pieced together.

"Sounds like William Robertson and his security guy"—Fíona waved her fork trying to remember.

"Gus." Skye supplied his name.

"Right. Sounds like they're in the clear and as stumped as we are about what these companies are up to."

Dana nodded, her mouth full.

"Maybe we should invite them into the fold. That man has money and influence," Fíona pointed out.

"And he's lost his son," Siobhán added. "He'll want to find out who's responsible and see them brought to justice."

"But he still thinks Primewell is supporting universal health care," Laurie said.

"True, but we can disabuse him of that notion right quick," Tadhg said.

The posse eyed each other and each gave a subtle nod. "Dana, you up for talking to him?"

"I'm probably not the best person to do it," she said. "I have to dance around confidentiality issues."

Jade motioned to Laurie, "You're current on everything. Why don't you talk to him?"

Laurie chewed thoughtfully, then nodded as she swallowed. "I'll call him tomorrow morning."

"Good plan," Siobhán said.

Skye and Jade put their forks down on their plates and sat back, wiping their mouths.

"Delicious as always," Laurie said, following suit.

Tadhg beamed. "Who wants blueberry pie?"

"Goddess preserve me. I'm stuffed to the gills," Skye said.

Dana chuckled, always amused by Skye's expressions.

Minh had no such compunction. "Yes," he shouted, then when he noticed his mother's raised eyebrow added, "please."

After everyone who wanted pie was served and the others enjoyed a warm cup of mint and chamomile tea to help digestion, Tadhg remarked on the other new piece of information. "Did you say these three thieving companies are supporting universal health care? That's a blooming miracle. Is somebody in Congress cooking up a bill for that?"

"Whitmore's been talking about it for decades," Jade said.

Everyone looked at Dana who just smiled.

Siobhán watched her face closely. "Ha, that's an affirmative. She can't say, but she knows."

"But we think there's something fishy going on," Skye said. "I mean, free universal health care—their companies would be defunct, so why support it?"

"Sounds like we need a tarot reading," Fíona said.

"Right." Fred's laugh was derisive.

Five sets of Yarrow clan eyes fastened onto him, some registering offense, others amusement.

Alarmed, he said, "Oh, yeah! That's exactly what we need. A tarot, uh"—he glanced around—"what is it?"

"Reading."

"Totally."

The room erupted in laughter and Fred's face turned crimson.

Tadhg clapped him on the shoulder. "Relax, son. We don't require you to believe anything. Not like some folks."

"Let's go over to our house. We can use my cards," Skye said.

Chairs scraped as the group got up. Plates clattered. A couple of cousins stayed behind to clean up while the main investigators walked over to Skye and Jade's cabin.

Rain pattered gently on the tin roof of the Red Fox Farm porch, a soothing rhythm against the mounting tension inside. The parlor smelled of beeswax candles, woodsmoke, and the faint citrus bite of tea simmering on the stove. Skye laid out her velvet reading cloth—a deep indigo scattered with tiny silver stars—on the wide oak table her grandfather had built. The cards waited, humming with possibility.

Laurie sat cross-legged on the floor beside Rosa, who'd returned from her romp, not having rolled in anything offensive, and was curled up like a cinnamon bun at her feet. Dana leaned against the fireplace, arms crossed but eyes alert. Fred fidgeted near the window, gaze darting between the steaming glass and the spread cloth. Tadhg and Fíona stood close together, silent and watchful. Siobhán settled into a rocker, shawl draped over one shoulder, while Minh lounged nearby pretending he wasn't fascinated. Jade stood behind Skye, grounding her with quiet presence.

Skye picked up the deck, closing her eyes for a moment. "I think I'll use my special five-card spread. The question is," she said softly, voice carrying with unnatural clarity, "what are Primewell Health Insurance, BioCure Pharmaceuticals, and Florence Hospital Conglomerate's hidden motives?"

Silence settled like a hush before the curtain of a play. She shuffled slowly, deliberately, her fingers deft and practiced. "In my layout, the first card represents the way things appear." Then she laid it face-up in the center of the cloth.

The Star.

"Hope," Skye said. "Healing. Renewal. They present themselves as saviors. Their messaging taps into the collective desire for change—offering something long denied."

Fred sat in a chair closer to the table. "Wouldn't that be great? Like finally we'd get what so many other countries have."

Skye nodded and said, "Hidden forces." She placed the second card to the left of the first.

Seven of Swords.

A collective murmur stirred the room.

Minh leaned forward. "That's the thief card, right?"

"Deception," Skye confirmed. "Secrets. Strategy. This is the card of someone slipping away with what doesn't belong to them—grinning politely all the while."

Dana narrowed her eyes. "This makes more sense given what we know about them."

"The public face is the Star," Skye said. "But behind the scenes, something's being taken."

Fred blew out a breath. "This stuff seems accurate. Amazing."

Jade flashed him a smile.

Skye placed the third card. "What lies beneath."

The Devil.

A hush fell over the room. Even the fire seemed to still. Rosa climbed into Laurie's lap, uneasy.

"They're bound by something," Skye whispered. "Addiction, greed, control. This isn't about providing care. Maybe it's about who holds the reins when the structure is in place."

Fred looked back at the cards. "I don't think they intended to make longevity and gene therapy available to everyone. If it ever works. The research has cost a fortune."

Dana's jaw clenched. "I found evidence of gag orders on the thumb drive Marcus left. That explains the sudden silence around former whistleblowers."

Skye waited for silence, then laid the fourth card. "Future possibilities."

The Tower.

Fíona sucked in a sharp breath.

"Disaster," Skye said. "Exposure. Collapse. If their scheme moves forward unchecked—the senator's plan will fail."

"We can't let that happen," Laurie said quietly. "Not again."

Skye reached for the final card. "A path forward," she said, and placed it above the others.

Queen of Swords.

Dana's mouth arched into a grim smile. "That's us."

"Truth-seekers," Skye said. "Strategic. Sharp. Not ruled by

emotion but unafraid of it. We'll need clarity and courage to cut through the illusions. Even when it's unpopular. Especially then."

Fred shifted in his chair. "So, we expose them?"

"No," said Tadhg, his voice low. "We watch them. We gather solid proof and hand it over to the legal team. Maybe the press."

"And we prepare." Siobhán spoke for the first time. "Because something is coming. Something big. And we need to be ready before it breaks."

Outside, a gust of wind rattled the windows. The candle flames wavered. Gandalf hissed and jumped down onto the table, his fur standing on end.

CHAPTER

SEVENTEEN

D ana stood at the top of the Columbia Center in the SkyView Observation Deck waiting for Senator Whitmore to publicly present her initiative for universal health care. Once again, Kevin's campaign stylist had won out and dressed Dana to the nines. The sleek, tailored midnight blue sheath dress made of structured silk crepe hit just below the knee and included cap sleeves and a high bateau neckline. Nicolette had added a slim black belt with a matte silver buckle which she'd cinched too tight. Dana had loosened it as soon as they'd walked away from Nicolette. Plus, she'd won out on her shoes. Low black suede heels with a V-cut vamp, practical enough to move in but sophisticated. At least there were no garters this time, but her hair: a sculpted helmet of dark waves, lacquered in place like she was ready to walk into court—or a hurricane.

She stood just behind Kevin, who flanked Senator Howard Langston, the Seattle mayor, and a line of polished state and local representatives. The head of Bayview Hospital stood near the end, his expression unreadable. Dana recognized him instantly from the research files—Bayview was in the crosshairs of the Florence

Hospital Conglomerate. He might not know what their plans were yet, but he would soon enough.

Senator Whitmore, radiant and composed, stood before a shimmering wall of cameras and microphones. She managed to exude both gravity and warmth with every glance, every word. Dana studied her, marveling at how she embodied both fierce leadership and maternal empathy—a political superpower if ever there was one.

They stood within the soaring expanse of the SkyView Observatory, the entire floor reserved for the occasion. Floor-to-ceiling windows surrounded them in a vast, sunlit ring. From this height, the whole of Seattle sprawled below, glittering in the rare clear light. Behind the podium, Mount Rainier loomed majestic and serene, like a sentinel watching over the day.

Dana had met with Whitmore just the night before. After hearing everything—Kevin's phone call, Marcus's files, the corporate shell games—the senator had insisted the announcement go forward. Publicly, it was full steam ahead. Privately, she'd unleashed her legal team and DC contacts to dig into what she called, "just what the hell these bastards are up to." Dana had laughed out loud at that. The rush of victory was still fresh. Evelyn Whitmore had joined the posse. Their little team had teeth now.

Inside the observatory, the energy was electric. Guests mingled with glasses of Northwest Pinot in hand, admiring the view and watching monitors flash pre-roll coverage of the event. The press clustered tightly around the podium, shoulders bumping as they vied for camera angles and clean audio.

Whitmore stepped up to the mic, the Cascade Mountains gleaming behind her like a painted backdrop. Her voice, amplified and sure, cut through the low hum of the crowd.

"Good afternoon. Thank you all for being here. Today, I stand before you not just as a senator, but as a daughter, a mother, and a citizen of this country who knows what it means to wait in a hospital hallway praying for help to come—not because the medicine didn't exist, but because the system wouldn't allow it."

Dana exhaled slowly, her tension easing just a notch.

Evelyn continued, her cadence precise. "We live in a nation of breathtaking innovation. But when it comes to ensuring every American has access to quality, affordable health care—our system is broken. That's why today I'm introducing the American Health Security Act."

A murmur of appreciation moved through the gathered crowd. Some clapped. Others nodded solemnly.

"This legislation guarantees universal access to health care for every American. It expands public options, stabilizes costs, empowers providers, and puts people—not profit—at the center of our system."

Dana noticed movement along the periphery—security sweeping discreetly. She saw Nicolette near the drinks table, phone in hand, nodding approvingly at Dana's immaculate appearance.

Evelyn's voice turned sharper. "Let me be clear: this is not a government takeover. This is about restoring balance. About ending the quiet suffering of millions who delay care or go without it altogether."

Then she paused.

"I know there are powerful forces aligned against this bill."

Dana stiffened.

"I've read the memos. I've seen the money."

Dana's breath hitched. Kevin's hand moved slightly, his knuckles whitening against the railing that ran along the windows.

"But let me tell you something—this country has faced Goliaths before, and the people have always prevailed."

The cheer that followed echoed off the glass.

Suddenly—a sharp pop.

A flash of red bloomed at Evelyn's shoulder. She stumbled. Her face contorted in pain.

Dana moved without thinking, pushing past a startled aide.

Evelyn's security converged, voices crackling in their earpieces. A protective formation closed around the senator, lifting her and moving swiftly toward the private corridor near the freight elevator.

"Gunshot," someone barked into a headset.

Dana turned instinctively—and saw him. The flash of a familiar face.

Hoa's stalker. He vanished behind a column, heading toward the emergency stairwell.

"I can't believe it," Dana whispered. "A professional assassin. Shadowing my daughter."

Kevin grabbed her arm. "We have to go."

She yanked free. "What do you know about this?"

Security was already locking down the observatory. Doors clicked. Metal barriers began to descend around elevator access. Officers moved methodically, weaponry drawn, sweeping the area.

The observatory lights snapped from soft ambient to glaring emergency white. Every exit pulsed with red strobes. A recorded voice announced: *"Security lockdown initiated. Please remain where you are. Law enforcement is responding."*

Dana's ears rang. Her pulse pounded in her throat.

Reporters screamed questions. Some were still filming. Others were already live, narrating the chaos. "Breaking news out of Seattle —Senator Whitmore has just been shot at a press event..."

Dana backed against the cool glass, mind racing, heart hammering.

No escape. Seventy-three stories up, trapped in a glittering cage of light and secrets.

"I'm not staying up here," she muttered.

"But they're locking the place down," Kevin said.

She scanned the room. The freight elevator was sealed, the main public elevators locked behind drop-down grates. Armed guards herded people away from the perimeter, but the press clustered stubbornly, cameras still rolling.

She turned to Kevin. "You should stay. Answer questions. Be a good gatekeeper."

He blinked. "What the hell is that supposed to mean?"

"I can't trust you." Her voice was quiet but flat. "Marcus told you he was worried some of your donors had a hidden agenda and then he was dead. You're part of whatever this is. Whether you know it or not."

"Marcus what?" His mouth opened, then closed. Color drained from his face. "Dana, come on. You really think I—"

"I think you're dangerous if you don't even know who you're working for." She didn't wait for his response. "Stay here. Spin the story. Play innocent. You're good at that."

Someone shouted Kevin's name and he looked away, distracted. That was all she needed. She shifted slightly, letting her body turn with the current of the crowd instead of against it.

Slipping sideways, three steps into a group of VIP guests, she ducked behind a tall man in a navy suit and a woman clutching a half-finished glass of wine. She dipped her head.

She didn't run. She just... flowed. Like a trickle of water slipping between cracks in a stone.

A voice murmured near her ear, "If you're planning to vanish, I know a way."

Dana turned.

Maxwell Briggs, her hacker and occasional field asset, stood there dressed like he'd wandered in from a tech startup in Palo Alto. His backpack hung loose on one shoulder, earbuds dangling.

"What the hell are you doing here?"

"I was monitoring network traffic. Figured I'd come in person. Good thing, huh?" He grinned like this was a thrilling game of hide-and-seek. "There's a private maintenance stairwell past the gift shop. Old-school keycard access, but I cloned it yesterday just in case things got spicy."

Dana grabbed his arm. "Spicy? The senator just got shot."

"Exactly. Let's go."

158

They ducked around the crowd, slipping past a panicked couple clutching champagne flutes. Maxwell swiped his phone over a maintenance panel near the wall—something Dana never would have noticed. The door buzzed and opened.

Inside, a narrow, industrial stairwell spiraled downward like the spine of the building itself. Metal grates underfoot, harsh lights overhead, and the faint echo of voices above them.

It was like descending into a furnace. The deeper they went, the hotter and more claustrophobic it became. Somewhere several floors down, a security team clattered in pursuit. Dana could hear their radios—short bursts of static and clipped commands.

By the time they reached the 50th floor, Dana's heels were in her hand and sweat dripped down her spine. The security team had gone quiet. Were they gone?

At 38, Maxwell paused and pressed another hidden panel. The wall slid open—an access corridor lined with server racks and cleaning supplies. A second exit waited at the far end, where he used a different card to trigger a door.

By the 30th floor, Dana's calves burned. They passed a door marked *Mechanical — Authorized Personnel Only* and kept going.

At 23, they turned into a narrow, gray corridor lined with janitor's closets and power meters. Maxwell led her through a battered steel door. "There's a service elevator just across this hallway. We'll take it to the sub-basement loading level."

Once inside, Dana leaned against the cool metal wall, panting. The midnight blue sheath dress clung to her, wet with sweat. Even her hair had drooped, the helmet melting with the heat and the effort of running down—she didn't want to think how many floors. She pulled off the black belt that had cut into her sides and dropped it.

Maxwell pointed. "Don't leave any evidence behind."

"Right." Dana picked it up just as the elevator doors opened.

Concrete. Fluorescent lights. A lone forklift sat idling near a stack of plastic-wrapped pallets. The chill of refrigeration units. She wanted to stand in the cool, but Maxwell kept them moving. Dana smelled stale coffee and grease.

Maxwell pointed to a side door, already slightly ajar. "Alley access," he said. "Nobody watching it. Yet."

She wiped the grit off her soles and stuffed her swollen feet into her shoes again, wincing at the pain. "I'm going to—"

He held up a hand. "The less I know, the better."

Dana shook her head. "Apparently, I've underestimated you. It won't happen again."

Maxwell gave her a wry look, the jaunty hacker back. Then he sobered. "I never met her, you know. The senator. But I totally support what she's doing. I read the whole file yesterday. I'm not surprised they came after her."

"Can you find out how she is doing and call me?"

"You need to ditch that phone. They'll track you." He held out his hand and Dana reluctantly gave it over. "Get a burner. Call me when you have it."

Maxwell opened a final door. A sliver of gray Seattle light beckoned.

"You're a ghost now," he said.

Just like Marcus, Dana thought, and stepped out into the alley.

CHAPTER
EIGHTEEN

William Robertson's hotel suite overlooked Puget Sound, the blue shimmer of the water stretching beyond the windows. Laurie sat in the wingback chair near the desk. Rosa sniffed around the corners, then came to lie at her feet. Laurie glanced at the room's subtle opulence—framed abstract art, tasteful lighting, a silver coffee service cooling on the sideboard.

Robertson, still in his shirtsleeves, leaned against the desk, arms crossed. "I appreciate you contacting me, Dr. Olson."

"Please call me Laurie."

Robertson nodded and glanced at his watch. "I don't mean to rush you, but I'm planning on catching Senator Whitmore's press conference."

"I'd like to see it as well. The information I want to share with you is related to her bill."

Robertson's eyes widened slightly. "I've been trying to get a straight answer out of Thomas Ellsworth for two days now. He keeps telling me he's supporting Whitmore's bill. I have some misgivings."

Laurie shook her head, pulling a flash drive from her bag. "He's lying. This is from Marcus Robertson—your son. Before he died, he uncovered a network of communications between Olivia Mercer at BioCure and Ellsworth from Primewell. The files point to a coordinated strategy to support the bill just long enough to make it law."

Robertson frowned. "And then?"

"That's what we've been researching. Marcus was beginning to connect the dots and saved evidence. After he died, he told Dana where he'd hidden the drive."

Robertson did a double take. "Wait, you said 'after he died.'"

Laurie felt a moment of panic. She was so flustered, she'd blurted out Dana's secret.

Just tell him, Rosa said.

She took a deep breath. "I know how this is going to sound, but my friend can talk to people who have passed over."

Robertson stared at her. Took a breath to speak but then stopped. A wistful look came over his face.

Laurie's breath caught. She hadn't expected belief. Certainly not from a man like William Robertson—sharp-eyed, rock-solid, not given to sentiment. Yet now he was looking at her like she'd just cracked open the sky.

"She can speak to my boy?"

The question was so raw it made her throat tighten.

"You believe me?" she asked, her voice small, careful.

Robertson didn't answer right away. He looked past her, toward the window, where the afternoon sun lit up the mountains in the distance. Rosa moved over and leaned against his leg. He reached down to touch the little dog's head, seemingly unconscious of his action. "I felt my mother after she passed. Tried to dismiss it as wishful thinking, but...let's just say there were signs."

Gus opened the door. "The press conference is starting." He moved to turn on the television, but Robertson waved him away.

"We'll have to watch the replay."

"Yes, sir." Gus walked out and closed the door behind him.

Robertson's gaze returned to her, and this time it was clear, no longer wistful but hopeful. "Would Dana try to communicate with Marcus for me?"

Laurie realized nobody had ever asked Dana to be a...medium. Was that the right word? She almost laughed at her friend, the serious attorney, opening a business as a ghost whisperer, but she bit down on her lip. The man had just lost a child. "Uh, we can ask."

"I'd be grateful." Robertson sat back in his chair. "So, this evidence that Marcus gathered that got him killed," he said, his voice rough. "You believe it's real?"

Laurie swallowed hard. Rosa trotted back to her place beside her human's chair. Laurie reached down to scratch behind the little dog's ears just to ground herself. "He's been trying to help us. Even after..."

Robertson nodded to himself. "Then let's listen to him."

Relieved to be on more solid ground, Laurie said, "We've cross-checked it. Fred Dickinson—he's a mid-level manager at BioCure—was gathering evidence, too. Fred was about to blow the whistle and according to Marcus's files, he was next on their hit list. When we got to him, he was about to flee to Mexico City. He has information about secret studies. They're hiding data when the tests go wrong. And there's more." Laurie decided to stop there.

Robertson scrubbed a hand down his face. "Jesus."

"As for why these companies would support the bill? Our best guess is that once the national system's in place, they'll start a propaganda campaign suggesting it can't keep up with demand. Sloppy government work. You know the drill."

He nodded.

"Then slide in with private options. Supplemental care, concierge tiers, fast-track coverage. People will flock to it once they believe the government version can't keep up."

Robertson slammed his hand down on the desk. "That's not reform. It's a takeover—with a patriotic paint job."

Before he could say more, the hotel room door burst open and Gus stormed in, breathless. "Senator Whitmore's been shot."

"What?" Laurie jumped up and Rosa started barking.

"Turn on the TV," Robertson shouted.

Gus grabbed the remote and flipped to the news. The image cut in mid-sentence: *"—repeating this breaking news. U.S. Senator Evelyn Whitmore has been shot at her press conference in Seattle. Sources confirm she is in serious condition. No word yet on suspects or motive."*

A shaky video replayed on the screen. Senator Whitmore standing in front of a sea of microphones, aides around her. Then the pop-pop of gunfire, chaos, people screaming. The senator collapsing.

Laurie's hand flew to her mouth. "Oh my God." Then she spotted Dana standing right behind Whitmore.

"She was going to push it through," Robertson muttered. "Why would they try to stop her if they're supporting her bill?"

The news anchor droned on: *"Authorities have not yet confirmed whether this was politically motivated..."*

"Of course it's politically motivated, you morons." Robertson turned to Laurie, jaw clenched. "We're not waiting anymore. If they were willing to shoot a sitting senator, we're past the point of subtlety."

Laurie met his gaze. "Then we expose them. All of them. BioCure, Primewell, Florence Conglomerate. They don't get to kill the truth."

He nodded grimly. "Count me in."

The news played the scene again.

"See her?" Laurie ran over and pointed to Dana who watched in horror as Whitmore fell. "That's our ghost whisperer."

"Dana Preston? Kevin Preston's wife?"

Rosa whined. *Is Dana still alive, girl?* she asked the little Havanese. Would she know?

Yes, but she needs help, Rosa sent back.

Laurie's phone buzzed. The display showed 'Unknown Caller.'

It's Dana, Rosa told her.

Laurie answered. "Dana? Is that you?"

"Yes, how did you know?"

Rosa sniffed.

"Never mind that," Laurie said. "Are you okay?"

"I had to ditch my phone—and Kevin. Can you pick me up?"

"Yes." She covered the phone and said to Robertson, "Dana had to run from the scene. She's alone on the street."

Robertson shot up from his chair. "Gus, get the car."

"We're coming to get you," Laurie told Dana.

"We?"

"Yes, I've got a surprise for you."

Dana sputtered. "I think I've had enough surprises lately."

"This is a good one."

Laurie got directions, then ran to catch up with Robertson and his security man.

After William Robertson gathered up Dana and then the kids, they drove to her house to pack a small bag—just the essentials: clothes, toiletries, anything they'd need to disappear for a while. Then he had Gus drive them all the way out to Red Fox Farm, a storm breaking over Seattle in relentless sheets of rain. On the drive to Duvall, Dana recounted everything—Evelyn's shooting, the chaos, her escape through the observatory's guts. Robertson listened in silence, jaw tight. Rosa climbed into Dana's lap and comforted her, something she'd been doing a lot recently.

At the farmhouse, Robertson met the family—well, some of it—and took in the reports of attacks on alternative health care across the country. He listened, asked a few quiet questions, and finally stood to go, raincoat in hand. At the door, he turned back to Dana, his voice steady.

"I'll be in touch," he said. "We're going to put a stop to all this."

LATER THAT EVENING, rain tapped the farmhouse windows in a steady rhythm, softening the late fall light. Inside, the living room was crowded with bodies and silences: Fred curled in the armchair with a blanket and a mug; Laurie sitting cross-legged on the floor, Rosa snoozing beside her; Skye leaning against the mantle, arms folded; and Siobhán standing at the bay window, peering out like she expected danger to crest over the hills at any moment.

Dana and Minh sat on the couch, shoulders touching, phones aglow.

"Okay," Minh said. "You ready for this? Social media has...lost its mind."

Dana blew out a breath. "Go on."

He scrolled, then read aloud. "Here's one: *'Whitmore faked the whole thing. Sympathy stunt. She'll walk out of the hospital in two days and claim divine intervention. Wait for it.'*"

Fred groaned. "Jesus. She was shot on live television."

"Here's another," Minh said, swiping. "*'This is what happens when you try to take health care away from the free market. The shooter was a patriot.'*" He grimaced. "Lots of flags and eagle emojis with that one."

Dana leaned in and read over his shoulder. "*#HealthCareHoax #FalseFlagWhitmore*—oh for the love of—Skye, come look at this."

Skye moved closer, her expression pinched. Minh flipped the screen toward her.

"This post says," Dana continued, "*'The shooter wasn't a person. Watch the footage—he moves too fast. That's military-grade augmentation. DARPA? Maybe biotech from a health care company?'*"

Fred's head thudded against the back of his chair. "And I thought I was paranoid."

Laurie twisted around, half-laughing. "You were. But these people have fallen down the rabbit hole."

Siobhán crossed the room quietly and stood behind them, her gray braid swinging as she leaned in. "What does that one say?" she asked, pointing to a meme.

Minh cleared his throat. "Um. It's... Senator Whitmore photoshopped next to a reptilian with the caption: *'Don't let the lizard win. Vote no on Health Act 203.'*"

Skye snorted. "A lizard. Really? I could almost respect the commitment."

Laurie's phone buzzed. "My turn. Here's a thread accusing Whitmore's staff of organizing the shooting to *'take her out before she flipped on them.'* As if Evelyn Whitmore takes orders from anyone."

Dana glanced up at Skye. "Is there anything we can do magically to deflect some of this? Disinformation is spreading faster than we can fight."

Skye tilted her head. "We'll ask Iona to check the grimoire. It's hard, though, when people *want* to believe it."

"Confirmation bias can be more powerful than any incantation," Siobhán said softly.

Minh sighed. "Even my classmates are reposting this garbage. One girl thinks the whole bill is a Trojan horse for implanting vaccine trackers."

Fred muttered, "That's not how microchips work."

Jade stood and rubbed her temples. "I wonder if there's a way to shift the focus. The more these theories spread, the more room the real conspirators have to operate unnoticed."

"Maybe they're behind these memes," Laurie suggested.

Jade looked over at Skye. "Are the wards holding?"

"For now," Skye said. "But I'd feel better if we reinforced them. Especially with what just happened."

"I'll help," Siobhán said.

"Me too," Jade offered, standing.

As the others drifted into motion, Dana said, "We'll keep monitoring. Let you know if anything gains traction—especially if it ties back to Evelyn or the companies."

Minh nodded, eyes already back on the feed. "I've got alerts set. We'll know if it spikes."

The fight wasn't just behind the scenes anymore or even in the streets.

It was here—in whispers and memes, algorithms and hashtags. Moving at the speed of three billion cycles per second.

CHAPTER
NINETEEN

At two in the morning, BioCure's downtown headquarters shimmered with cold light and silence. The building's modern glass facade reflected the city's restless energy, but inside, all was clinical stillness—white walls, steel accents, and the low hum of servers.

The skeletal night shift rarely noticed the cleaning crew. Tonight, that was the plan.

Dana adjusted the janitor's jumpsuit, trying not to flinch at the clashing scent of industrial cleanser and a sage bundle Skye had tucked into her boot "for protection." Laurie's hair was tucked under a cap, and Skye—strawberry blonde hair charmed mouse-brown and glasses to look slightly too large—pushed a mop cart like she was born to do it.

Rosa trotted at Laurie's side in a tiny service dog vest with a forged badge and more intelligence than most people in the building. She sniffed at corners, the hem of office doors, and told Laurie there was a strange metallic scent of fear that lingered on air ducts and elevator seams.

This company thrives on intimidation, Laurie sent back.

"Security will rotate in twelve minutes," Skye whispered. "Confirm."

The posse had been equipped with earbuds so they could hear and respond to each other, gratis Maxwell.

"Affirmative," Laurie said.

"Roger that," Dana said.

Skye rolled her eyes at her friends' spy talk, then tapped a glowing glyph stitched into the inside of her glove. "The access badge enchantment will hold if we don't ask too many questions out loud. Just look busy."

No problem for us, Rosa said to her human.

Laurie rolled her cart past the executive elevator, casually swiping the stolen card Maxwell had gifted them. It blinked green.

The elevator doors opened with a whisper.

They piled in, clumsy with nerves. The wheels of Skye's cart got stuck in the groove between the elevator and the outside floor and the door bounced on it twice before she and Laurie got it unstuck. The door closed and Skye leaned against the wall. "Geez. Great start."

"Rosa says you were born to be a janitor," Laurie teased, and Rosa ran over to Skye, turned around and barked at her human.

"I'm thinking she did not say that," Skye muttered.

Dana and Laurie burst out laughing.

By the time the elevator opened on the 47th floor—BioCure's executive suites—they'd collected themselves. Skye led the way past frosted glass doors labeled *Advanced Strategy Division*. Dana slid a USB stick into a terminal behind the receptionist's desk and nodded. "Maxwell's in. We've got twenty minutes before the real cleaning crew shows up."

"Let's spread out. See what we can find," Skye said.

Laurie headed down a hall festooned with closed office doors, each bearing the name and title of the employee. She read the titles—Executive VP of Research, President of Strategy, Lead Strategist and the like—until she came to the end of the corridor and faced a double door with the name she'd been looking for: Damien Blackwood, Chief Executive Officer.

Laurie swiped the stolen card across the keypad and the lock clicked open. Inside, Rosa sniffed around while Laurie rifled through the drawers which were mostly empty. Business cards. A few dusty paper clips probably twenty years old. No file cabinet. No bookshelves. Only Scandinavian style sofa and chairs arranged to take in the view of Seattle's skyscrapers and a sliver of water. The dominant feature seemed to be the liquor cabinet.

She admired the cut crystal glasses and decanter. Blackwood didn't stint on his alcohol. Pappy Van Winkle Special Reserve Bourbon, Macallan 18-year-old Double Cask Single Malt Scotch Whiskey, Clase Azul Tequila Ultra, 2001 Screaming Eagle Cabernet Double Magnum. Several bottles of Dom Perignon Brut Champagne worth a few thousand were shoved to the back as if they were an afterthought. Drinking seemed to be the only work Blackwood did in here.

She wasn't familiar with the names, except for Dom Perignon, so she snapped a photo. She and John could look them up online later just to see how much they cost. Laurie preferred a good local vintage over all this bling.

You done drooling over the alcohol? Rosa asked.

Am not.

Were, too. I've got his scent. Want to find the secret room?

There's a secret room?

Just as Laurie walked out of Blackwood's office, Skye's whisper came through her earbud. "Somebody's opening the front door."

Quick, we gotta get out of here, she told Rosa.

Laurie waved her card in front of the adjacent office door, and the two detectives ducked in just as two flashlight beams pierced the dark of the hallway.

A man's voice came from the end of the hall. "The motion detectors went off in Blackwood's office."

Shit, Maxwell had missed that. Laurie closed the door to the room they were in but stopped it just before it latched. She couldn't risk any noise.

"Where's your key card?" The man's voice was gruff.

"If you turned on the damn lights, I could find it faster." The door opened and light from Blackwood's office flooded the hallway. "Nobody here."

"We have to check to see if anything's been moved."

"I don't know how we'll know that. Boss only holds meetings in—"

"Just look," the other man snapped.

Laurie listened to footsteps in the other room, the occasional shuffle of paper. Then a voice right outside the door they were hiding behind. "Can't figure it out."

"Maybe it was a false alarm. I'll tell the nerds to check their computers."

"We done?"

"Yeah, beer's on me."

The heavy footsteps moved away. After another few minutes, Laurie heard Skye's heavy sigh of relief. "Coast clear."

Laurie opened the door and Rosa made her way down the hallway, nose to the floor. Laurie followed the little Havanese through the main room where she finally sat in front of a section of the wall.

"Rosa says there's a hidden room behind the wood paneling," Laurie said. "She followed Blackwood's scent."

He goes in here a lot. So do other people. Not the killer, though.

Good to know, Laurie said.

Skye ran from the other hallway and arrived, slightly out of breath, Dana behind her breathing normally. Laurie remembered her intention to start jogging. She swiped her card around the panel and something clicked. The panel moved slightly away from the rest of the wall. She pulled it open and found a room. "Bingo."

The group slipped into what turned out to be a conference room —empty but for a wall-length whiteboard, the kind you could write the future on and then pretend it was just a brainstorm. But this wasn't a brainstorm.

It was a blueprint.

Flowcharts sprawled across the surface like a spiderweb: *Policy Implementation* fed into *Legislative Influence* fed into *Phase II—Population Management*. Arrows looped and doubled back with unnerving precision. Beneath one node marked *Behavioral Prediction Algorithms*, someone had scrawled "Start with Medicare crossover populations" in red ink.

A list of initials ran down one margin—likely senators and representatives. Dana recognized at least three from committees that had publicly opposed the bill, now bracketed with dollar amounts and 'LTP access confirmed.'

Skye pointed. "What does LTP stand for?"

Laurie and Dana scanned the mass of writing. "Wait, here's a label in the research section. 'Longevity Treatment Protocols.' That matches," Dana said.

And in the middle of it all, circled in thick crimson marker like the eye of a storm: OneHealth.

Dana stepped closer.

Beneath the name was a tagline still being workshopped, the kind marketers threw around in pitch decks: "One system. One standard. One solution."

A smaller scribble in the corner: "*Universal care becomes proprietary protocol post-transition.*"

Her breath caught. Post-transition? They weren't just lobbying for the bill. They were preparing to inherit it—**to** let the government carry it to term, then snatch it away once the baby could crawl.

Dana stared. "They're planning what happens after they get the bill passed."

Laurie snapped photos. Skye riffled through a filing cabinet with an anti-intrusion alarm, but her charm-disruptor bracelet fizzled through the protection like it was cotton candy. She pulled out a red folder marked *Phase III – Consolidation Protocols*.

"Got something," she said, flipping pages. "Payoffs to senators and representatives—specific ones. Promised off-book longevity treatments if they vote yes."

Dana clenched her fists. "Bribery in the form of immortality. Subtle."

"There's more." Skye read aloud. "Reduction of what they're calling *'disease load on society'*—aka denying expensive treatments to people deemed economically unproductive. It's all algorithmic—age, income, education level. They've built actuarial profiles for controlled attrition."

Laurie's voice was flat. "Medical murder through omission."

Skye handed her a second folder. "Read the timeline."

Inside, a chart showed the merger: *BioCure + Primewell + Florence Hospitals → OneHealth, Incorporated.* The next page had a diagram of the ownership structure. Twenty-five percent stocks belonging to four major players from these corporations, names they already knew. Damien Blackwood, Olivia Mercer, Thomas Ellsworth, and Garrett Monroe.

Becoming one entity with total vertical control of insurance, pharmaceuticals, hospitals, research.

Rosa gave a soft bark and pressed her nose to the far wall.

Laurie went to the little dog, ran her fingers along the paneling. "There's something more here."

Dana found a magnetic latch behind a frame. The wall popped open to reveal a hidden compartment. Inside: flash drives, marked envelopes, and a black leather folio embossed with a silver "K."

Laurie opened it on the conference table, hands shaking. They all gathered around. Inside were emails, meeting notes, and internal memos—some signed by Kevin Preston.

Dana's stomach dropped. "He's not just helping. He knows everything. Gatekeeper wasn't metaphorical."

A sudden voice echoed through the floor. "Cleaning crew, report to executive elevator bank."

They froze.

Skye whispered, "Pack up. Now."

Dana shoved the files and drives into her utility bag. The went into the conference room and Laurie snapped the wall shut. Rosa pressed close, eyes sharp.

They made it to the elevator just as the doors opened and two sleepy janitors stepped out.

Skye smiled. "You're early. North employee elevator was being worked on—we looped around."

The woman grunted, already annoyed. "Whatever. Long night."

They slipped inside the elevator.

As the doors closed, Dana stared at her reflection in the metal panel, eyes dark with fury.

OneHealth was real. Kevin was deep in it. And people were going to die unless they stopped it.

She placed a hand over the bag slung across her chest. They had the evidence.

Now they just had to survive what came next.

THE WINDING ROAD back from BioCure had been shrouded in pre-dawn mist, the sun just below the horizon doing little to warm Dana's clenched shoulders or the chill that had settled in her bones. But it did cool her fury, so hot in the moment of their break-in, leaving only exhaustion in its wake. Skye waved to her as she walked to her own cabin. Dana trudged toward the house, her boots quiet on the hardwood floors. The roomy weathered farmhouse, wrapped in early morning silence, smelled faintly of wood smoke, lavender, and cinnamon—comforting and surreal after the chaos of the night.

She dropped the bag of stolen intel on the long oak table in the strategy room—Minh's makeshift war room, where the crime board now spilled across three walls—and retreated to their suite upstairs. Her room was tidy, too tidy, as if it were staging itself as a place of refuge she didn't feel she deserved. It felt like they'd moved in permanently, like they were fugitives from their own lives.

A few hours later, sunlight streamed through the lace-curtained windows, and Dana awoke to the familiar tension of sleep interrupted by unfinished business. She showered under scalding water that didn't quite erase the night's grime, then pawed through her bag for something clean to wear. Nothing. Just more dirty jeans and wrinkled shirts.

She'd have to go back to the house eventually. Face Kevin. Retrieve her things. Invent some plausible story about why they weren't staying there. Why Hoa was being chauffeured around by Evelyn Whitmore's staff. Her mind recoiled from the idea like a hand from flame. When would she tell him what she knew? Should she?

Pulling on the least offensive t-shirt and jeans combo, Dana padded barefoot down the creaky farmhouse stairs, chasing the promise of caffeine. The kitchen was deserted, the usual chatter absent. She poured herself a cup of dark roast so strong it could strip paint and wandered into the back room.

There, bathed in soft light from the east-facing windows, stood Minh. He was motionless, staring at the black leather folio on the table—the one embossed with a silver "K." His shoulders were drawn tight, his jaw set. The folder might as well have been radioactive.

Her breath caught in her throat. Stupid, stupid, stupid. She'd left it out, right in the open. Letting her son stumble into his father's betrayal alone.

"Minh," she began, the word catching somewhere between guilt and apology.

He turned, his expression raw, his usual sharp wit nowhere in sight. "How could he?"

"I'm sorry you found out like this. I should have—"

He shook his head. "No, Mom. I sort of suspected. I mean, I checked out all his donors. Blackwood, Mercer, Ellsworth..." He tapped the table, searching for the last name.

"Monroe," she said quietly.

He nodded. "Yeah. That hospital guy. They were all top contributors. And then we started getting the evidence. I wondered."

Dana sank into the chair beside him, wrapping both hands around her mug as if it might ground her. "We don't know everything yet. Not the full extent."

Minh gave her a look—gentle, sad, but certain. "Come on, Mom. I think that ship has sailed. Dad's willing to let people die if it means he wins."

Across the room, Marcus stood at the edge of the table, translucent and solemn. His spectral presence seemed to draw the room tighter around itself. He looked at Minh with quiet sorrow, then at Dana, but offered no words. No comfort. Just his steady presence.

Then, like sunlight through a storm cloud, Hoa burst in, her feet barely touching the ground as she skipped across the floor. "I love it here! Can we stay all summer?"

Minh opened his mouth, but Dana lifted a warning finger. "Go easy," she whispered.

"Dad's an idiot," Minh snapped.

Hoa didn't miss a beat. "Tell me something I don't already know."

Minh blinked, caught off-guard. "No, really. He's taking bribes from seriously nasty people," he said, lowering his voice but not the intensity.

"It looks like your father might have gotten in over his head," Dana translated, the words tasting like chalk.

Minh snorted at the understatement.

Hoa's face shifted. She glanced between them, her brows furrowing. "So...are you getting a divorce?"

Dana leaned back, sighing into her seat as if it might swallow her. "You know I love you kids. And I love your father...but we've grown apart."

Minh raised an eyebrow in disbelief but kept quiet.

"I've been thinking about divorce," Dana said finally. "But first... we'd live separately."

"Two houses?" Hoa asked. "Will we have to live in D.C.?"

"If he wins, it complicates things," Dana admitted.

Minh huffed. "He's not going to win. Not with all this evidence. He's going straight to jail. Do not pass Go. Do not collect two hundred dollars—or however much those bastards are offering him."

Hoa's eyes widened. "Jail?"

Dana sat forward. "No. He's not going to jail."

Minh gestured at the mountain of data on the table. "Seriously?"

"For crying out loud," Dana muttered. She took a breath, the deep kind they told her to do in yoga, but it did nothing. "People like them don't go to jail. Not really. They cut deals. Or end up in luxury 'detention' centers with tennis courts."

"But what did he do?" Hoa asked, her voice small now.

"Nothing yet," Dana said. "It's what he's planning."

"Pretty sure they've got laws against that too," Minh muttered.

Dana noticed then that his eyes were filled with tears. She opened her arms and motioned them both in. Somehow, Minh managed to fold his lanky frame into the hug. She held them tight, her heart aching with the impossible wish to shield them from everything.

"I'm here. I'll always be here," she murmured. "And your father still loves you. You're going to be okay."

"Yeah, as long as you catch my stalker," Hoa sniffed.

Dana kissed the top of her head. "We will. I promise."

Could she promise that?

A cool breeze swept across her neck, the telltale chill of Marcus's ghostly touch as he folded his energy into the family knot of limbs.

You got this, he whispered, his voice like rustling paper and memory.

Minh stood, squaring his shoulders. "Guess I can live without a father."

Right then, John Newman poked his head in. "Need some help? I hear there's a shit ton of...uh"—he glanced at Hoa—"a lot of files to go through."

Dana's breath caught. Since the reunion, John had filled more of the "dad" role in Minh's life than Kevin ever had—taking him out to see the whales, offering advice, even giving him a shot at a future with an internship. Minh listened to John in a way he never had with Kevin. Maybe it was the integrity. Or the kindness. Maybe it was because he just wasn't his parent.

Laurie followed John into the room, Rosa padding beside her like a little fawn sentinel. The Havanese mix circled the room, then hopped up onto a chair and placed her paws on the table. Laurie helped her up.

Rosa sniffed the evidence—every file, every drive, and the black folio.

"She says," Laurie announced, "she doesn't smell the killer."

Hoa groaned. "I thought you said you'd *find* him!"

Rosa trotted over, hopped into Hoa's lap, and licked her cheek.

"She says not to worry. They will. And she'll help with your stalker, too."

The room softened, for just a moment.

And Dana, for the first time in days, felt like maybe—just maybe —they were going to be okay.

CHAPTER
TWENTY

"You do realize none of this material is admissible in court," Vivienne said, throwing down a thick report on the longevity research and glaring at Dana. "This theft could get you disbarred."

Siobhán jumped in before Dana could respond. "We don't have time to subpoena for reports, though."

They were gathered in the conference room of Vivienne's law firm with the stolen files, flash drives, marked envelopes, and the black leather folio that condemned Kevin all spread across their long polished table. It was a lot. Laurie had started to print out the pictures she'd taken of the wall-length whiteboard with its damning flowcharts, but Minh pointed out that uploading them to the laptop was better. "That way you can enlarge any section you want. Really see what's there." He'd been right.

"Would Fred's data be enough?" Skye asked. "Or what Marcus was able to pull together?"

Dana folded her arms across her chest, already knowing the answer. Marcus stood beside her in much the same position.

"No provenance, unfortunately." Vivienne pushed her large

black-rimmed glasses back up her nose. "The only clean evidence we have are the depositions coming in from people who were paid to file false claims against alternative health care providers. No offense, Siobhán, but the public is not going to get outraged about traditional medicine going after herbal healers and such."

"Yeah, especially with the new officials in D.C.," Laurie added.

"Why couldn't they pick somebody with real expertise for that job, like the president of Wellspring?" Siobhán threw her hands in the air.

"Right?" Skye said. "These people don't know chamomile from echinacea."

Dana jumped in before they went off on a tangent. "They're moving too fast for the courts to stop them. We have to go another route."

Vivienne took off her tailored midnight-blue blazer and hung it on the back of her chair. Dana admired the subtle velvet lapels and silver thread stitching along the seams, wondering if it would pass muster with Kevin's prissy campaign stylist.

Vivienne rolled up the sleeves of her stark white blouse, put both hands on the table, and spoke to Dana, the other person with a law degree present. "Senator Whitmore's bill hasn't passed yet, so there's no law to work with. I don't want any of this coming back on Grant, Everhart & Vale. We're a small firm and would get squashed in a flat second by these big boys."

"Agreed."

Vivienne stared at the documents scattered across the table. "So, these assholes want a monopoly on all areas of health care in the United States."

"And that's just the beginning," Dana said. "It's clear they're buying votes with the promise of longevity treatments."

"Which don't even work," Siobhán snorted.

"And hiding the evidence of their failures," Fred said from his seat at the end of the table.

And here I thought they only wanted to take over the billion-dollar health care industry. Marcus shook his head. *They want to extend the lives of the worst of humanity and let the rest die off.*

Dana nodded. *That's what it looks like. Good thing you discovered all this.*

Vivienne exhaled through her nose, tapping a fingernail against the table's glossy surface. "The courts won't save us. And the press won't touch this without a vetted source."

"So, what do we do? Just sit on it and wait for them to take over the entire system?" Minh asked, his voice filled with the outrage only a teenager could still muster.

"No," Dana said slowly. "We go around them. Let the cat out of the bag."

Vivienne looked at her. "Go on."

"We leak it," Dana said. "Not from you. From someone anonymous. Public drops. Strategic releases."

Minh nodded, catching on immediately. "A media dump. We give it to online journalists, data transparency networks, watchdog organizations. Package it like a whistleblower leak. If it hits enough platforms at once, they can't scrub it all."

"And the public goes wild." Laurie spread her hands above her head. "The fake complaints, the merger plan, the names of officials on their payroll—people will connect the dots."

Vivienne arched an eyebrow. "You're talking about coordinated disinformation warfare."

"Coordinated *truth* warfare," Dana corrected. "We're not falsifying anything. We're just not pretending we got it through proper channels."

"It's not a courtroom win," Skye said. "It's a public one. If we can stir up enough backlash, we can force an investigation. Gather public support for—" she snapped her fingers. "What's the senator calling her bill?"

"American Health Security Act," Dana answered.

"She needs another name," Minh mumbled. "Something amped."

Siobhán leaned forward. "What if we tie the exposure to a broader health freedom movement? Herbalists, naturopaths, home birth centers—everyone who's been targeted by these people."

"And let them speak for themselves," Laurie added. "Not just statistics. Personal stories. Faces. Lives."

Minh tapped rapidly at his keyboard. "Maxwell and I can create a clean digital front. Anonymous submissions, mirrored archives, embedded visuals. No trail back to the firm."

Dana came up short. "Wait, you're working with Maxwell now?"

"You already knew that, Mom," he said.

She wasn't sure how she felt about her sweet teenage son who wanted to save the oceans teaming up with the snarky hacker who possessed questionable ethics, but a crusader's heart reluctantly pointed in the right direction.

Marcus leaned closer, a wave of cool air washing over her. *Stop worrying. You raised him right. He's growing into a good man.*

Thanks. Dana resisted the urge to ask the ghost if he could see Minh's future.

Vivienne still looked unconvinced—more out of self-preservation than principle.

Dana met her eyes. "You're not involved. No firm letterhead, no comment, no trace. We'll say it came from inside the future OneHealth—leaked by someone who saw too much."

Vivienne stared at her for a long moment, then nodded once. "You'll need a mouthpiece. Someone not tied to any of you. Someone credible, angry, and ideally dying of something treatable."

Fred raised his hand tentatively.

Everyone turned.

"I think I might know a whistleblower," he said.

The room erupted in laughter.

"You're perfect, Fred," Skye said. "Only catch is, you're not dying."

Fred gave a dry smile. "No—but they sure want me dead."

SKYE HAD ASKED her little cousin Iona MacAllister to find a spell, a ritual, something to counter the social media reaction to Senator Whitmore's shooting while they showed Vivienne the information they'd uncovered—well, stolen—last night. "We thought things would be calmer this morning, but the social media circus is still in full swing," Skye had told her.

Glad for the opportunity to use her new position as family historian and keeper of the grimoires to help in this crisis, she climbed up to the ritual room after they left for their meeting.

The attic at Red Fox Farm wasn't dusty, despite what newcomers always expected. It had the rich scent of old paper, wax, cedar, and the faintest trace of lavender. The shelves curved with the slope of the roof, one big section packed tight with leather-bound grimoires in shades of umber and black, rust and green. Each one was etched with runes and initials—hundreds of years of Yarrow and MacAllister hands, passing knowledge forward like flame.

Iona MacAllister sat cross-legged in the center of the room, her thick auburn braid coiled at the nape of her neck, sleeves rolled past her elbows. Around her lay open volumes, layered like petals: a heavy, iron-clasped tome bound in dark, cracked leather, its vellum pages etched with fading ink and sigils that seemed to shimmer faintly when touched; a vellum-bound ledger from the 1870s; a spiral-bound journal with ink from five years ago; and a digital tablet propped up on an enchanted bookstand, blue screen glowing with her own annotated grimoire app.

A storm of thoughts swirled behind her dark eyes.

She opened the iron-bound grimoire first, turning each page carefully so as not to tear anything. The volume had ancient spells, ageless and some antiquated rituals. In the margins her ancestors had made notes, suggested changes, indicated a different herb for a recipe. "Should the mandrake take to sulking—or shriek at handing —mind not its tantrum."

Toward the middle she found spells for quelling disputes. One page was titled '*To still the tongue of a neighbor much given to dispute.* Another '*For the binding of a wagging tongue that stirs ill winds 'twixt households.*' Another related to relationships: '*To silence the ceaseless prattle of a troublesome companion in close quarters.*' On the next page she found something promising.

Charm for Binding a Quarrelsome Tongue
To be employed discreetly, and only when all civil remedies have failed.
Components:
A scrap of linen or muslin cloth
A ribbon of black thread, no longer than a yard
A dried thorn from a hawthorn tree
A small slip of paper with the neighbor's name written in iron gall ink
A pinch of valerian root (for calming)
A silver coin (to seal the charm with fairness)
Instructions:
Wrap the name and valerian together in the cloth, whispering thrice:
"By root and thorn, by thread and breath,
Let peace walk where once was wrath.
Still the tongue that strikes like storm,
Let silence now be kindly born."
Prick the bundle once with the hawthorn thorn—lightly, with respect. Bind it tight with the thread, knotting it nine times.
Bury the charm beneath a stone at the edge of your property— preferably near the boundary with the neighbor in question—and place the silver coin atop the stone as offering to the spirits of peace.
Note (in margin, slightly faded): *Should the quarrel grow anew, renew the charm under a waning moon.*

Iona chewed her lip, considering. This might come in handy, but how where to bury something to influence the whole world? What name would she use? Her mom might have some ideas.

She flicked a page in the 19th-century grimoire, lips moving as she translated the Gaelic scrawl. *'To sway the minds of many, one must first sing to the river of thought.'*

"That's it. This is one of the old collective influence spells," she whispered.

Behind her, Ashe padded softly into the room. She licked Iona's hand and curled beside the pile of recent entries—ones her Aunt Siobhán had contributed in her youth. Iona smiled faintly, then returned to the pages.

Voices filtered up through the floorboards. Downstairs over late morning coffee, Fíona trying to calibrate what "enough evidence" meant, Cormac reading aloud another meme comparing Whitmore to a cyborg.

"Ridiculous," Iona muttered, flipping a page. It seemed the more irrational something was, the more people believed it.

She reached for a modern grimoire—her cousin Brigid's work from the late '90s, filled with sigils designed to work through radio waves and early internet protocols. "She was ahead of her time."

Near the back, Iona found it: *'Ritual for Mass Persuasion Through the Veil of Media.'* Her fingers hovered over the page. It used a blend of thoughtform direction, mirror-path weaving, and voice imprint amplification—a subtle glamour sent through waves of influence: social, emotional, even digital. Not mind control. More like turning up the volume on truth and compassion so it could rise above fear and fiction.

She flipped backward to the older book and cross-referenced a 1734 ritual designed to turn village sentiment against a corrupt land-lord using blessed river stones and whispered intentions during the full moon.

"We can modernize this," she said aloud. "Thread the emotional current through livestreams. Blend the enchantment with language, imagery, repetition. The old ways and the new."

A thrill ran through her. She stood and pulled the pieces together —sigils from the oldest volume, updated cadence from Brigid's work, the amplification charm from her own notes. She sketched a rough glyph on the whiteboard mounted near the dormer window.

Ashe tilted her head, watching with her eerie ice-blue eyes.

"They want to believe something," Iona told her softly. "Let's give them something worthy to believe in."

She closed the books one by one with care, touched her hand to the cover of the oldest and whispered a blessing in Gaelic.

"I have a ritual," she announced to the space and any ancestors listening.

CHAPTER

TWENTY-ONE

T hey gathered in the ritual room at the top of house just as the sun reached the tops of the trees bordering the west of Red Fox Farm. Skye swept the floor with saltwater and rosemary. The air pulsed with intention. Outside, wind stirred the orchard, and in the kitchen, candles flickered in every window.

The camera was already set—an old DSLR linked to Minh's laptop, ready to livestream across every platform he could access. "We'll embed the glyphs into the video overlay," he explained, fingers flying. "Sigils as watermarks. Invisible to most, but not to the unconscious mind."

Dana lit the main candle, a tall white pillar wrapped with red thread in a spiral. "To speak truth to power," she said softly.

Skye stepped forward, barefoot and focused. She wore a dress the color of dusk, and in her hand was a woven cord of yarrow, rosemary, red thread, and a scrap of ribbon from Senator Whitmore's campaign launch.

"Iona," she said, "you have the invocation?"

Iona stood at the center of a circle they had chalked and blessed. Beside her, Fíona held the ancient grimoire, its cracked leather cover gleaming faintly in the candlelight. Iona had her own handwritten notes—updated cadences, rhythmic to match the algorithmic flow of media.

Fred, Laurie, and Siobhán stood along the outer ring. Rosa sat at Laurie's side, tail still, ears alert. Ashe kept watch on Iona.

The room felt...awake.

Iona began, her voice calm and resonant:

"By the ink of the ancestors,
    By the breath of the wind that carries word to ear,
    By firelight and fiber-optic thread,
    Let truth walk the roads of the many.
    Let compassion ride the current.
    Let fear be as fog—seen, then burned away by clarity."

Minh cued the livestream. The camera light glowed red.

Dana stepped into frame. Her voice was low, steady, personal. "Senator Whitmore is still alive. She is healing. And her dream—of a health care system that puts people first—is still within reach. But the noise is deafening. Lies are rising like floodwater. And so we ask —listen with your hearts. Help the dream become reality."

As Dana spoke, Minh layered in the video: scrolling images of Evelyn shaking hands in clinics, sitting at veterans' hospitals, speaking in storm shelters and food lines. Faces of supporters. Nurses. Children. Doctors in rural towns.

Behind it all: a pulsing sigil. Soft, almost invisible. Designed by Skye and Iona together—a spiral within a spiral, topped by an open palm with an eye in the center.

Iona continued the spell, one hand lifted:

"We speak not to bind the will—
    But to clear the fog from eyes.
    Let hearts remember what justice feels like.
    Let ears turn toward the wounded, not the wealthy.

Let the song of truth echo through the glass halls of power."

Skye added herbs to the cauldron—a mix of thyme, sage, and dried apple blossoms from the orchard. She lit them with a taper.

Fragrant smoke rose. On-screen, the candlelight seemed to shimmer. Viewers wouldn't know why it stirred them. Only that it felt real.

Minh whispered, "People are watching. It's spreading."

"Good," Iona murmured. She raised her voice once more.

"By the roots of the old ways
> And the code of the new,
> We name what must be seen:
> Life is sacred.
> Healing is a right.
> The truth does not kneel."

The flames flared.
The camera blinked.

AFTER THE RITUAL, they gathered in the farmhouse to watch the cyber storm they'd cooked up. Every couch, cushion, and crooked wooden chair was occupied—most by the Yarrow clan, others by the posse. Rosa made the rounds for ear scratches and any treats to be had. The air buzzed with too much tea, not enough sleep.

Already there was speculation on feeds about the ritual they'd sent out.

#Witches rule and #Whitmore is dope popped up. Some decided she served the devil.

"Typical," Jade scoffed.

Minh sat cross-legged on the rug, laptop open on the coffee table. Tabs were stacked like bricks—news outlets, watchdog forums, encrypted chatrooms, whistleblower threads. Maxwell had sent an advanced packet to an underground journalist he knew and a livestream from her site had already started scrolling phrases like 'unredacted,' 'BioCure internal,' and 'project OneHealth.'

"Just wait until we go live with our plan," he told them.

Grandmother Brigid passed out blueberry scones without comment, as though pastries could brace a person for systemic collapse. Iona scrolled through feeds at triple speed, muttering translations under her breath when old sigils showed up unexpectedly in protest memes.

At 8:03 p.m., the first drop hit.

A low murmur spread through the room as people read silently, phones glowing like fireflies. Laurie leaned against the mantle.

Rosa pawed her arm. *What's it say? What's it say?*

Hold on, Laurie said.

Minh's voice cut through the quiet. "Maxwell put together a bunch of files revealing their scheme. I got to help." His eyes shone with a mix of pride and disbelief.

"We scheduled drops over the rest of the night and all through tomorrow," he added, voice trembling just slightly. "Different angles, different platforms. It's like opening floodgates in pieces, so they can't plug it all at once."

Dana stood near the window, arms crossed, watching the reflection of the flickering screens behind her. Marcus was beside her, more solid than ever. *Looks like my work is done.*

Almost, but you should stick around for the grand finale. Dana was surprised that she wasn't ready to let him go yet.

A ping echoed from Iona's phone. Then another from Siobhán's. Then ten more. Mentions, alerts, tags, quotes.

"The longevity treatments are trending," Laurie said, scrolling.

"Whitmore's name, too," Fred added. "They're already accusing her of leading a secret health cult. That's...not the worst spin they could've put on it."

Skye raised an eyebrow. "We could do worse than a health cult led by Evelyn Whitmore."

Laughter rose from around the room. The tension was breaking up.

On screen, an anchor at a small local affiliate read off headlines like she was trying to contain fire. *"The source of the leak is currently unknown. We reached out to representatives at BioCure, Primewell, and Florence Hospitals—none have responded to requests for comment. Meanwhile, sources say Senator Whitmore will be released from Baywater and make a short statement tomorrow."*

Vivienne's voice echoed from the kitchen, phone pressed to her ear. "Sorry, we can't comment on ongoing litigation."

She walked back into the living room. "A Seattle Times journalist just tracked me down. He's made the connection between the fraudulent claims against alternative health care providers and all this." Vivienne waved her hand, indicating all the people watching different feeds around the room.

"That was fast," Minh said. "We haven't even released that packet yet."

Dana turned back to the group. "They're going to come after us."

"They already are," Skye said. "But now they're chasing shadows."

"More like a hydra-headed monster," Laurie said with satisfaction.

Fred leaned forward, gaze steady. "And for once, the truth gets to move faster than they do."

Vivienne and Dana headed back to the war room. She gave the crime board a quick glance. "Impressive work."

Marcus put one startlingly solid hand behind his waist, the other in front, and executed a formal bow.

Dana bit her lip to stop herself from laughing. Marcus had certainly started the ball rolling—and paid with his life—so he deserved the credit.

"I think we should leave everything here. I don't want any contraband in the office."

"Agreed," Dana said.

Vivienne covered a wide yawn with her hand. "I'm headed home. Talk tomorrow?"

"Yes. We're eager to see how things have developed in the morning. I just hope I can convince Minh to get some sleep."

"Good luck with that. I don't have kids, but you've raised two good ones as far as I can tell."

Dana felt a rush of warmth. "Thank you. I worry, so it's good to hear what other people see in them."

Vivienne patted her arm. "I'll try to get back here before Senator Whitmore gives her press conference."

"We'll look forward to it."

"We," Vivienne repeated, then looked directly at the spot where Marcus stood.

Dana tried not to panic, then realized she didn't need to. Vivienne was a practicing witch. She'd probably understand.

"I don't know who your guides are, but I'm glad you have them," Vivienne said in a low voice.

"Oh." Surprised, Dana opened her mouth to tell her about Marcus, but then decided the night was late. She could divulge her secret tomorrow.

CHAPTER

TWENTY-TWO

The living room at Red Fox Farm was packed again, this time with coffee mugs instead of laptops and cell phones. Everyone had claimed a spot—Fred in an overstuffed chair, Gandalf curled up on an ottoman, Skye perched cross-legged on the hearth, Laurie sitting backward in a chair with Rosa curled under it like a lion in waiting, John standing behind her holding a mug decorated with a Mini Mouse face.

"Who's got popcorn?" Minh joked, refreshing the stream on the big monitor.

"It's a little early for that, but I brought lemon rosemary scones and some blueberry from last night." Grandmother Brigid set down a tray with enough butter to soothe a wounded nation.

"I loved those blueberry ones," John said.

"You're in luck. I still have a few." Brigid handed John a small plate with a scone and a mountain of her lavender infused butter. Others started shouting orders.

Dana sat on the edge of an armchair, arms folded. Her shoulder twinged—residual stress, not injury. She missed her morning runs. "Vivienne said she was going to be here. Anyone see her yet?"

"No sign," Iona murmured, flicking her fingers across a charm to strengthen the Wi-Fi.

The screen finally stabilized. A sea of press flanked the Federal Building. The podium stood stark against the steps, the crowd in front of it murmuring with anticipation.

"I thought she'd do this outside the hospital," Laurie said in a quiet voice.

She doesn't want to look weak, Rosa said.

But she'd gain sympathy.

"There she is," Dana whispered, as Senator Whitmore stepped into frame.

She seemed thinner, paler—but looked absolutely unshaken. Gray suit, no nonsense. The kind of presence that didn't just command a room; it disciplined it.

She didn't look fragile. She looked *forged.*

As the chatter fell quiet in the farmhouse, Whitmore stepped up to the mic and began. The bullet wound had left her with a sling and a deeper line between her brows—but her voice rang clear. "Thank you all for being here.

"Two days ago, I stood before you to introduce legislation I have spent almost three decades fighting for—the American Health Security Act. I did not expect to leave that stage in an ambulance. But let me be perfectly clear: I will not be stepping down. I will not be intimidated. And I will not apologize for believing that in the United States of America, health care should be a human right."

Applause from advocates, staffers, and several watching from nearby balconies echoed faintly before the cameras resumed rolling.

Whitmore continued, eyes steely. "This bill is not about party politics. It is about survival. It is about making sure that veterans, teachers, single parents, and small business owners do not go bankrupt because of a diagnosis. It is about restoring dignity to the act of seeking care and ending the quiet cruelty of a system that profits most when people are sickest.

"I have heard the arguments against it. I have seen the lobby money. And now, I have felt the violence of those who would rather silence me than debate me."

She paused, letting that settle.

"I'm still here." Her voice rang out like a bell striking straight to the heart—clear, defiant, impossible to ignore.

Reporters began shouting questions. She pointed to a woman in a blue blazer near the front.

"Senator Whitmore," the journalist called out, "what's your reaction to the documents supposedly coming from BioCure, Primewell, and Florence Hospitals? Your public records show they've been some of your strongest backers."

Whitmore didn't hesitate. "If that information is genuine—and I believe it could be—then those companies were never backing *me*. They were backing the bill for their own ends. Not to serve the public good, but to consolidate power, inflate profits, and take over what should belong to the people.

"I won't stand for it." She leaned forward, her face determined.

"If they think their campaign contributions bought my silence, they are sorely mistaken. I have already returned every dollar. My office is cooperating with investigators, and I will personally support any effort to revoke the medical licenses, nonprofit status, or corporate protections of any entity that seeks to prey on Americans under the guise of care.

"This is not just about corruption. It's about betrayal. Of patients. Of doctors. Of every family who skipped groceries to cover a copay. And I will make damn sure the public knows who sold them out."

Hoa hooted. "She said 'damn' to the press."

"She sure did. And she just declared war." Skye raised her tea mug to the Senator and everyone in the room followed.

"She threw down the gauntlet," John agreed.

More questions flew. The senator's aides stepped forward to shield her as she turned from the mic, her message delivered, her chin high.

Senator Whitmore had survived the bullet. Now she was coming for the empire behind it.

"What's next?" John asked.

"We watch the feeds. See how the tides are running," Laurie said.

John smiled at her nautical metaphor.

"Can't miss the reactions to that speech. Maxwell and I are cooking up some things," Minh said, his fingers flying over his laptop keyboard.

"Maxwell?" John mouthed.

"One of my part-time employees," Dana explained quietly. She stretched and, catching a whiff of her shirt, crinkled her nose. "I think this is a good time for me to go retrieve some clean clothes." She looked up and stammered, "I don't mean to assume...that is, if we can stay for a little while longer."

"Of course, you can stay, dear," Fíona answered. "As long as need be."

"I'm doing a few loads of laundry this afternoon," Aunt Róisín. "Just leave your things in a pile outside your door."

"Oh, that's too much to ask."

"Ye be helping us, now, haven't ye?" Grandmother Moira said from her rocker in the corner. "Where'd we be without ye, then?"

Dana blushed. "You've got plenty of help." Then pointed to the kids. "Want to come?"

Minh barely looked up from his laptop.

"Can I stay? Brenna and Jamie are harvesting honey. Jamie says we need to share the farm news with the hives.

Dana didn't know what to say to that, so she stuck with traditional mom advice. "Just don't get stung."

"She sings special songs to the bees and she's going to teach me." Hoa's eyes shone with excitement.

Siobhán patted her shoulder. "Honeybees are gentle souls, but they have to be kept up on the family news."

"Bring Lele," Skye suggested. "She's all alone and Gandalf won't mind, will you boy."

The orange cat gave her a dubious look and Laurie sputtered a laugh.

"I don't want to know," Skye said.

"Okay, then." Dana searched her purse for her keys and walked toward the kitchen door only to run into Joey, who dangled his own set of keys in front of her.

Dana blinked. "You're back already?"

"Yeah, just turned around and got on the next flight back with my passport. No sightseeing for me," he said with a shrug. "Now let's get you those clean clothes."

She sighed but nodded. "Fair enough."

THE DRIVE WAS QUIET, the silence broken only by Joey whistling something she couldn't place. The rain from earlier had dried, leaving the streets with that damp, glimmering sheen that always reminded her of Seattle's many masks.

When they pulled into the driveway of the house she used to think of as home, she hesitated. The porch light was off. The blinds were drawn.

Joey reached for his door handle.

"You don't have to come in," Dana said.

"I wasn't going to," he replied, then added gently, "but I'm not going far either."

The key stuck in the lock, like always. Dana jiggled it and pushed the door open. The door creaked as she stepped inside, inhaling the scent of her old life: lemon oil, old wood, and something faintly bitter. Maybe regret.

She didn't expect him to be there.

But as she turned toward the hallway, Kevin appeared from the kitchen, holding a mug in one hand, barefoot in an old campaign t-shirt. His expression was half guilt, half relief.

Dana froze.

Kevin moved just past the kitchen archway, arms folded, mug forgotten on the counter behind him. He looked tired. Unshaven. ""I figured you'd come by eventually. How did you know what Marcus had?" he said.

Dana held her ground. "Hello to you, too."

"You said it at the press conference. After Whitmore was—" Kevin went still, his eyes losing focus.

"Shot?" Dana supplied.

He shook himself. "Yes, then you ran away. You said Marcus had files. But nobody ever said what was on them. Not publicly."

She shrugged off her coat, buying time. "I read between the lines."

"Bullshit." His voice was low and hot. "You've seen them. You got your hands on something."

"Marcus talked to you about them, then he was killed. Whitmore announced her health care plan, then she was shot."

"How do you know Marcus told me what was in his files?" he shouted.

"Because he told me," Dana said. "Satisfied?"

Marcus appeared by her side, a reassuring ghostly presence. She glanced at him.

"Seeing ghosts again, wifey? Like that crazy cheerleader?" Kevin leaned close and sneered. "Or are you the crazy one?"

Dana drew back. "You know what? Go to hell." She turned and ran up the stairs, but he chased after her. She slammed the door to her bedroom and flicked the lock.

Marcus sat on the bed. *You'll get through this.*

Dana nodded. *Thanks.*

You're almost done now.

She tried to focus. What did she need? Grabbing an empty gym bag, she stuffed clean underwear and bras—comfortable ones—in first.

Kevin's voice came from the other side of the door. "Dana, be reasonable. Open the door."

Jerk.

She grabbed sweats, then jeans, and a couple of t-shirts.

I never realized he was so deeply involved, Marcus said. *Otherwise, I wouldn't have shown him what I discovered.*

I could never have imagined he'd sink this low. She swiped a tear from the corner of her eye. Taking a deep breath, she walked to the closet and took a work suit that was still in its dry-cleaner bag.

"Come on, Dana. I just want to talk."

She opened the door and found Kevin, arms on either side of the frame, blocking her way. "Move. I need to get some things for the kids."

A flash of anger crossed his face quickly replaced by the aggrieved husband look. "I hired a security firm to protect you and the kids, but you run off to Skye's farm? It's not safe out there."

She pushed past him and went into Hoa's room first, then Minh's. Gathered up a change of clothes for each. Kevin was messing with her concentration. Flashes of their life together played through her mind. His jokes that lightened their study times. Sailing on Lake Washington, the wind catching the loose curls of his dark-brown hair. Sitting in a rocker holding Minh as an infant, his face lit with wonder. The enthusiasm when he decided to run for local office. How he'd wanted to change the world. But that man seemed to have disappeared, replaced by a calculating, greedy politician.

She came back out into the hall to find Kevin's tall frame blocking the hallway.

"Would you stop?" Kevin grabbed her arm.

She shook him off and headed down the stairs. She didn't believe he'd actually hurt her.

Kevin followed. "Tell me what is going on. If word gets out that you're hallucinating, well..."

Would he?

She dropped the two bags on the living room floor and whirled to face him. "What? You'll have me locked up like some nineteenth century wife?"

"Dana," his voice softened.

"I don't trust you anymore."

He stepped forward, just enough to cross that invisible line of comfort. "I deserve to know what the hell is going on. You're my wife. I've been walking blind while you and your coven pulls strings from the shadows."

"You want to talk about shadows?" she said. "You were the one having phone calls in the middle of the night. Talking about 'gate-keeping' and 'keeping your hands clean.' I was just connecting dots you left lying around like bloody breadcrumbs."

"How did you—" His face was a mask of shock, but he recovered quickly. "You don't understand what this is, Dana."

"Then explain it to me."

He looked at her like he was waiting for her to fold first. When she didn't, his voice dropped into something almost pleading. "The government can't run something this massive. Universal care? It'll collapse in a year. And then what—total chaos? Rationing? People dying in waiting rooms?"

She snorted. "You mean like they're doing now?"

Kevin's composure cracked. "You think you're so noble, so pure. But you don't get the scale of it. The strain. The population numbers alone—"

"Don't," she warned.

"We've *talked* about this," he snapped. "Over dinner. In bed."

She winced.

"At every damn fundraiser. The system can't survive this many people draining it dry."

She stared at him. "So what? You throw them away? Let them die quietly while the rich inject themselves with fake eternal youth?"

He didn't answer.

Her voice dropped into a whisper. "That's mass murder, Kevin."

His jaw tightened. "It's survival."

"You sound just like them."

"And you sound like a child," he shot back. "Taking the moral high ground while the world burns. The earth cannot sustain this many humans."

Dana took a step closer, fury rising like fire in her chest. "It *could* if the billionaires paid their fair share. If we stopped hoarding resources. Not cooking up some half-baked scheme to evacuate the rich to—what? Mars?"

He looked away.

"Oh my God," she breathed. "You actually believe this. You believe in this nightmare."

He opened his mouth—then stopped as another voice cut through the hallway.

"You all right?" Joey stood at the front door, one hand inside his jacket, calm but coiled. "I heard yelling."

Dana didn't take her eyes off Kevin. "Yeah," she said, voice like ice. "We're done." She scooped up Lele, who didn't protest, and walked past Joey without another word. Joey lingered just long enough to give Kevin a look that said, *I know who you are now,* then grabbed the bags and closed the door behind them both.

Dana took out the keys to her SUV. "I don't want to leave my SUV here, so—"

"I'll be right behind you," Joey said.

CHAPTER
TWENTY-THREE

By the time Dana and Joey returned to Red Fox Farm, the afternoon sun had burned through the clouds. Chickens strutted in the yard like they owned it, and someone was baking something sweet in the kitchen—probably Brigid or Iona. The scent of chocolate chip cookies wrapped around Dana as she stepped onto the porch. She took a long, grounding breath. Joey stayed behind her, leaning against the rail, pretending not to keep watch.

Inside, the living room buzzed with quiet energy. Laurie, sprawled on the area rug with Rosa curled beside her, gave her a thumbs up, then went back to watching her iPad. Minh sat at the corner table with his laptop, earbuds in, muttering, "Hashtag surge is holding." Close by, Iona monitored her own laptop. The television showed the news on mute with closed captions. Fred snored softly on the couch under a quilt, his phone still clutched in his hand.

Lele squirmed to get down, so Dana handed her off to Hoa. "Can you take her up to our suite?"

"Yeah, Jade put a litter box up there. Plus some water and food."

"Thanks, sweetie." Dana kissed the top of Hoa's head, which was getting harder to do now that she was getting so tall. Hoa took off up the stairs, Lele's tail squishing back and forth with impatience. Then Dana walked back into the kitchen.

Skye looked up from her place at the table, a steaming mug of something herbal in her hands. "Hey. You okay?"

Dana stood still for a moment, then shook her head. "No. But I will be."

Skye set down her mug. "What happened?"

Dana pulled out a chair and sat across from her. "I saw him. Kevin. He was at the house."

Skye's expression darkened, but she stayed quiet, giving her space to speak.

"He knew something was up—he asked how I knew what was on Marcus's drives." Dana rubbed the heel of her palm against her temple. "He's not just involved, Skye. He believes in it. All of it. Population control, privatized health care, the whole damn plan."

Skye's eyes softened. "That's hard."

"It's worse than hard. He thinks it's pragmatic. He looked me in the eye and said the earth can't sustain so many humans." Dana gave a bitter laugh. "We've had that conversation before and he's right, but now his solution is to let people die."

"I'm sorry." Skye reached across the table, touching her hand.

Dana didn't pull away. "He's not the same person I married. How could he have changed so much and I didn't notice?"

"Both of you were busy with your careers. Raising two kids."

Dana huffed a breath. "I did most of the child rearing. And cleaning."

Skye shook her head. "You needed more help."

"I was thinking of a separation. Not official if he won the election. The kids would live with me during the school year. Spend some holidays with him, although I doubt we could pull Mink off John's boat in the summer." She looked at Skye who watched, her hazel eyes sympathetic. "But now I know. Our marriage is over."

A cup of steaming tea that smelled like chamomile and rose

petals plopped in front of her. She didn't even look up to see who'd put it there, but took a sip, blinking back tears.

They sat in silence for a while, then Skye changed gears gently. "Senator Whitmore's coming this afternoon."

Dana blinked. "Here? To the farm?"

"She's going to slip by the press camped outside her house. She wants total privacy. Just one aide. Her security guy." Skye waved her hand. "Says it's safer."

Dana nodded. "That tracks. After everything, she probably doesn't trust anyone outside the circle."

"I already set up Minh's war room," Skye said. "Once she arrives, the elders will lay down some heavy wards around the farm. We'll know if anyone breaches them."

Dana exhaled. "Good. She'll want to strategize. She's not the type to retreat."

Skye smiled faintly. "You two have that in common."

The two wandered back into the living room and Iona looked up with sad eyes. "Some of these posts are awful. Family members dying because health insurance denied their claims. People going bankrupt, losing their homes and life savings to pay for treatments."

Skye walked over and gave Iona a hug. "If these companies get their way, we'll see a lot more of that."

Iona pulled back, her face fierce. "We have to stop it."

"I have some good news." Minh told them that social media was moving in the senator's favor. "People are riled up. The trending hashtags are *#HealthCareIsAHumanRight*. That one's boring." Minh scrolled. "Then *#WhitmoreWontBackDown*, *#EndTheDisease-Business*—"

"Ooh, I like that last one," Dana said.

"And my personal favorite, *#OneHealthOneLie*." Minh sat back in his chair and smiled up at his mother.

"Great work," she said.

"And you should totally divorce Dad if he's down with this." Minh waved his hand at his computer screen.

Dana snorted in surprise. She studied her son, but he didn't seem sad. More defiant. She wondered if that would last when the divorce really happened.

Laurie appeared between Minh and Dana and changed the subject. "I've been tracking responses to the longevity plans. This part really pisses people off."

Minh leaned toward her. "What are the hashtags?"

"#LiveForeverGate, #ImmortalityForThe1% and—this is my favorite—#MartiansForMedicare."

They entertained themselves reading through the social media feeds and making up some new ones that Minh sent off to Maxwell who was helping them out from what he called 'an undisclosed location.' Then they watched the talking heads bloviate.

In the middle of their general hilarity, Senator Whitmore arrived wearing a dark green coat and sunglasses, her arm still in a sling. Joey took the keys from Carl and drove the car away somewhere so nobody would spot it. Carl took up position on the porch beside one of Skye's uncles who sat with an old-fashioned shotgun over his knees. Ashe and Taran lay beside him, eyes on the woods.

Everyone wandered back to Minh's war room as he'd christened it. Brigid delivered a platter full of warm chocolate chip cookies. "Tea? Coffee?" she looked at Minh. "Milk?"

He favored her with a grown-up look. "The dairy industry is cruel. I don't drink milk."

"I'll take coffee if you'd be so kind," Evelyn said, then glanced at Minh, "with milk."

"It's from our cows. We don't separate the babies from their mothers. We rotate who calves each year," Brigid huffed.

"Sick," Minh said, his eyes brightening.

Brigid's spine stiffened. "None of them are ill."

"Oh, he means that's cool," Dana explained.

Brigid looked between them, then shook her head muttering something about kids these days as she walked back to the kitchen.

Whitmore settled into a cushioned chair with a wince. "It's good to be here. I trust this house more than any office in D.C."

Dana stood near the head of the table, palms flat on the worn wood. "We're glad you came."

The senator looked over the crime board. "Impressive work, whoever did this."

Minh preened.

"Now we have too much to go up there," Skye said, "but we've organized the material on the table by topic."

"But I must ask, is the internet secure here?" Whitmore asked.

"Maxwell sent us a super secure VPN. One he designed himself," Minh answered.

"And who is Maxwell?"

"He's my hacker," Dana said. "Very talented. We can trust his work."

"Second question, has Vivienne arrived?" Whitmore asked.

Skye shook her head. "Not yet."

"She was supposed to be here," Dana said. "We spoke last night. She was prepping her statements, going through the latest drops with Minh."

Whitmore frowned. "She's not the type to flake. When's her press conference scheduled?"

"Tomorrow morning. Aren't you two doing it together?" Laurie said.

Whitmore checked her schedule. "Right. I usually have Mary helping me keep up, but I didn't want to put her in any danger."

William Robertson suddenly appeared in the doorway, windblown and rumpled in a tweed coat. He looked older than he had two days ago—but sharper, too. Sharpened by grief and rage.

"I've got my own copies now," he said without preamble. "Marcus's files. BioCure's roadmap. The whole plan for OneHealth. You were right."

His voice dropped. "Those bastards killed my son."

Dana looked at him, surprised by the rawness.

"I'm in," he continued. "Fully. I'll fund whatever you need—media campaigns, whistleblower protections, hell, even private security. Whatever it takes to stop this."

Whitmore gave him a grateful nod, then turned back to the group. "We keep pressure on the system. Legally, publicly, and privately. Dana, I want you to help coordinate the legal end. Siobhán and Skye—your network's going to be important. We're not just fighting in the daylight anymore."

They rolled up their sleeves and went to work. An hour later, they had a detailed plan of action. The aroma of dinner tempted them to wrap things up.

Laurie glanced at her phone. "Still no sign of Vivienne."

Dana's gut tensed. "This is not like her."

Skye pulled out her phone, texting fast. "Her office?"

Dana pulled out her phone and pressed a button. She identified herself to whoever answered and asked, "I'm waiting to hear from Ms. Grant. She's quite late for an appointment. Can you tell me—"

"Yes."

Silence.

"I see." Dana ended the call and looked around the room, eyes wide. "Her assistant said she left this morning for the farm."

Robertson frowned. "That was hours ago."

A long silence stretched across the room.

Skye met Dana's eyes. "We have to start looking."

Each of them called their contacts, spreading out into the living room and kitchen so their conversations wouldn't overlap.

The sun had started to sink behind the trees on the west edge of the pasture, casting long shadows over the porch and soaking the fields in amber. But inside the farmhouse, there was no golden hour —just the sharp hum of worry.

"She left her office mid-morning," Dana said for the third time, pacing near the living room fireplace. "Vivienne told her assistant she was coming straight here."

Senator Whitmore sat stiffly in an armchair, her face unreadable, her injured arm carefully cradled. "She's never late. Never."

William Robertson stood by the window with a tumbler of untouched whiskey, jaw clenched. "If someone got to her..."

Skye touched his shoulder. "Let's not go there yet."

Laurie stood at the table with Minh, fingers flying across his laptop keyboard. "Can we trace her phone?"

"Already tried," Minh muttered. "Signal died just outside Wood-inville. No pings since."

"I can request a location trace," said Jade quietly, stepping forward. She wore her badge clipped inside her coat, hidden from view. "But I need to be subtle. I'm already on someone's watch list."

Dana paused in her pacing. "Can you do it without triggering alerts?"

Jade nodded. "It'll take finesse, but yeah. I'll route it through a cold case database and scrub the inquiry after."

She stepped outside to make the call, voice low and tense.

Dana turned to Minh. "Get Maxwell. We need his eyes."

Minh nodded and tapped out a series of encrypted messages. A few minutes later, Maxwell's voice came through the speaker, rough and annoyed. "This better be a ghost with juicy intel."

"It's Vivienne," Dana said. "She's missing. Left Seattle hours ago and never made it here."

His tone changed instantly. "Send me the plate number. I'll check traffic cams and pull backup feeds."

Minh got to work.

"If they grabbed Vivienne, it's not just retaliation. It's strategic," Skye said. She crossed the room with a bowl of soup and placed it on the side table next to Whitmore. "Potato leek. Brigid says you need to keep up your strength."

"Thank you, but—"

"There's soup and bread in the kitchen if anyone's hungry," Skye announced, soothing Whitmore's concern she was the only one eating, but nobody moved.

208

"We all knew they'd hit back," said Iona quietly. "We just didn't know how fast."

Minutes passed in tension. Dana poured herself half a cup of cold tea and didn't drink it.

Rosa paced the floor, sniffing the air, ears alert. *I need to go out,* she sent to Laurie.

Laurie went into the kitchen and opened the door. Ashe and Taran waited at the bottom of the porch steps and took off toward the woods once Rosa joined them.

When she came back, Minh's head jerked up. "We've got something."

He turned the laptop toward the group. A grainy still from a highway cam flickered on-screen—Route 203, just before the turnoff to Duvall. The image showed Vivienne's black car pulled to the shoulder of the road. Two figures stood beside it. One of them—a woman in a deep red blazer—was being pushed out of frame.

Dana leaned in. "That's her. I'd recognize her fancy blazer anywhere."

"Pulling the video," Maxwell's voice came over the speaker. "Give me a second."

The feed stuttered, then played. It showed Vivienne stepping out of the driver's side, raising her hand—maybe to wave, maybe to shield her face—before a man came up behind her, grabbed her arm, and shoved her roughly toward the ditch. The video cut off seconds later.

Gasps broke around the room. Whitmore muttered something low and furious under her breath.

"I'm forwarding this to Jade," Dana said.

But Minh wasn't done.

"Wait—Maxwell just sent two more things. First, a text exchange between two of our favorite conspirators." He taped a key and two texts appeared, dated a few hours after Whitmore's shooting.

OM: *What happened? This wasn't the plan.*

DB: *I've got my team trying to identify the shooter.*

OM: *Somebody is messing with us. I want them taken care of.*
DB: *As soon as we figure out who we're dealing with.*

Robertson pointed to the screen. "Who are OM and DB?"

"Olivia Mercer and Damien Blackwood," Skye answered.

He blinked. "How can you be so sure?"

"Because Marcus had texts between them in his files and this matches," Dana said, trying to keep her eyes off the ghost who stood watching his father.

"I haven't read everything yet," Robertson said.

Whitmore waved this away. "So, who shot me?"

"There's more," Minh said. "Maxwell cracked a private server on a darknet network. Super locked-down, barely any traffic. But he's seeing new chatter."

A string of anonymous messages appeared:

> Anon553: She wasn't supposed to survive.
>
> BladeMoth: Whitmore wasn't the real target.
>
> NullGate: Then who was?
>
> Anon553: Doesn't matter now. The leak's out. The clock is ticking.
>
> SpectreVault: Phase Two begins.

Dana's blood chilled. "There's someone else," she whispered. "Maybe another group we haven't identified yet."

Robertson looked over at Whitmore. "You need to double your security."

"I'm not leaving this farm," the senator said, then flinched and looked up at Fíona, who leaned in the doorway. "That is, if it's okay with your family. I don't want to put you in any more danger."

Fíona scoffed. "We were in danger before you got here."

"I think we should stay together until we figure all this out," Skye said.

Jade re-entered, face pale. "They found her car. Empty. Her brief-case and purse were still in it. Phone on the seat, but the battery was dead. They're sending out a search team."

TWENTY-FOUR

"I think it's time we checked the scene," Carl said. "Gus and Joey can stay for security."

"Let us know as soon as you find anything," Whitmore said.

"Don't let the police see you," Jade shouted as Carl headed out the door.

"No problem," he said over his shoulder.

His smile was somehow menacing. Not for them, but for whoever took Vivienne. Skye glanced out the window. Uncle Douglas waited in his truck, shotgun on the rack behind him. Carl jumped in and they peeled off, spraying gravel.

"I have an idea," Whitmore said and took out her phone. She waited a few seconds for the call to connect. "Mary, I'm sorry to bother you at home."

She listened. "Yes, yes. I'm fine. Taking good care of myself. Have you gotten any messages from Vivienne Grant today?"

A pause.

"Nothing? All right, thank you. I'll be in touch." She ended the call and shook her head.

Rosa, Ashe, and Taran ran into the room.

Laurie braced herself for the smell of whatever they'd rolled in, but the dogs were clean.

Rosa stood in front of her, body rigid, focus intent.

"Oh, my God." Laurie jumped out of her chair.

"What did she say?" Skye asked.

"What did who say?" Robertson asked.

Skye shook her head. It was too much to explain.

"The dogs say they've scented Marcus's killer in the woods," Laurie said.

Everyone stopped and stared at her.

"Here?" Dana's voice was low, cold. "Now?"

"They say he's moving. Fast."

"The dogs are telling her this?" Whitmore asked in a low voice.

Fred shook off his surprise and stood. "Then what the hell are we still doing inside?" He ran toward the kitchen.

Fiona darted up the stairs, pulling Brigid with her. Dana followed Fred, fishing for keys. Whitmore pushed herself up and took a few steps.

"Wait. We might be safer in here," Skye said.

Jade's hand moved instinctively toward her sidearm—except she wasn't carrying it. She was off duty. And they'd agreed not to bring more weapons into the farmhouse than necessary.

Rosa gave a low growl and stared at the door.

They were too late.

The back door burst open with a crash of wood and wind.

A man stepped in, gun raised, eyes dead and flat. The stalking shadow that had followed Hoa for weeks—his face unremarkable, pale, and smug with the power of a predator who'd finally cornered prey.

Dana recognized him immediately—the man who had watched Hoa. The man who'd killed Marcus.

Behind him came another—taller, wirier, younger. Possibly ex-military. Definitely ex-human in the eyes.

"Everyone into the living room," the lean one snapped. "Now."

No one moved at first.

He pointed his snub nose revolver in a wide circle toward them. "I said now."

Slowly, they obeyed. Gus helped Senator Whitmore back into her chair as the men herded them into a cluster—Jade, Skye, Dana, Minh, Robertson, Laurie, and Fred. Hoa tried to hide behind the bookcase in the corner. The second man kept his gun aimed, eyes scanning constantly.

"Where's Carl?" the killer asked.

"I sent him out to find you," Whitmore said in a menacing voice.

The man sneered. "Looks like I found you first."

Gus, standing in the corner, didn't reach for anything. He just watched—calculating, reading the room, waiting for an opening.

The younger intruder moved toward Minh. "Are you the little social media brainiac she's got working for her?"

"Leave him alone," Dana said, voice sharp.

"You should've stayed in your law office," the killer snarled.

"And you should've stayed away from my kid."

Something primal flickered in his eyes. He raised his pistol toward her.

Dana faced him down.

Skye reached slowly for the edge of the side table, eyes flicking toward the spell drawer—too far.

Minh swallowed.

Rosa growled low in her throat beside Laurie but didn't lunge. Then she noticed Ashe and Taran were nowhere to be seen.

But they were outgunned. And outflanked.

The killer stepped forward, pistol sweeping. "Which one of you leaked the files?"

Silence.

Then Skye heard a vehicle approaching. It stopped short of the parking area and the engine turned off.

The younger man went to the window and flicked the curtain so he could peek out. Then looked back at the lead man and shock his head.

Are they waiting for somebody? Skye wondered.

Robertson squared his shoulders. "You're making a mistake."

"Wrong," the killer sneered. "I'm cleaning one up."

He turned toward Minh—intent clear.

Dana moved in front of him. "Over my dead body."

"That's no problem," he said, but he didn't fire.

Gus took a step forward.

Skye caught a sliver cf movement out of the corner of her eye— Carl slipping through the yard, silent as fog.

And that's when her warrior cousin Finlay McAllister burst in through the kitchen—mud on his boots, a hunting knife in one hand, wild red hair tied back in a leather thong.

"You picked the wrong farm," Finlay said.

The second intruder turned, but too late. Finlay threw the knife —not at the man, but at the curtain rod above the window. It crashed down onto him and Rosa launched herself from the ccrner with a snarl, jaws snapping. Ashe and Taran ran in behind Finlay, joining the fray.

Chaos erupted.

"Move!" Gus shouted.

Fred yanked Minh to the floor. Skye shielded Whitmore with her body.

The intruder recovered from the curtain rod and lunged toward the side of the room, clearly aiming to grab Whitmore.

But Rosa was faster.

She launched from the floor like a streak of lightning, slamming into his side with a feral snarl. Her jaws locked around his forearm, yanking him off balance. He let out a guttural cry, stumbling sideways into the wall as Ashe and Taran darted in behind her, snapping and flanking like a coordinated pack.

Rosa shifted her grip, dragging the man off balance as he swung wildly with his free arm, trying to crush her against the wall. He might've succeeded if Ashe hadn't lunged and sunk her teeth into his calf.

He buckled with a cry.

Then Finlay was there.

He vaulted over an overturned chair, slammed his boot down on the man's wrist, and yanked Rosa back by her scruff. The attacker hissed in pain, tried to scramble away—but Taran growled low and stepped in front of his face, snarling.

"Move again," Finlay said, knife gleaming in his hand, "and the dogs won't stop this time."

The man froze, bloodied, breath ragged.

Rosa backed away to Laurie's side, tail stiff, eyes fixed, and Laurie dropped to one knee and stroked her head.

"Good girl," she whispered. "That's my girl."

Meanwhile, Gus had moved to the lead man like a whisper turning into thunder, his punch landing with a crack. The man fought back hard—jabbing with his elbow, twisting to break free, trying to bring the gun up—but Gus was already in his space, smothering his momentum with sheer, brutal efficiency. He slammed the man's wrist against the doorframe once, twice, until his weapon clattered to the floor.

Jade dove for the dropped pistol.

The man swung wildly, catching Gus with a kidney punch.

Gus crouched with the pain.

Carl suddenly appeared and surged forward, catching the man around the middle and driving him backward into the wall with a thud that rattled the windowpanes. The intruder grunted and dropped low, trying to hook Carl's leg, but Carl shifted weight like a brawler who knew exactly where his center lived.

A knee to the gut. Another strike to the throat—not enough to kill, just enough to choke the air from him.

The man staggered, tried to recover—and Gus rose back up, caught him with a blow to the side of the neck that dropped him like a sack of meat.

The two men stood over the heap of him, Gus's chest heaving, blood running from a split in his eyebrow

The whole room had gone silent.

Until Dana shouted, "Everyone out! Minh, grab Hoa!"

Fred helped pull Robertson behind the kitchen island. Jade reached the dropped pistol just as the second attacker began to rise beneath the curtain rod. She didn't shoot—but she held him at gunpoint, hands steady despite the tremor in her jaw.

Finlay grabbed the man's collar. "You're going to tell us where Vivienne is. And if you lie—" he yanked the curtain rod up with a grin "—I'll find another use for this."

Skye spit out a laugh. Her little cousin had an imagination.

Carl had the leader pinned, bleeding and cursing. "You get one chance," he snarled. "Tell us where she is."

The man just smiled. "Doesn't matter. She won't live to see tomorrow. And neither will you."

Joey burst in through the front door, gun raised, too late. "Are you—"

"We're fine," Skye said, breathless.

Robertson stood slowly. "Where is Vivienne?"

Dana stepped forward, staring down at the younger man as the dogs kept him from moving.

"Talk."

The man shook his head.

Finlay stepped in, knife in hand.

"Oh, I'll make you sing, lad. Don't worry."

And then—footsteps on the porch.

The front door opened.

Derek Robertson stepped into the farmhouse like he owned it—dark coat open, a faint, bitter smile twisting his mouth. Behind him, two armed men dragged Vivienne forward. One pinned her arms while the other pressed a sharp blade against the soft skin below her ear.

Her eyes were clear, but her lip was split.

Skye's stomach turned at the sight.

Derek took in the room—Skye, Dana, Gus frozen by the window, Whitmore sitting stiffly in her armchair, eyes blazing. Rosa growled low beside Laurie, teeth bared but waiting for a signal.

The killer came to on the floor and reached for the knife Finlay had dropped. He and the younger intruder slowly got to their feet.

"Everyone stay calm," Derek said, voice smooth—the former CIA analyst's son morphing into his final shape—cold ambition laid bare. "Nobody else has to bleed tonight. You're going to do something for me."

No one spoke.

The only sound was Vivienne's breath—steady despite the blade at her throat.

"You're going to go online right now," Derek continued. "Every channel you've got. Every feed. And you're going to say the longevity trials and OneHealth plan were a hoax. That Whitmore's shooting was an inside job by rogue radicals. That you were misled."

Minh's laugh cracked through the tension like glass breaking. "You think we're just going to—"

Derek cut him off with a glance at the man holding Vivienne. The knife bit closer, drawing a line of red. Vivienne flinched but didn't make a sound. "Do it or she dies."

"Derek, Robertson's voice was ragged. "What are you doing?"

Derek's eyes flicked to his father—empty and sharp all at once. "What you never had the stomach for."

"You're my son," William said, voice breaking. "You don't—"

"I'm not your son anymore."

No one moved. The second armed man scanned the room, his gun sweeping from Gus to Skye to Dana.

Dana pointed at Derek, connecting the dots. "You're behind the shooting. You weren't trying to stop Senator Whitmore. You were trying to frame someone for her murder. Make her a martyr."

Derek nodded. "Yes, then her bill would pass, no question. Sympathy vote. After that, the right people will rebuild it."

"The right people," Laurie scoffed.

Robertson took a step toward his son, even if that son rejected him. "And what have you built?"

"The company that will implement OneHealth's plans after they've been discredited. I'll be a billionaire." Derek's eyes took on a fanatical gleam.

And that's when Skye heard it beneath the sound of Derek's voice.

A faint creak on the old stairs. A door nudging open near the back hall.

Fíona Yarrow appeared first—barefoot, an old wand clutched in her hand like a branch cut from the first tree that ever grew. Her eyes glowed with anger older than the house.

Next came Grandmother Brigid, hair pinned up, apron on over her nightgown, gripping her rolling pin like the cudgel it had always secretly been.

Then Uncle Douglas, moving in from the pantry door, one hand curled casually around the grip of an old rifle he'd oiled every winter since the last big storm.

They didn't say a word.

Derek followed Skye's gaze and saw them. For the first time, a flicker of doubt crossed his face.

And in that flicker, Gus moved.

He lunged for the man with the knife—one arm hooking the wrist, the other jamming a knee into his side. The blade jerked away from Vivienne's neck as she ducked instinctively. Carl, waiting hidden behind the woodstove, tackled the second armed man, knocking the rifle sideways just as a shot barked into the ceiling.

Vivienne stumbled clear, hair wild, eyes blazing fury.

Finlay came from nowhere—a blur of red hair and fists, cracking Hoa's stalker, Marcus's killer, across the temple. The knife skittered under the sofa. Gus followed him and with a decisive blow, knocked him to the floor.

Derek pivoted, hand diving inside his coat for a sidearm—but

Rosa was there first, a flash of fawn fur and snapping teeth. She locked onto his forearm, dragging his arm away from his weapon. Ashe and Taran sprang at Derek's legs, snarling, herding him backward into the center of the living room.

Fíona raised her wand and murmured something low and sharp in the old tongue. The lights flickered. The fireplace roared back to life in a gust of embers that danced dangerously close to Derek's boots.

Brigid stepped forward, rolling pin raised high. *Crack.*

Derek's head snapped sideways. He went down hard.

Outside, sirens wailed—a chorus behind the farmhouse walls. Blue and red lights flooded the windows. Deputies poured into the living room—weapons drawn. They looked to Vivienne, who pointed out the criminals. Barked commands mixed with the barking dogs. They swept up Derek, his men, and the bleeding, cursing killer. Handcuffs snapped shut, boots thudded, radios crackled.

Robertson stood at the edge of it all, shoulders sagging, watching them drag his son out in plastic restraints.

Vivienne sat on the sofa, hair askew, a bandage someone had grabbed pressed to her neck. She caught Skye's eye and gave a small, grim nod.

Outside, the clouds gave way to clear stars—unbothered, unchanging.

Inside the old farmhouse, the Yarrow clan, Senator Whitmore, and the ones who'd chosen to stand with them all exhaled together. One long breath.

TWENTY-FIVE

One week later, the world watched as Senator Evelyn Whitmore stepped up to the podium, her arm finally out of the sling, her eyes clear, sharp, unflinching. Vivienne Grant stood at her side—neck bandaged but chin high, suit pressed.

Behind them, a wall of American flags framed a screen scrolling headlines:

HEALTH TRIAD CEOS ARRESTED

DEREK ROBERTSON IN CUSTODY

Cameras clicked. Microphones crowded forward.

"Today," Whitmore said, voice ringing with that iron warmth that made crowds lean in and listen, "we take back what always should have belonged to the people. Health care is not a privilege for the wealthy. It is not a bargaining chip for corporations. It is the foundation of a free, thriving society."

A ripple of applause built, raw and genuine.

Vivienne stepped up beside her, voice crisp. "These arrests are only the beginning. There will be trials. There will be revelations. But this is our line in the sand: no more selling human life to the highest bidder."

Whitmore smiled faintly. "And if you think we're done—" She glanced sideways at Vivienne, who returned the smallest nod "—well, you haven't met my team."

The crowd broke into cheers. Somewhere in the back, a single sign lifted above the rest: *#PeopleOverProfits*

THAT NIGHT, the bells on the old green door of Old World Apothecary chimed like laughter as people drifted in from the fall dusk. Herbs hung in fragrant bundles from rafters brushed clean of dust. Fresh beeswax candles flickered in mason jars on every shelf.

The big worktable had been polished to a soft glow—its wood grain warm and welcoming. Siobhán stood behind it, sleeves rolled up, chatting with a customer about allergy teas. Laurie leaned near the front, sipping cider, talking with Skye. Rosa wandered the crowd, shamelessly begging for treats and adoration.

They were celebrating the grand reopening of Siobhán's business, and by all reports, similar events were happening across the country. The fake claims against all types of alternative health care practitioners had melted away, like fog under a strong sun.

But best of all in the posse's opinion was the passing of the American Health Security Act, Senator Whitmore's legislation. But it had been christened Whitmore Health in social media and the name had caught on, no matter how hard the senator tried to correct it.

Sure, there was a lot of work to be done. It would take a few years to implement. Dana would be working side by side with Senator Whitmore to make that happen. But tonight, a celebration was in order. And that's exactly what they were doing.

Minh perched on a stool near the window, showing Hoa how the new donation tracker worked for a local clinic—each sale from tonight funding free herbal care for anyone who needed it.

Dana watched her kids. They would heal from their disappointment that their father had played a part in this fiasco. In one fell swoop, Kevin Preston had lost his election and lost his wife. The divorce would go through with no argument. He'd gotten off easy. No arrest. The charges against Blackwood, Mercer, Ellsworth, and Monroe overshadowed any part Kevin had played.

Just as Dana had predicted, the relationship between Kevin and Nicolette, the campaign stylist, seemed to be heating up. Nicolette could pester him to wear uncomfortable clothes, although she doubted men had any items in their wardrobes that compared to the torture devices of five-inch heels, underwear bras, and those ridiculous garter belts. Nicolette only cared for appearances, not content.

In a way, their budding affair was a relief. Kevin wouldn't be around badgering her and soon the kids would be old enough to decide what kind of relationship they wanted with their father. She did grieve for the man he had been. Remembered the good times. But that was gone, and just like her kids, she would heal.

Speaking of healing, William Robertson sat in a corner, quiet but steady, talking to Fred. The knowledge that his son Derek had played a part in the murder of Marcus had laid him low, but he seemed better tonight. A full recovery would take time, but they'd be there for him.

Unbeknownst to both of them, Marcus stood beside his father taking in the festivities. Dana felt the ghost was taking his leave soon. In fact, she kept checking back to see if Marcus was still there. His form was thinning, but he glowed like another beeswax candle. She wondered if anyone else could see him. Surely one of Skye's clan had this ability, but nobody had said anything to her.

Whitmore's security detail lingered outside in the garden but didn't interfere. Tonight, the senator had insisted on no speeches— just the clink of cups and the low murmur of people daring to hope.

Vivienne arrived late, stitches still under her collar but eyes alight. She squeezed Dana's hand, then slipped a folded piece of paper into Skye's pocket. "I had some work to finish up. For the apothecary. A permit for expansion. Just in case," she said with a wink.

Someone had propped the front door wide, so the scent of blooming lavender drifted in. Brigid moved through the crowd with fresh scones. Uncle Ewan played a fiddle and his nephew Jamie accompanied him on a frame drum in the corner, their music weaving through the laughter like a soft spell.

Rosa trotted outside, lifting her head, ears twitching at the breeze. Laurie joined her. No shadows tonight. Just the hush of night settling easy over a healing center that felt alive again. A group of people, a country, with hope again.

Inside, Dana raised her glass, catching Whitmore's eye across the room. "To Whitmore Health," she said.

"And to justice," Skye added.

And the room answered as one: "To health and justice."

Dana felt a pull and looked over at Marcus, who had turned into pure light. He nodded and with a smile, he vanished.

She knew he was gone now. No fanfare, just a nod. She would miss him, but he had other things to explore. Just as she did. Her friends, her kids, the Yarrow clan, and the prospect of a fresh future.

YULETIDE MAGIC, missing relics, and a witch on the edge—what could possibly go wrong? Skye Yarrow's back in *Crystals, Crooks, and Chaos* —festive, funny, and full of magical mayhem. Click here to keep reading the third book in the Emerald City Paranormal Cozy Mystery series.

WANT TO READ ANOTHER LAURIE, Dana, and Skye adventure? Claim your copy of "The Antique Shop"and get my newsletter. Not spamy and you can cancel any time.

THANK YOU FOR READING *Ghosts, Garters, and Grimoires*. Your honest review will help future readers decide if they want to take a chance on a new-to-them author. Just click here to leave a review.

ABOUT THE AUTHOR

Best-selling author Theresa Crater writes compelling supernatural suspense and paranormal women's fiction. Her series include the Spirit Springs and Emerald City paranormal women's fiction series, the award-winning Power Places supernatural suspense series, and the Mystic Assassin series. She has published several individual novels, many short stories, and a spiritual memoir (the story behind the stories) which can all be found on her website. She lives in Boulder with her Egyptologist partner and their cat who is naturally named Cleo. www.theresacraterbooks.com

ALSO BY

Theresa Crater

Spirit Springs Paranormal Women's Fiction

The Crone and the Stolen Orb

Emerald City Paranormal Women's Fiction

Murder, Mystics & Menopause

Ghosts, Garters, and Grimoires

Power Places Series

Under the Stone Paw

Beneath the Hallowed Hill

Return of the Grail King

Into the City of Light

Power Places: The Complete Series

Yuletide Tales: Holiday Short Stories

Stand-Alones

The Star Family

Three Awakenings: A Spiritual Memoir

Other Books from Crystal Star Publishing

T.L. Crater

Mystic Assassin Series

Assassin Awakens

Breached: A Mystic Assassin Novella

Louise Ryder

God in a Box

School of Hard Knocks

ᴀCKNOWLEDGMENTS

Thank you to all my fabulous readers. You make it possible.

A special shout out to my advanced readers for their eagle eyes and helpful suggestions.

Special thanks to Stephen Mehler and Cleopatra Iset.

www.ingramcontent.com/pod-product-compliance
Lightning Source LLC
Chambersburg PA
CBHW051506260626
47162CB00008B/2850